DEVICES AND DESIRES

DEVICES AND DESIRES

by

E. ARNOT ROBERTSON

He gave them their desire, and sent
leanness withal into their souls.

PSALM 106

JONATHAN CAPE
THIRTY BEDFORD SQUARE
LONDON

FIRST PUBLISHED 1954

PRINTED IN GREAT BRITAIN IN THE CITY OF OXFORD
AT THE ALDEN PRESS
BOUND BY A. W. BAIN & CO. LTD., LONDON

CONTENTS

1

THE GOOD PLACE

THE child had seen her father afraid so often that now it seemed strange — more strange than anything else at first — to watch him from the shelter of the bushes on the edge of a clearing, lying out in the open with machine-gun bullets spurting up the dust a little way beyond him; lying still and unafraid at last, and dead, staring at the evening sky.

She crouched where she was until the firing slackened and came from further away. Then, carefully, she crawled over to him, to look at the wound in his face and feel his heart, before crawling back into deeper scrub — a small, undernourished, enduring creature of thirteen, with a flame of respectability in her heart.

Now, with only herself to consider, she would somehow get back to the country to which only a quarter of her belonged by blood; but for as long as she could remember it had been for her 'the Good Place', the home of well-being. Now she might even manage to go to the sort of school she had read about, in England. She had been too young for school when she lived there, but she knew the life quite well through books, picked up in Jamaica, South America, in ships and boarding houses — wherever her father's enterprises had taken her.

She crawled on, along the Bulgarian hillside, in the fading light of an autumn day — the bitter, early autumn of 1946 — and presently rose when the bursts of firing, rare now, sounded from the other side of a ridge of wooded ground. Following a faint trail, leading downwards, among taller trees, she relied on the sound of a river running in the valley on one side of her to assure her of the direction when the path forked, and came at last to an encampment where there were lean-to shelters of boughs, and a small fire which had recently been scattered and almost stamped out. Here three men and a woman were sitting. They peered at her anxiously through the twilight. 'Where's your father? What happened?'

'He's dead. I waited to make sure.'

She looked at them with contempt. They had been together when the shooting started, but they had run at the first sound of it. Homeless people, in her experience, always ran. Refugees, displaced persons, fugitives from justice or injustice — it did not seem to make much difference to their behaviour which they happened to be, once they had given up hope of return to their own 'good place', wherever that was. These were a mixed bunch from south and eastern Europe, driven from their countries not directly by the war but by its various aftermaths of social and political change. Her father had been shepherding them to Salonika, and some of the job would now be hers. She would try to get them across Greece: it was not a long journey, as such trips went, and she had been in this part of the world before. They or their relatives had paid for them to be taken to a port and put in touch with one of the ship-owners who handled illegal immigrants. And that would be the end of them so far as she was concerned. It did not matter to her that it would probably be the end of them so far as they were concerned, too: it was likely enough that in Salonika they would not find a ship to take them on safely to the various places where they hoped to settle — because they had friends, or because, not knowing where else to go, they had simply picked out a name on the map. They were not Jews; no powerfully backed organizations were on their side. They were likely to be sent back, eventually, to Poland or Rumania or wherever they came from, and would die of exposure or starvation or sheer unwillingness to live, on the way. Many hundreds had died like that, as Hebe knew. That would be their affair. Fishermen rarely pity fish, or shepherds the sheep that go to market, even if at heart they are kindly people. Hebe's father had made his living too long out of such people's need of sanctuary or of moving on aimlessly, if they could not find sanctuary, for the fate of travellers without passports to trouble his child. With luck she would be far away, living in that beautifully ordered monotony of routine of which she had read, among girls who wore gym-dresses, and admired the games-mistress, believing that the only thing which really mattered was getting into the hockey eleven — the most surprising books fetched up in remote tropical ports. That life would not seem dull to her. Later, if their ways crossed again, as she intended, she would marry André, the only person she had known who shared that flame in the heart, a driving desire for the world's quiet favour. Then they would settle down decorously in France, and perhaps run a café, in some small town. That too could not seem dull to her: not after the childhood, or the lack of it, which she had known with the man lying dead in the clearing on the hillside. The wildest dreams are not dreamed in wild places but in suburban domesticity. Theirs — hers and André's — were the longings of all unwilling adventurers, for a time when nothing happened, except the expected.

'Dead! Ai, ai, ai!' Lisabet, the peasant woman from Transylvania, who had lost her husband in Hungary and her child on the journey south, rocked backwards and forwards, but her voice was toneless as she accepted another misfortune. She paid it the tribute of outcry, that was all.

The two younger men, townsmen from France and Rumania, newer to the life of international exiles, clamoured to know what the shooting had meant. Nothing — anything, Hebe told them. They were ex-Resistance fighters, under suspicion in their own countries for various reasons: a remnant of vanity made them believe that any firing must be connected with them: someone was looking for them. But it was nothing to do with them, Hebe insisted. On this Greek-Bulgarian frontier there was always shooting.

Probably the affray had been no more than a clash between border police from one side and guerilla troops from the other, the Greeks having crossed the frontier on a marauding expedition. The child's father had died by accident, killed by the habit of stealthiness, and fear. A figure, moving with suspicious care, had been sighted by armed men on the watch for other stealthy passersby. They had fired, and drawn fire in return, and the running fight had ended far from the clearing. Those responsible were unaware, as yet, that a man lay dead there.

'We needn't have scattered the fire then,' one of the younger men said to the other, who had started the job. They went down on their knees, trying to revive the embers. It grew very cold here at night, at this time of the year. They could stay where they were until just before first light; but then they must cross into Macedonia as soon as possible: when the body was found it would draw attention to the existence of the handful of illegal travellers.

'I'm sorry, my dear. My dear!' The oldest of the party, the man whom they called the Professor, put his hand on her arm. He was from Poland, and had the face of a wizened monkey. She hunched her shoulders: there was so much to be sorry for.

They shared with her the last of the food they had, hearing without comment her statement that she knew the safe ways over the frontier and remembered, from the former trip, the route through the Macedonian hills. After she had finished the stale bread and goat's milk cheese, for which she was desperately hungry, she began to cry a little.

The Professor quoted to her, '. . . and when they had eaten they grieved for their companions,' from Homer; and listening to his soft, broken voice talking in English, which only the two of them now spoke in the party, explaining to her how natural it was to feel little emotion until bodily needs were satisfied, she found after a while that the tears had stopped. He had other, more recent illustrations of this principle to give, from the concentration camps of eastern Europe: it was after the morning soup, he said, when you felt life coming back into a half-frozen body, that you minded most about the man who had been dragged out of your cell in the night. This was in Russian camps, in winter. He had been in various prisons from before the beginning of the second World War, until a few months ago. First as a left-wing Polish intellectual, he told her, in the concentration camps of his own country. . . .

His voice died away; the child did not seem to be attending. The two younger men, Jean-Paul and Mihael, were speaking softly and haltingly together, in a tongue which sounded almost as unfamiliar to them as to him, while they blew and blew at the re-made pile of wood ash. The one who knew it best, Mihael, repeated a sentence several times in an effort to make himself understood. French was the common language of the party, though all of them spoke it badly, even the one they called the Frenchman, Jean-Paul: he was only the most French, of mixed blood like the rest: Alsatian-Czech, while the others were Rumanian-Croat, Hungarian-German, Polish-Lithuanian, and in Hebe's case, Dutch-English-French.

'Go on talking,' she said in English to the Professor. 'But slowly, so I can listen through what you say.'

In a Polish prison you were apt to be tortured, he said, and paused, in order that she might take in what Mihael was repeating. Then when the Germans invaded that part of Poland, he went on, he was shifted to a German concentration camp. There was not much difference, he said, and paused again.

'The Russians liberated the district towards the end of the war. I thought I would be free, then. I had lived on that hope for five years. But they took me into Russia, and put me back into a concentration camp.'

He looked at her inquiringly as a small flame shot up from the rekindled fire, illuminating their faces. She nodded, satisfied that she had heard enough, and he went on talking. In the Russian camps you were not likely to be tortured, unless you happened to be of political importance, and obstinate — then God help you, he said. But he was lucky; he was unimportant. Just a schoolmaster who wrote books, not a professor at all, really. You suffered desperate hardship, from hunger and cold — but then you knew all the time that outside the walls there, men suffered desperately from hunger and cold too. And if your companions died like flies, others did as well, though they had done no wrong, such as being born to the wrong people or in the wrong place. They had not even the wrong ideas: but they died, with the same suffering. So in a way it was not so bad, being 'inside' in Russia, the sad, un-impassioned voice explained to her, to distract her from her own sorrow. He did not add, lest she should begin to cry again, that in the hands of the people from whom he had expected liberation, all desire to live had died in him because of hope betrayed: in other ways, therefore, torture or no torture, it was worse.

But he need not have refrained, she would not have cried. The fate of only two people, herself being one, could really move her now; and the other was far away — safe through action of hers, she could believe. Still, she liked the Professor better than the others. It occurred to her, with something like satisfaction, that as one of the results of this afternoon's shooting the people with whom she travelled would be more likely to come to their journey's end, in the Lebanon or Egypt or Transjordania. If her father had lived, at some stage of the trip he would almost certainly have let them fall into hostile hands.

'They think, those two, it would be safer to leave us! Tomorrow, if they get the maps,' she said. 'The maps my father carried, and the names of contacts in Salonika. They could move faster, they say.'

Jean-Paul and Mihael sat silent, watching the fire burn up anew.

'Why did they put you back into the last lot of prisons?' she asked the Professor presently. 'You were on their side really, weren't you?'

The monkey face grimaced, lit by the growing flames — it was dark now, under the trees. But the voice was as detached as ever: 'It wasn't just myself. There were quite a lot of us, awkward people. I think they felt we had been in concentration camps so long, it was better we should stay there. Men get unaccustomed to freedom. Maybe they were a little right in thinking we were not likely to make good use of it, having been so long without.' He looked across at the two younger men. They had not been in prison, but for the most important years of their early manhood they had been under the rigid discipline of intrigue and deception in the Resistance movements: they had known little freedom of thought or action. 'Maybe, I don't know.'

The younger of the two, the Rumanian Mihael, came across to Hebe.

'Your father had maps on him.'

She lied quickly, having made up her mind what she would do. 'Not of this part. Not of the Struma valley. Only of the roads into Salonika. Just the last bit of the way.'

'Where are they?'

'What?'

'The maps he did have. And the list of people to go to in Salonika.'

'I took them off him. It's all right.'

'Where are they?' he repeated, thinking she had not understood his heavily accented French.

'If I remembered to take them, isn't that enough? Since I'm the only one who has been this way before. And I know the way across the frontier.' She had not travelled exactly this route with the previous party, which had made its way into Greece further to the east; she knew only the general direction of the great Struma valley — the stream nearby was a tributary of the main river — and through her father's description, certain places on the frontier where he had hoped that they might cross unobserved. If only, she thought, she had remembered to take his papers off the dead man!

Mihael hesitated, uncertain whether she was pretending or not. But in any case she alone knew where the body lay on the hillside: he might search all through the moonlit hours of the night without finding it, and by dawn, with patrols about, they must be on their way. The war over the border in Greece was at that time still a war with boundaries: the Macedonian frontier had not yet ceased to exist, as a frontier, though armed bands were crossing it, more and more often — the party must reckon with the probability of heavy patrolling for a considerable area on both sides. Mihael walked back to the fire, now burning merrily, banking it up with earth so that the glow should not show through the trees. It would burn till morning: at intervals, when the autumn cold crept into the shelters, they could crawl out to its comfort and thaw a little.

'What were they talking just now, when you listened?' the Professor asked.

'Dutch.'

'You have quite a lot of languages, Hebe!' he said, with the air of paying a kind compliment to a child. She was sitting upright, with her arms tense about her knees, staring ahead of her, nerving herself for further effort.

'No, no,' she said angrily. 'A few words of this, a few words of that. Picked up in the country because we just passed through it, he and I.' She jerked her head backwards towards the open ground, where the still man, so unlike the father she remembered, stared calmly at the sky, waiting for her return by moonlight to fetch the papers left in his pockets. The list of contacts in the port was unimportant, save as a weapon in her head, to make the others remain with her. Compiled to impress, it was out of date anyway: probably half the people on it were in prison or dead already, because of the civil war; at any rate they had almost certainly gone from Salonika. But the maps she must have: they covered, in fact, all the northern territories; one, a rough sketch-map made by her father, showed the places on the frontier which were thought to be least guarded. She must study those maps, memorize them and destroy them, so that the others could not take them from her. Fear sharpened her voice: 'That's not "having languages",' she said. 'I would like to learn French, though. Learn it properly. Not the way we talk it.' She meant, not to speak it of necessity, but to get by heart long strings of verbs, and grammar without human context, as children older than herself had done, grumblingly, in the early life of security enshrined in her memory. Suitably brought-up children did not understand many foreign tongues, they worked at one, reluctantly, without mastering its use. The Professor had no understanding of her resentment.

'So? So!' he said soothingly.

'My mother used to say, when I lived with her, that people who know a lot of languages never talk any as if that language belonged to them. *He* had a lot of languages — bits of them.'

When the dead are newly dead, especially if they are your own and die in your presence, they have little of the terrible, remote quality which comes later. But once you have left them, they become really dead, and then to come back to them, alone and at night — flesh and spirit alike shrank from the idea. Yet if she did not at least appear to know the way, better than anyone else, the others would leave her; probably not the Professor, she thought, but Jean-Paul and Mihael, and possibly the complaining peasant woman Lisabet. They were talking again now, all three of them; with Lisabet shaking her head dismally while the men argued. Judging by their fluency they were using French: it did not matter then, what they were saying, and she would not trouble to listen.

'They musn't leave us here,' she said to the Professor in English. 'Mihael speaks Greek well enough to get by. No one else does. He worked with the Partisans round Athens for a bit, after things got troublesome for him in Rumania and Italy. We must keep him; keep them both.' She had other reasons for wanting to know what happened to Jean-Paul and where he eventually settled.

Catching his name, Mihael looked across the fire at them questioningly. She made a gesture towards the lean-to he shared with the Professor, as though she spoke of camp matters. 'It doesn't matter if he leaves us when we are well into Greece. It's in this next part that nobody'll help us if they think we've come across the border, and there isn't a Greek in the party. We must keep him to get through.'

'Does it matter so much, getting through?' he asked,

She did not think it worth while to reply: the Professor was old, older than her father had been. At least forty. He did not care enough about living to endure more than he need for it. Unlike the rest of them, so desperate to live — anywhere, anyhow — that none of them cared what was abandoned in the effort, he came with the party only because it was easier to move than to starve in one place. He might, she felt, decide at any time that it was less trouble to starve. She would not ask him to do this thing for her, or even to come with her on the unspeakable errand. This was a world where you did not ask favours if you were weak: it emphasized too dangerously how weak you were. But she was going on — going back, rather, to the Good Place, first of all, and then going on.

She crept into the shelter which she had shared with her father, to wait there until the others slept. For an hour or two she herself slept until awakened by the moon shining full on to her face near the entrance, through a gap in the boughs above; she had carefully arranged herself so that the light should reach her, after a last-minute bargain with panic that if it failed to wake her — if the moon went behind clouds, by chance — she would let things take their course, and not go back to the man on the hillside.

But when she opened her eyes she moved at once, without hesitation, pulling on a thick Italian army shirt which her father had somehow acquired, over her other layers of clothes, and emerging to stand with determination for a moment, getting her bearings in the wood, noticing the direction of the wind in the tree-tops, not here, near the ground, where it would not be true, before she began to retrace her way along the path by which she had returned after the shooting. She was very capable; her body rather younger than her years, her mind of varying ages, but usually much older, and for the moment almost wholly adult.

The wind, snow-laden, sweeping down the valley, rustled the trees so that the sound covered that of her going. Against it, the noise of the stream came more and more faintly to her ears, as she climbed out of the closely timbered valley into the sparser wood of the hillside. Water flowing — surf on the Palisades at Kingston in Jamaica — André, whom she had known there, over a year ago, with whom she shared something which she shared with no one else . . . She must keep her thoughts steadily, if she could, on a remote object. Here was something satisfactory from the past, a memory which stretched forward, too, into the future; as a thin, improbable promise, perhaps, but at least an idea reaching beyond this moment: there was a long way to go through the speckled dark of the trees.

She could not have said why it was that André, after less than a month of not very close association, remained in her mind as the person because of whom she must bear whatever came to her, in order that eventually they should come again — together or alone, but together for choice — into the world of good standing and neighbours' respect, from which they were both exiles. It was a bond of shared interest, not affection. She had no illusions about him as a particularly kind or particularly attractive young man: he had taken no care whatever to protect her from the consequences, had there been any, of the action she had taken on his behalf, to save him from joining in one of her father's ill-starred projects. Fortunately, no one discovered that it was she who had warned him. But the bond, because she now had no other, was very strong.

A pigeon terrified her, bursting out of a tree beside her, with what seemed a deafening clap of wings. She stopped, panic stricken, on the edge of the open ground, and then went on, telling herself that it would be better when she could see the whole sky, not just the moon at intervals, and the shadows it threw. But immediately she emerged from the wood, although the body was still about half a mile away, she was in the presence of the dead.

Why had she forgotten the maps when he died? — No, André ... she would think only of what she had done for him. A strange action it seemed to her now. And in the company of the living André — for she was sure he was all right somewhere — she could face the dead.

He had been nineteen when she was twelve, and had taken no particular notice of her for the first few days in which, with her father, they had shared a table at a seaman's eating house in Kingston. It was to her father that he had wanted to talk, a man accompanied by a very ordinary looking little girl; apparently, people from the world out of which André himself had just fallen. Father and daughter stood out as an unusual couple in the sailors' dive, where more than half the customers were coloured, and seeing them together brought back to him that atmosphere of the family café at Lille, for which he was desperately homesick.

Shaken by the magnitude of his recent trouble, André had poured out his story to them. A deck-hand off a French cargo boat, he had been implicated in a dockside robbery at Port au Prince, though only to the extent of helping a friend, a member of the crew with whom he had gone ashore, to shift a few crates on behalf of yet another member of the crew. This was the man who had actually carried out the robbery: what André did not know at the time was that he had also killed a night watchman while getting away. Both the men who had planned the robbery had well-planted alibis, in bars and brothels throughout the town: André had none. Not caring for the social amenities of Port au Prince, he had been alone all that evening, save for the short period when he had been induced to bear a hand, in loading a small boat with loot. But it was not until he found that the killing was being planted on him that he had realized the seriousness of his position. Then he had slipped out of Haiti by native ketch. For some years at least, he would not dare to go back to his own country, where the police would be told to look out for him. It would all blow over in time; but meanwhile, how homesick he was, how pleased to find people reminiscent of the clientele of his parents' café in Lille. In looks, anyway.

Hebe's father had suggested that he should join their South American venture, running immigrants into Brazil. As outlined, it appeared to be an excellent scheme, even for the immigrants. Hebe had wondered at the time if the stranger would notice one thing about the official prospectus her father showed him, dealing with the settlement of homeless European farmers in clearings of the Brazilian forests — it had been written before the second World War. A convincing description was given of their opportunities in virgin soil, among untapped natural resources and vast potential markets; such settlements had been Government-sponsored in the period when the first Nazi persecutions in Germany had led various South American states into short-lived efforts to find room for unwanted people. Even then there had been a strict quota. But why, it could be argued by people like her father, should these great advantages not be shared a little more widely, by men with enterprise? There was naturally nothing in the prospectus to show that the settlement plan had been from the beginning a grim and costly failure; it had been officially abandoned for years. No more such immigrants were being admitted.

André had not noticed the slight internal evidence of the date of the prospectus: it was in German which he could only just read, and most of the German-speaking refugees on whom it was used, displaced persons or political suspects, did not notice this either. Hebe's father had brought a boat-load of them as far as Kingston, in an overcrowded, ill-found ship, without too much difficulty; but he wanted his crew increased for the last part of the journey. These people always made most trouble towards the end of the trip, whether conditions warranted it or not — and even though they did not know what was waiting for them.

André had agreed to work his passage, and land with the rest. To be on the safe side, he ought to put in as much as seven or eight years somewhere on the borders of lawlessness: it was easy to persuade him that they might as well be spent in farming, in a community which asked no questions about the past. But inevitably there were five days of refuelling and inadequate replenishing of stores before the expedition could move on, and while they lay low in the native slums of Kingston, he talked to Hebe of his ambition to run a café himself in some small provincial town of France: it would be called *Le Bien-Venu*. He talked so much of it that at the last moment Hebe had advised him not to come with them. Knowing what she lost by doing this — the companionship of the person with whom she had common ground — she had made him realize the fate ahead of the human cargo in the ship her father had chartered. By stealth and heroic endeavour some of these illegal immigrants would succeed in joining those who had been settled on the land when the first clearings were made, hopeless groups of sick men, already dwindling in the pest-ridden depths of the forest. It could not be kept out by their small-scale European methods of tree-felling and agriculture. All that the prospectus said about the richness of the soil was only too true, and soon this would be slightly increased by many more of their bodies.

(The scrub-covered top of the next ridge stood out blackly against the moonlit sky. Just beyond it was the barer patch of ground where her father waited. . . .)

André had scarcely thanked her for her warning, being too much incensed against the man who had nearly inveigled him into disaster. When or if they met again, he might not recognize her, she reflected, but they moved steadfastly towards the same goal, and for the moment that was enough, since it had to be. One day, though, through her present action, they would walk upright about the earth, instead of cringing or running or hiding. They, or she — no, for this night at least it must be 'they' in her mind. They would go in by front doors, everywhere, not round by the back, choosing the unnoticed moment. This entering by front doors had become an important feature of the Good Place, in her early memories of sheltered days. It was almost as desirable as having a passport with which to cross frontiers, while people were watching — a possession to be valued from pride, more than for use: it was not likely that once in possession of the café, she or André would wish to travel again. Theirs would be a life full to the brim of nodding to neighbours and giving well-considered views on local events: and of esteem; immense esteem in their own small circle. Possibly she would add to it a little lustre of her own, too, having been, by then, to the good school in England.

Jean-Paul, in her party of international trespassers, was André's cousin: the contact had been made through a recommendation given while André and her father were still planning the trip together. Eventually, because the conception of the family and all it stood for counted so much with André, he would get in touch with all his near relatives. He would never dare return actually to his home town: it would be no use looking for him in Lille; nor, of course in the West Indies: but somehow Jean-Paul would know where he could be found. She had lost touch with André; she must not, if she could help it, lose touch with Jean-Paul: he could not be allowed to desert her.

Now she could hear movement, she thought, not only the passing of the wind over the scrub. In her terror, which grew and grew, even when it felt as though it could increase no further this side of flight, it seemed to come from a little distance beyond the ridge: but she knew that it might be only her own blood beating as she stopped to listen.

In a moment she realized that it was a mistake to have stopped. Going on became much harder afterwards, though she had not believed that it could be. But the wind helped her here — it was so cold, that from sheer animal discomfort she found it impossible to stand still for long in the full force of it, near the top of the ridge; she moved forward, up and over the ridge, into sight of the dead.

Something on four legs ran from the body as she approached: probably one of the half-starved dogs which roamed ownerless about these hills. They stayed in the neighbourhood of the miserable farms which had been their homes before these were looted by bandits. There was supposed to be wild pig, too, in the Struma forests, descended from livestock which had escaped in raids, and she had seen plenty of foxes even by day; but only the dogs were dangerous. They were especially so, of course, when there were several of them together. She waited with stones in her hands, a few yards from the darker patch on the ground, at which she would not look fully; but the creature did not come back. There appeared to have been only one, and it could not have been in the clearing long; from what she could take in by the corners of her eyes, the body had not been disturbed. Beyond help now from any thought in the world, wondering at her feet for obeying her, she moved through the last few steps, still avoiding her father's face with her eyes as she knelt down to feel for the maps. With her hands numb and clumsy, it took her some time to find that his papers were not in the pocket where she had expected to find them, and almost accidently, as she moved round him to get to the coat-pocket on the other side, her gaze came near enough to his eyes for her to notice again the alien air of unconcern. She could look at him then. His expression — his whole attitude — was almost confident, at last; and after that she was not desperately afraid of him and of the night any more, but only longed to have done with this errand and to get away.

2

THE HOLLOW

IT was over, and it had not been quite as dreadful as she had expected. The realization that few events measure up to the fears or the hopes felt of them beforehand struck her on the way back to the encampment, as the ridge rose like a barrier between her and the man who no longer had reason to be afraid of anything. That, she thought, was something to be added to your armour — the poor, thin armour of understanding: all you had.

She and the Professor had discussed, a few days before, the importance of making discoveries which added to that poor, thin armour — this had been his description of understanding, and she had liked it. He seemed to think that for her there were even some advantages to be found in their present way of life. She did not suppose he meant that these outweighed the disadvantages, or came anywhere near to balancing them; but still, he thought they existed. Certainly you made discoveries in understanding, like this one about events being smaller than their shadows, quicker than you would be likely to do in the Good Place; or even in a somewhat better place — Well, you had to: and this one was valuable because fears, not hopes, were the usual shadows thrown by happenings in her world of today. But then the Professor had confused the issue for her by going on to talk about nightingales and their eggs: speaking as he occasionally did, harking back to the days of his real freedom, as though she were one of his pupils and could be expected to follow his thoughts: something about knowledge which

> . . . lay hidden,
> As the music of the moon
> Sleeps in the plain eggs of the nightingale.

She was misled by remembering that there were nightingales in their thousands in these Balkan hills; they had made the shining nights loud with their song on her last journey, in spring; and vaguely she had imagined that he must be referring to these actual birds.

The nightingales were silent now: both they and owls abounded, but in sound it was the season of the owls only: they were hooting everywhere in the woods on three sides of her. She carried her father's maps and torch and the few other crumpled papers which had been in his pockets, three quarters of a mile or so back along the goat-track to where the scrub-oak began. Here, a little way off the trail, there was a hollow full of leaves and moss. When she came this way after her father's death she had noticed it, with a brief reversion to childhood, as a spot that would have been nice for playing 'house' in the old days. She scrambled in and crouched down: it was sheltered, and relatively warm; out of the wind, at any rate. The last of the moonlight, streaming down through the scrub, filled about a quarter of it with a milky brilliance.

Disliking them, because they were wanderers' lure, Hebe had all the same an excellent memory for maps. So few drawn or written things had yet made any demands on her power of learning by heart that she could repeat to herself whole pages of *The Omnibus Book for Girls* and *Stalky and Co.*, word-perfect but not always sure of the meaning: tattered copies of these two books had been in the lodging house at Kingston. The contours of the frontier, the roads and rivers across the plains of Thessaly and the lists of names not likely to be of any help — all these would join them in her head before she lost the bluish-white ray of light which crept faster and faster up the overhanging bank of the hollow as the moon sank: hardly aware of shifting her cramped position, she moved up after it at intervals. The torch battery was weak, almost run down, it reinforced the moonlight, no more, but flicked on for only a few seconds at a time, so that the beam seemed brighter after a rest, it served to let her read a name, or trace the thin line of a track. (There were few roads through the Macedonian hills ahead.) When the moonlight had gone it would be useless alone.

Tired as she was, kept going solely by the urgency of the night's business, she would remember not only the shape of the ground to be covered, but what that shape might mean, in woods and human habitations, or in bandit areas where the approaches were naturally guarded by water or steep mountain faces. The Struma valley, and all its neighbourhood, had been fought over with little respite for far longer than anyone living could remember. Great wars in the outside world made little difference to the local activities of raid and feud and counter raid, except that now, more than a year after the end of the second World War, the presence of the Russians in Jugoslavia and Bulgaria, and the British and American military missions in Greece, ensured the bandits a better supply of arms, stolen or issued, and new political names under which to carry out age-old oppressions. In or near the towns, men might bear arms for strictly contemporary ideas; hereabouts they did merely what their fathers had done before them, and for the same reason — that a man with a gun in his hand could get food and shelter with less monotonous hardship than one who relied on the ground to grow it for him. Most men handled both a gun and a plough in this region, but at different seasons. Hebe marked in her mind places which were likely to be centres of bandit activity, because of their inaccessibility from the roads, and also the detours which would take the party clear of them — they should need her, those two men in the encampment, while she needed them.

When she was satisfied with what she had memorized, she tore up the list and the maps: an owl hooted mockingly near by, making her pause to look up and shiver again, before she buried the pieces in the moss.

She looked through her father's other papers, while the last inches of the moon-bar narrowed on the bank. Papers were all he had: the expedition had run out of money some days before; ill luck had followed it from the start. Suddenly her present surroundings faded away; the owls hooted unheard. From an envelope containing also an old and probably fraudulent customs receipt, dated in Colombo, she pulled out a snapshot of the house on the west coast of England where she had lived for the three most important years of her life, the longest time she had ever stayed in any one place.

It was a small, snug villa, where much care was expended daily in concealing from three fat dogs, by insincere abuse, that they were really the centre of the household — Hebe remembered her father irritably summing up the atmosphere of the house in some such way just before he left for South America for the first time. Of Dutch origin himself, he was not inclined to look kindly on the extreme zeal with which his wife's family, half-French, had taken on colour from the English seaside community in which they lived. The house belonged to her parents, and they resented him about equally for being wholly a foreigner, and a failure. But it was the one home where his child had known security. This was 'the Good Place'.

All Hebe's most satisfying recollections were punctuated by relations shouting to other relations in that house to look out for Boxer, the curly-coated black retriever who lay for choice at the bottom of the stairs, in a poor light, on a curly black rug exactly like a retriever's coat. It would have been easy to break a leg on him — much easier than to get agreement in this family to the moving of the rug or the dog.

This was stability. Here she had been a rightful enterer by the front door, even if only on sufferance — she had known very early, in the way children sense such things, that her mother's people looked down on her father, and were glad when he left. And here she had been Laura, not Hebe, which was only a nickname acquired casually, not very long ago. It had been given patronizingly, too, which made it distasteful, by the officers of a ship in Colombo harbour, when she waited on them and washed dishes for a week, in their rowdy club ashore: 'Our Hebe' was a joke, because she looked so childish to be working in the kitchen regions of a house with a number of peculiar activities. And it had stuck because her father took it up at once. She had noticed that he caught gladly at anything which separated him still more from the life to which that house belonged; the house whose snapshot had faded and creased in the years in which he had carried it about, till now the details would have been difficult to make out, in the diminishing Bulgarian moonlight, for anyone who remembered them all less clearly. So Laura had become Hebe: but why had her father kept with him all these years the picture of a place where surely he had known nothing but heartbreak? Perhaps the most interesting discoveries were those you could never make — certainly this was something that now, no one could ever know, she thought, coming back fully for the moment to the hollow and the owls and the presence of the thing in the clearing, over the ridge. Had the four-footed creature which was probably a dog returned yet, alone or with others? By this time the unconcerned eyes might no longer be staring up into the sky . . . It was drawing towards dawn: she must get back to the encampment soon. But for a moment more she could not move.

Associations flooded into her mind again, mingling with the immediacies of the night, lightening them so that they became a little more bearable: it was cold and she was alone, and at the same time, Boxer lay companionably but less dangerously invisible than usual against the bottom stair — because for once it was possible to see his pink open mouth against the blackness of himself and the rug, as he panted in August heat. Nobody needed to shout. Memories came in no sensible order, but were the echoes of events and days, often long forgotten, which had become jumbled together. In some way, André was connected with the house in her mind, though he had never seen it; but her efforts to describe to him the funny porch, which she could just make out by lifting the photograph higher, into the last light, and using the torch, had opened the way for his own childhood memories of Lille — there had been a still funnier gable, it seemed, above his parents' café.

She had gone to live in the house of the photograph when she was five, and had left it when she was eight. Where she had lived before, or where she had been born, she had no means of knowing: there were dim recollections of many flittings. It was just before her ninth birthday, she remembered, that she had been taken to South America. She had lost a bicycle as a present by going. Against

much family advice, given in the snug villa, her mother had decided
to sample life again with her husband, in Brazil this time, taking the
child with her. To sample life was all that Hebe's mother ever did
with it. A dark, impatient, handsome woman, hungry for anything
new — so Hebe recalled her across the distance of years. Her image
brought none of the sense of regret and longing which the picture
of the house aroused. She had never seemed so much a part of the
solid foundation of life as the dogs and the stairs and the atmosphere
created by the voices raised against the peril of Boxer. Indeed, such
a reckless creature could have brought no sense of security to anyone. Yet when she finally drifted away, it was as if Hebe's father
felt that his luck had deserted him too; and it was after this that fear
came into Hebe's life: the most shaking kind of fear, for a child; not
her own but the constant foreboding of someone on whom she was
dependent. Her father took her with him on more and more of his
journeys: a man and his little daughter made an unsuspicious-look-
ing couple, to others besides André. The scope of his undertakings
increased, and the hazards of them, too, as the backwash of war
stranded, in many lands, growing numbers of dispossessed people
who would try at any cost to defeat the ever-tightening international
restrictions on their movements: the greater their need to drift, the
more efficient became the regulations to stop them. Of late, Hebe
could recall him most typically in moments of frenzied dread, when
disease broke out in the ship off Brazil, and afterwards, when coast-
guards surprised a landing at night. There had been moments of
slipping control on this trip, too, besides the last, fatal occasion of
over-caution. She would remember, henceforward, that it did not
pay to be afraid. But she could be glad, at least, in the midst of
desolation, that fear was over for the man lying out on the hillside:
in his own way, her father had been kind to her.

Memory had come full-circle. The light had lifted above the edge
of the hollow, with the moon nearly set. Hebe stood up, dropping
the now useless torch, for which there were no refills. Turning her
back to the bitter wind which was still blowing, she tore up the
snapshot, making a little hole for the pieces under the lip of the

bank before she climbed out. The remains of that photograph should not lie with the remains of the maps, part of this life of crouching and hunger. But she did not want to keep with her something so weakening with longing as the picture of the house. It would not help her on her chosen path, the long road back to the kind of security that her people had thrown away.

3

THE FRONTIER

THE others were stirring, but no one asked where she had been when she came back to the shelters and squatted down beside the fire, grateful for the warmth on her outstretched hands and suddenly too tired to care that there was no more food to be shared.

The Transylvanian, Lisabet, who was always worrying about omens, was just returning to the encampment, too, after a moment's absence, settling her heavy skirts about her and complaining that a hare had crossed her path, running from left to right; and the younger men were intent on an argument that broke out in one form or another every morning, while they waited for the Professor to dispose among his clothes the useless personal oddments he insisted on carrying. He clung with equal stubbornness to mending material for shoes past repair, a shaving mug and mirror, though none of them now shaved, eating utensils, a half-empty pot of some medicament, a pipe for which he had acquired no tobacco throughout the trip, and a packet of letters of introduction to people who would not be pleased to see him, in lands he was unlikely to reach.

Every morning he kept the others waiting while he loaded himself ingeniously, having no pack and no pockets which had kept their linings; and during the day, if they came by more food than they needed to eat at once, he protested against carrying a fair share with the rest, because he was already burdened. Nothing could convince him that he was not entitled to special consideration in this way: yet as an unassuming man he often protested against being called professor, to which he was not entitled either. To him it was a term of the greatest possible honour: and nothing could convince him either, that to anyone else it might be a term of contempt.

No one in the party besides himself owned more than they wore when the weather was cold; they were ready to move without delay at any moment. Before each start, in their irritation at the slowness and care with which he fitted the pipe into the handle of the tin mug, tying them and the letters to his belt with the shoemaker's thread, the younger men fell to bickering about their days of glory.

'Your leader in the Marseille sector in '44 — the one who was responsible for shipping arms to us in Italy — '

'The Bear. What of him?'

'He had no guts,' Mihael said emphatically. In the Resistance *patois* they used, a kind of international slang, the term was not 'guts'. One day, thought Hebe, reaffirming hope — one gym day, wearing a school badge on her tunic, like the dumpling-girls in the illustrations to the book she had memorized in Jamaica — she might find difficulty in forgetting much of what she now knew: words and their meanings, sights and sounds and implications which could not be admitted to the Good Place. But she would manage. Women, her father had told her sourly, after her mother had left them, were clever at forgetting things at will. She would be exceptionally good, with any luck. Luck — it was all luck, the road she would travel, but people made at least half their own luck.

'The Bear? He had guts! And how!' said Jean-Paul. 'I, who worked with him, I tell you he had them. You never met him.'

'No, but our lot had dealings with him. We sent him men, when our own district grew too hot for them — and he let two of them be caught. He had no guts.'

'He let two be caught — why? Because no doubt he had to choose between getting them away to safety and getting away a party of five or more. Those were the times when we all made decisions like that . . .' Now that nobility had deserted their ways, they re-lived constantly the period in the war when all the courage and devotion of which they were capable had been bent up to one end, and a brief significance given to their lives by the belief that any sacrifice was worth while. At first it had seemed a bond between them that one had worked with the Italian and Greek and the other with the French underground movements: recently it had meant nothing but disputes. They were no longer men of full stature and they boasted of their old prowess, real enough at one time, and that of their friends, their sectors and anyone with whom they had been associated in their pride.

'Of course he preferred to save his own men. Ours could not give away his network when they were captured!'

'I will tell you what he did, that man! To get the information he wanted, he slept with the sister of the Gestapo chief in Marseille. Yes, and got her into trouble.'

'What with?' The Rumanian laughed at his own unusual wit: he was a slow, simple man.

'I say he had them! In his time we passed prisoners along the escape route under the nose of the enemy. Under his very nose.'

'Oh, as to that, once we took our own men in a German police truck — yes, with the official driver! — through Athens, during the occupation. Partisans! He thought they were Albanian forced-workers for the cement factory at Eleusis.'

'You have been to Eleusis, Mihael?' the Professor broke in. He was almost ready at last.

'For two months I worked within five miles of it — while the Germans were in Athens!'

'Then you saw the site of the ancient Mysteries?'

'We did not go sight-seeing at that time! We had other things to do. No, I did not go to Eleusis just because I was working five miles away. We passed wanted men. Flyers. Patriots. Anyone on our side who needed to get away. And we worked close! Till of the lot with me, hardly anyone else was left. Yet look at me now. Greece, for whose liberty, I a Rumanian, fought — Greece of today would not even give me the right to pass through, if I asked!'

'You did not work as close as the Bear! Right under the nose —'

'We worked close!'

'You were heroes! Men of the Resistance! Partisans.' Lisabet spoke with sudden, heavy anger. 'How fine to say, "These shall live, these shall die." You liked to pass prisoners out of the country under the nose of those who would kill them if you failed. It was more fun, working close. You were bigger heroes. Smoke a cigarette with the enemy police at the road-block. Say, "Why not look in my hay-waggon — maybe it's full of spies!" When it was full of something else — not spies — just escaping men who did not want to risk their lives. My man was not so very brave. He hoped to live, for himself and me and our child. When he escaped from a prison camp a boy of seventeen took him half way to safety. One of your sort. Working close. Shooting when he got the chance, not when he had to. Being a man. Just like your Bear. They were both killed.'

There was a long silence, and then the Professor said, 'I think I would not have been as capable as either Mihael or Jean-Paul in the Resistance. I should not have wanted to work close. Or use the Gestapo van. But I am sure I would have seen Eleusis.'

Hebe rose from the fire. The old man had all his gear slung about him at last: they would go now, putting — if they could — a frontier between themselves and the body on the hillside before full day had broken and there was any chance of its being discovered. Not that one shot man the more on the Bulgarian-Greek border was likely to cause much interest at that particular time, with civil war flaring up in Greece and guerilla activities on all her frontiers taking on international importance. But their demands on life had grown humble: they asked no more than to pass unnoticed. It occurred to no one even to discuss stopping to bury him: they must get on, and somehow acquire food.

For the first moment, as they started downhill under her direction, a feeling of breaking ties rose chokingly in Hebe. This was the real parting with the only person in her world who bridged the gap between these and better days. One end of her memories of her father rested upon security. In the dimness, unseen brambles and undergrowth tugged at her feet and legs: it was as if even the things of earth tried to hold her back, as soon as she turned away from the bare little encampment which was the last thing he had made. She stumbled, ripped free from their clutches, and went on.

C

The lie of the ground, seen in the half-light, did not conform at first to her expectations, based on the maps: it ran too steeply towards the river — were they, perhaps, not after all at the bend of the Struma tributary from which her route was planned? Immediate anxiety about the way absorbed all her attention. Soon, however, as the dawn showed it to her through the thinning timber, the path flattened out and took a more reassuring direction, following the map in her mind; the hidden river swept away from them, judging by the fading sound of its waters. She could think again of her father, when weariness allowed; he had become someone safely banished into the past.

The Struma itself, he had said, was not to be followed. It crossed the frontier, but through water-meadows, where they could be easily observed. Further to the east, the frontier lay along the tops of the hills: there was a particular valley running into these hills which he had once described to her; seen from the right spot for the approach, the mountains closing it on the Bulgarian side grouped themselves into the shape of a rabbit's head, with long, erect ears. That resemblance had made it seem safer to Hebe as soon as he spoke of it. If the ears were kept apart while they climbed out of the valley, they would reach the frontier at a place about half way between two important patrol-points, and apt for this reason to be neglected by guards scamping their duties. This valley could not be more than three or four miles ahead.

When she was no longer worried about the way, Hebe walked with Lisabet. Everyone felt warmer towards the Transylvanian after her outburst: it was the first time she had shown any warmth of her own, any evidence that she, like the rest of them, had known a happier state, or indeed any emotion beyond a sturdy peasant preoccupation with keeping alive, no matter how miserably and no matter who died. It made no difference to their fellow-feeling for her that her man must have been fighting on the opposite side from Mihael and Jean-Paul, and it was their comrades who had killed him. But it was not easy to get on with Lisabet. Her feelings were restricted: she had no interest in anyone she could not serve, and was always censorious in small matters. 'Now that's not right. No, no! It's not reasonable at all,' she would say, of some minor aspect of war and the human greed, cruelty or indifference which had set thousands like herself wandering, homeless, over the earth: when in fact, as the Professor suggested, nothing was right and nothing was reasonable which had led up to their condition. But on the larger injustices from which they suffered she never commented at all: it was as though she could not resent great wrongs, she had grown too much accustomed to them. In everything to do with folk-lore she was learned and credulous. Today she pointed out over and over again the unwisdom of going any distance after the hare had warned them.

Not for this reason but for another, Hebe determined that they would not walk far that day, even if they managed to find a farm, or some other means of getting food, quite soon.

Without sleep she could not go on remembering minutely the windings of the great hills. They would look for some kind of human habitation just clear of the frontier patrol area, and there — it was a prospect that seemed relatively blissful, in the empty discomfort of the morning — besides having something to eat she might be able to cut her toe-nails. It seemed odd to her that no adventure story which she had yet managed to read, nor any in the Professor's much wider experience of books, had ever mentioned this constant problem of the real wayfarer. Hand-nails wore down or broke, easily enough; they could be bitten or picked at the worst. But feet were more important, when travellers walked from one country to another, and attending to their nails was far more difficult. She talked quite cheerfully of this to Lisabet, in their faulty, fluent language, full of words from half a dozen tongues.

So many thousands of footsore people there had been, wandering through the world, the Professor had said: from the time of the Crusades, and even before that, down to the present day. Most of them must have longed for just this relief, a moment of safety and leisure, and something sharp, but not too sharp, with which to ease the pressing of toe-nails against shoes. How remarkable that though there had been plenty of people to write of their wanderings, not one of them had ever recorded this desire, so far as he knew. Hebe and he had discussed the subject at length. 'Isn't it strange, Lisabet? He thinks it just as strange as I do. Don't you?'

Lisabet was not responsive: she made vague assenting sounds. When she spoke it was of the problem of food, and the difficulty of getting it. Hebe's father should have made better provision. So much had been promised, and none of the promises had been kept.

There was nothing to be gained from answering this, and reminding Lisabet that running out of money was only one of the party's many misfortunes, like the delays due to bad weather, and the detours made necessary by new police methods. Hebe was unforthcoming, in her turn, but Lisabet persisted —

Why did Hebe suppose — why had her father thought before her, apparently, since he had not turned back when funds gave out — that in these terribly poor, tumble-down farms of the border region, they would find anyone who would give them food for nothing?

That, too, was not worth answering: they had gone on because there was nothing to which they could turn back.

'If there were just you and the old man alone,' said the peasant, speaking with certainty of other peasants, 'then maybe they would give you something. A little oil and bread. Because you are young and old. But why should they feed five? When three of us are neither young nor old. *I* would not.'

'They're said to be like that, the Greeks of Macedonia. They give easily.'

'Who says that?'

'I don't know,' Hebe told her weakly. 'But I am sure I have heard it said.'

'They are small farmers here. We were small farmers in our country,' said the other, and added, after a while, 'If only we were Jews!'

Times had changed indeed for such groups, struggling towards sanctuary across southern Europe. The Jews, so recently and for so long the most persecuted of the dispossessed, now had the only well-organized escape routes, held open by money from overseas beyond the resources of individuals; and in extremity, a ruthless fanaticism on their side — their belief in the importance of their survival as a race. Such others as these had nothing, not even the idea that they ought to survive, apart from their wish to do so.

'Do you think, Hebe, it would help if we said we were Jews?'

'Here? No. Why should it?' In the childish mind, contemptuous of all refugees, there were yet grades of acceptability. 'Anyway, I will not say that, whatever happens. And there is going to be food.'

Behind them the young men still bickered, but more amiably, because they were moving, not waiting. The path through the trees wound on and on, while the light grew, but still the valley leading to the frontier failed to appear. Again doubt rose in Hebe's mind: was it possible that somehow they had missed it? — 'That was the time when we took on nothing but lost causes! When to fail once was to lose everything. But — we did not fail! I sometimes wonder —' the Rumanian's voice changed, and sounded almost shy — 'if our side could have been *meant* to win?' Mihael had lately become obsessed by the possibility of the existence of God, having had no contact with religious belief in his short and violent youth. The rest, brought up in various forms of faith, remained indifferent to the whole subject.

'For any man, to survive even one lost cause,' said the Professor, 'is enough to poison the rest of his life. Because life always seems at its best when he no longer cares whether he is killed or not — something else matters so much more. Nothing can compare well with that. Afterwards, with safety, comes the smallness of living once more. You two — neither of you will ever do a decent job again, wherever you go. From the age of — what? Eighteen with you, Mihael, and twenty-one with Jean-Paul? — you had power of life and death over other men, and continual excitement. It would be hard now for either of you, wouldn't it, to imagine anything that could appear important enough to do with all your heart? Or anything you could want as you wanted things in those days?'

'Oh, I don't know about that,' Jean-Paul protested mildly. 'I thought, once, if I could see my part of France free of invaders, what more could I ever want? I should never hate anyone again. But it's wonderful how quickly one relearns. Among one's own people. Both to want and to hate — When one sees the types that come to power after a stir-up like that! As soon as it's safe for them. Oh, well, it's always the slim fish that float to the top of the stream when a stick of dynamite goes in! Still, it's enough to sicken a man.'

'When you aren't among them at the top, you mean!' said Mihael. 'Your own people! Who do you call your own people? Weren't you for Resistance and then for collaboration by turns? Isn't that why you're here? Too many people with a grudge against you?' For himself, Mihael had the excuse of the overrunning of his homeland by the Communists, to explain his exile Return there now was obviously unwise for a man whose sympathies were known — in Rumania — to be royalist. In Italy and Greece during the war, he had been no supporter of kings, and had in fact fought for their overthrow, but it would be rash to expect a Soviet-controlled administration to remember this, from one country to another.

'It just depends who survives in greater numbers, your friends or your enemies, whether you are called *maquis* leader or collaborationist at the end of an Occupation.' The Frenchman spoke without rancour: he knew — they all knew — that among the Rumanian's suspected activities were some which were only remotely political, and in these the police were interested. Mihael had never had much regard for money, having always lived hard: for this reason he had never bothered to learn any means of earning it. When hostilities ended, he remained faithful to brisk partisan ways of raising the little he needed.

For recriminations of this kind Jean-Paul would bear no malice, unlike Mihael, who was touchy, and brooded on any wrong that had been done to him. 'My friends were the fighters, you see, Mihael! Because of it, they died while the others lived. Therefore it was said I had turned informer.'

'I did not say you had turned informer.'

'No? Perhaps. But others did. Because — this bit is true, certainly — I had no love for the type who was put over my head to run the network in Marseille when the Bear moved on. The sensible thing would have been to let me run it. Anyway, he was caught by the Gestapo, and he talked. There's one for you that had no guts! Not the Bear, I mean, of course, but this other who succeeded him and was taken. Oh, I know, in their hands it was hard not to talk. Still, he talked. Then others talked — why had he fallen into their hands? So I am here. Wherever that is. Which only Hebe seems to know.'

Here is something I must understand about people, she thought. I will try later, when I am not so tired. Because it is only by knowing why people do things that you can make them give you what you want. She had learned through André that Jean-Paul had been not only a devoted and gallant underground worker, in the middle of the war, when things went ill with the Resistance, but a useful source of intelligence to the Gestapo towards the end, when the tide had turned against his new masters. A queer and, on the whole, good-natured little man, André had said of him: one who merely loved action for its own sake, and tended to take it, entirely by chance it seemed, on the losing side.

It was not surprising to Hebe that courage and self-sacrifice, treachery and malice could inhabit the same carcass, in the way that such human variety remained constantly noteworthy, and deplorable, to Lisabet. Hebe had met them together often enough before, in South America and the West Indies; all her life, in fact, outside the house with the dogs, where in her memory at least, people were comfortably consistent. Simply, she must be able to tell, if possible, when a man was to be moved by one or another of these curious strings attached to his mind — strings that could be twitched, by which he might be dragged to fantastic lengths of kindness or brutality. For her, the value of this knowledge would have none of Jean-Paul's delight in doing or knowing things for their own sake. She was intensely practical, of necessity: this way lay safety.

The Professor said in his mournful voice, 'You make me think, Jean-Paul, of a man I knew, in my home town in Poland. An accountant, he was.'

'Oh, an office-type! Me, I don't work sitting down. What is there worth doing that can be done sitting down? You can't fight or make love sitting down!'

'No, but this was a rare kind of office worker. He seemed to enjoy his job, he smiled to himself so much. Once I asked him why he smiled, but he wouldn't tell me. And when he died, suddenly, it was found that for years he had falsified the accounts of almost all the businesses in Cracow.'

'For his own profit?'

'No, for the pleasure of it.'

'Go on!' said Jean-Paul. 'This is something!'

'To the head of one firm he would say, "This year you have made ten thousand zloties".'

'When he hadn't? When perhaps he had made a loss?' asked Jean-Paul eagerly, and cackled with approval at the Professor's assent.

'Yes, and to another, who had done well, he would say, "Be careful. This has been a bad trading year for you." And a third he would tell that for him, profit and loss came out about even. Which might be somewhere near the truth, for once. Whole balance sheets he worked out in false detail from imagination, to support the results he gave. He was so much respected as an accountant, men never questioned what he said about their businesses. Why should they? He did not make a penny out of what he did beyond his salary as accountant. And there was chaos when he died. I think he smiled right up to the end.'

'I could have liked that man! How I could have liked that man. Well, well, and so I remind you of him,' said Jean-Paul with satisfaction. They walked on, through the hungry dawn, more friendly together as a party than they had ever been in the company of the man left behind, whose fears had worked in them a continual irritation.

To Hebe, the recognition of the valley at last — a mile or more beyond her furthest estimate — came with a sense of aching and almost magical relief. She could manage it. The rabbit's head was unmistakable, seen through half closed eyes.

They stopped at the edge of a dense patch of scrub wood, and looked down into the open valley, with the frontier facing them, unmarked but obvious in its position along the sharp ridge of hills on the other side. It was already too late in the day to cross without finding out, if they could, how closely this area happened to be patrolled. There were men moving in the valley. The smoke from two wretched-looking farms made plumes in the cold clear air, but it was too dangerous to approach them. They settled down, sitting or lying just within the cover of the trees, to wait and watch.

Hebe's eyes — but not, at first, her sleepy mind — followed one of the many small hawks which were hunting in the valley: they seemed to be as common in the open space as the owls in the woods. This one had found a fair-sized snake, probably a harmless grass-snake but a cumbersome thing for the bird to kill. With a great struggle the little hawk had lifted it from the ground and was flying a few hundred yards up while the creature writhed in its talons. Then the hawk dropped the snake on a stony patch of ground below and, turning closely on one wing, swooped down to repeat its attack before the half-stunned prey could wriggle away. Her attention was wholly caught now, and sleepiness forgotten. Twice the bird dropped the snake exactly on the same stones, diving beside it as it fell, and after the third lift the long body swung limp from one claw, while the hawk flew a triumphant circle in the sky, before settling in a near-by tree and beginning to eat. Hebe let her breath go in a long sigh. It had been mercilessly fine in its precision, this act of hunger, and something stirred in her which was not hunger, or was hunger of a different kind and akin to the feeling that had come to her once before, in Jamaica, watching flying-fish in the sunshine, with André forgotten for the moment beside her.

It was the most unexpected feeling, this conviction, strong though passing, that there was more to be desired than to walk about the world without cringing, going in by front doors, even with a chosen companion to savour the satisfaction, too. That first of all, of course. To be respected would remain the dominant passion throughout her life; but at intervals there would come as well the other wild, inconsolable longing, to share in some way the quality which at present resided only in a memory of a shoal of fish and a bird in the air.

After a few moments of observation, in which nothing of interest to him occurred, Jean-Paul concentrated his attention on the farms, hovels with middens in front and a small area of cultivated land behind, enclosed in high walls. Could anyone see if there were chickens roaming about outside, he asked, for if so, risk or no risk, the party should not stay empty much longer. If they could not go up to the doors, it should still be possible to get somewhere near, unseen.

'There'll be no pickings here,' Hebe told him. 'If there had been, better bandits than you would have got them first. Remember this is the bandit region. It always has been. I know it.'

'So you say. But all the same I would like to see the maps, even if they're not maps of this frontier. Where are they?'

Now it had come, the weighted moment.

'Where have you got the maps?' Jean-Paul said again, and ran a hand over her flat little chest and stomach. She could have hidden them here, under the bulky U.N.R.R.A. shirt picked up in Italy.

'I destroyed them last night. And the list of names, too. The Salonika contacts.'

The others stared at her in consternation, except the Professor, who was re-arranging his pack.

'Ai, ai, ai!' Lisabet made the toneless outcry which had greeted the news of the shooting.

'I have told you, I know the way. And the names and addresses. Why should I carry papers? Or give them to you?'

'If you were a little younger,' said Mihael, in helpless rage, 'I would beat you sick for this. And if you were a bit older —'

' — we should know if they were just boasting or not,' said Lisa-

42

bet sharply, 'all those stories of yours of what you can do with women!' In fact, the Rumanian did not boast much of his sexual prowess, beyond telling of the escapes contrived for him by women: or not more than Jean-Paul, who was ugly. But Mihael was so excessively handsome, however unshaven and unwashed, that every Partisan tale of his which mentioned a girl-comrade sounded inevitably like the recounting of a conquest. Lisabet was younger than she looked, under fallen-in fat and dirt. To be unkempt did not become her as it did the man, and he had made no advances towards her. In her view that was neither right nor reasonable, in the circumstances.

He looked at her with bewilderment, jolted out of his anger by hers. Jean-Paul suddenly gave his irresponsible cackle. There was a long pause, in which it was realized that there was, in fact, nothing useful to be done: they could only hope that Hebe was capable of remembering as much as she believed she could. Accepting this, they spoke, finally, of other things, while they waited to see who passed over the frontier, and how they fared.

'I see no sense in what he did, that man the Professor knew,' said Mihael, harking back.

'If it brought him no advantage,' he went on, Jean-Paul having only grunted in reply.

'Supposing it had been for money, or for a woman, then I could understand.' Mihael had a habit of stating something obvious and continuing to affirm it as though his hearers were arguing with him.

'You — from the underground movement — ' the Professor said in his gentle, exhausted voice — 'You should know that people do much queerer things from pride or curiosity, than they will ever do for money or self-interest. Betrayals and so on.' He glanced inquiringly at Jean-Paul, but the Frenchman was too busy to notice: he had begun to stalk two of the active little tortoises which rustled through the dead autumn bracken on the hillside, looking for somewhere to hibernate.

The tortoises were intent on their search, considering and deciding against tussock and hole and bracken-clump, one after the other, and Jean-Paul caught them in an unwary moment, keeping them inside his shirt while he scooped out a small pit with over-hanging edges, borrowing the Professor's mug as a shovel. He transferred them to this prison in order not to have to kill them before he knew whether the little fire he set about building, further back in the wood to hide the smoke, would burn well enough to cook them, despite the dampness of the rotten wood lying about the hillside. He was, as André had suggested, a man not devoid of unreliable feeling: and the party had not quite reached the state of eating the creatures raw.

The fire kindled, but before the dead leaves and twigs with which he nursed it were well alight, one of the tortoises, in trying to escape, fell over on its back, and rocking on its highly curved shell, could not right itself by its own efforts. After a while it lay still, and apparently thought about its predicament, with extremities tucked well inside its shell: suddenly a long wrinkled neck craned out, to let the head study the position, with an expression of distaste so marked on its bony face, seen the wrong way up, that the watchers round the pit began to laugh. Shared laughter, though it was little more than the reaction from anxiety, loosened all their tense nerves: not only the practical results of what Hebe had done were accepted: they felt increased confidence in her for having decided on an act much more ruthless on her own scale than the sort of thing they were apt to do themselves.

At the sound of their laughter the tortoise withdrew its head, as if in injured dignity, to think further. Putting out one exploratory hind leg, it rowed itself half round its prison, levered its weight against the shell of its companion and by co-operative heaving from both of them, turned itself right side up, before looking all round with a small air of self-congratulation.

The clumsy acrobatics of the pair appeared overwhelmingly absurd, in the charged atmosphere of waiting to attempt yet another frontier, until sudden clouds swept across the sun and a flurry of the long-threatened snow came down, setting the party shivering again. Then the tortoises were killed without further delay and —

the fire having caught — baked in their shells. A mouthful apiece, they had a sweet and welcome oiliness which clung to the teeth.

By the time they were finished, the travellers could even joke a little, or almost-joke, with a feeling of grim truth not far off, about the episode of the papers which might have ended so differently if tempers, strained almost to breaking by misfortune, had been strained just a very little further. 'I see it would be no use trying to get maps out of anyone's head by force,' said Lisabet. 'But we could still make you tell us who are the people your father had dealings with in Salonika.'

'No, because I should lie,' Hebe pointed out, still wary of her words, in spite of returning sleepiness. They must not guess how valueless that list would be except as a weapon in her head.

'That's what I realized,' Jean-Paul put in. 'That's why I didn't do it.'

' "Ionides, Lycannos Street" — There *is* a Lycannos Street in Salonika,' said Hebe. 'How do you know if I'm making up the name of a contact or not?'

'What you do know,' she went on after a few seconds, with assumed lightheartedness, 'is that if you go to someone who may be called Ionides, and may live in that street, and ask him to ship you illegally, and he isn't in the business, first thing he'll do for his own sake is to tell the police. Then you'll be in a D.P. camp before you can turn round!'

For all such groups of people, on the move without passports, the disaster of being rounded up into one of the huge camps for Displaced Persons, then springing up throughout southern Europe, was a possibility which was always in mind, as something to be avoided while any will to freedom remained. Because officially they had no right to be anywhere, once inside it would be years before they were let out again, if they ever were. And when or if they emerged, almost certainly it would only be in order to be deported to their place of origin, despite all the efforts they had made to escape from it, and the dire personal reasons behind those efforts.

'Ai, ai!' Annexation of her land by a Police State had lost Lisabet her home: she was terrified of the police in any country, they were indeed birds of ill-omen. No one contradicted Hebe's statement.

'I still think,' said Mihael, frowning as he picked his beautiful teeth with a tortoise's leg-tendon, 'it was a stupid thing that man did, the one who made muddle without cause. Really, there is enough confusion in the world.'

'And I would have called him brother. I am complimented that the Professor sees a likeness —'

Hebe drifted off into uneasy sleep. As the morning advanced, there were more and more signs of life in the valley on this side of the frontier, with men going from farm to farm, or bringing down a load of wood from the opposite hill, but no one crossed the line of the ridge. If her father's body had been discovered by this time — well, it could not be helped. They would make a dash for the frontier should danger threaten from the Bulgarian side, and chance a few shots behind them, or a challenge on Greek territory from patrols alarmed by the firing. Meanwhile, she could rest, with her face against Lisabet's broad back to keep the occasional snowflakes off it.

When she awoke the situation had not changed, except that the sky had cleared for the moment. Jean-Paul was saying, 'I wish we had something to read — And don't tell us, Mihael, "It would be better if we had something more to eat", because that is plain to us all. It would be better. But all the same, I wish we had something to read. I like reading. I used to read a lot before the war. It was part of my *métier*. A very uncommon *métier*. I had false teeth made for a living.'

'You mean you made them?'

'No, I had them made for me. Dozens and dozens of gold-topped dentures. To fill up this gap in my front teeth which came from a small accident I ran into with a boot, when I was a lad. I may well be the only person who ever made a living by this means. Taking the teeth away to wear, on the advice of the dentist, to see if they needed adjustment, and then selling them before the time of the next appointment. Good, expensive dentists — and I never used any other — they don't expect you to pay until the teeth are comfortable. Sets don't fetch much, they use very poor gold, but if you have several being made at the same time, you get by. And the expenses are low. You have shelter, you have warmth provided in the waiting rooms. And always plenty to read. I used to write letters too, each week, to nearly every member of my family, down to the distant cousins. Even my wife thought I was a commercial traveller, from the way I moved from town to town. Well, so I was, in a sense.'

'It's not reasonable that people should trust someone like you with false teeth, knowing nothing about you,' said Lisabet. 'That could only happen in a town. In the country everyone would have a good idea of all your circumstances: they could tell if you were likely to pay or not. Anyway they would say, why do you want the teeth? If you're married already you don't need them to look smart, in order to go courting, and you don't chew with the front ones.'

'Oh, they welcomed me in the waiting-rooms. I was popular, you see, because if someone came in with the tooth-ache I would always say, "Go on, have my turn. I'm in no hurry." I learnt a lot about dentistry, too; I could talk to the dentists about their work, and they liked that. Most people can't.'

'You met no trouble?' said the Professor wonderingly — he who had brought on himself so much more, by doing so much less, merely by thinking.

'Never actually, but once very nearly. Oddly, through sentiment. My wife did not want to be alone over her confinement. I knew it was unwise to work Marseille again so soon, though of course I was careful to choose different districts. Still, I did it. One must sometimes be human. Who would have thought that two well-established dentists, charging top prices in the best part, would have had their work done behind the scenes, on the cheap, by the same miserable little mechanic in the Old Town? One of those who never forget the furnishings of a mouth once they've worked on it. Something warned me not to go to the last appointment but one, with the fellow who was to have the teeth ready first. No reading for me that afternoon: I watched the dentist's house instead from the street. And it was as well, because the police — Hallo! Those men, there, are they going to cross, do you think?'

'No,' said Hebe. 'I'd been hoping that too.'

'They're nearer the frontier than anyone else has been.'

'But the way they're heading, there's a track that curves back into the valley. They must be making for that further farm.'

'If you call it a farm,' said Jean-Paul disgustedly. 'What a place to make for. Well, I wish we had something to read.'

'Once I read a book about a woman,' said the Rumanian. 'The man who wrote it said she had a mouth like a wound. Mind you, one could see he desired her himself, by the way he wrote of her. Almost I desired her myself, too. But with such a mouth —'

'No doubt it was meant as poetry. I like that all right. Just a little at a time.'

'No, but a mouth like a wound! That was what he put.'

'I expect he had never seen a wound,' said Hebe, recalling the hole below the cheekbone in the face which had stared at the sky. Shattered bone had shown through the puckered, mushy edges — no, indeed, whoever wrote that line belonged wholly to the world of excellent ignorance which beckoned her. With admiration un-damaged by the contempt in Mihael's voice, she thought of some-one — a man and a writer, probably twice her age or more — who had managed to avoid knowing what he was talking about in this matter. That was the proper way to live, far from such realities. What could they tell her of desirable things, these more experienced people around her, chasing the taste of tortoise about their back teeth with their tongues?

'You have brains, you know, Hebe!' the Professor said quickly, as though sensing where her thoughts had turned.

'You would not have put that into one of your books, would you?' Mihael asked him. 'As a professor, you must have written books?'

'I wouldn't have written that description, no. But I was never a professor, as I keep telling you, just a schoolmaster, and I only wrote two books. One was a comparison of Polish and English literature in the nineteenth century — that was what probably started the people in power believing I had a corrupting influence on the youth of my town. Foreign writings were suspect at the time. And the other was a Life of St. Theresa of Avila. Foreign goodness has always been suspect, of course. So you see, Mihael, it could hardly have come in — Do you know, Hebe, what she said, that sharp Spanish saint, when mothers brought their daughters to her convent, recommending them to her as being so devout and diligent? "We will make them devout and diligent," St. Theresa told them. "The question is, have they got brains?" That is how highly she valued your possession, you see!'

'But as a saint, she must have valued still more a belief in the existence of God?' said the Rumanian.

'That she took for granted.'

'How could she take it for granted?' He spoke with deep concern. 'I don't understand how anyone can take it for granted. You don't take it for granted?'

'No,' said the older man. They had been over this ground many times in the past three weeks, without coming appreciably nearer to any solution of Mihael's doubts of the non-existence of God.

'That's comforting, in its way. Because lately, you know, I have come to consider seriously things I have done, which might make it unfortunate if after all there turns out to be something of the kind, in the end. Of course, when I did them I hadn't thought this possible. I still feel it is unlikely, on the whole. And better not. On all accounts, I mean, not only on mine. For if there does happen to be something — ' the note of diffidence came back into his voice, 'surely it makes certain another life after this one? Going on and on.'

'Of course,' said Jean-Paul, and Lisabet nodded, but the Professor said, 'No. I don't see why.'

'You don't? Ah! For who could want to live for ever? That seems a dreadful thought, doesn't it — for ever? You have lived the longest of us, and plainly you have the least wish to go on living.

But of course I see that it makes no difference to the existence of God, if there is one, whether it would be a good thing or not. I don't know —' His troubled tones died away. The strain of such a degree of impersonal thought appeared to be great — too much to be borne for long at a stretch by a mind accustomed only to decisions of expediency.

They watched a party of men approaching from far up the valley on the Bulgarian side, driving sheep towards the frontier.

'You see, if there happens to be a life beyond the grave —' Mihael began once more, with an effort.

'Oh, *not* that again!' said the Frenchman, throwing himself flat on his back from a sitting position, in exasperation. 'Me, I don't care if all the people with a proper grudge against me are waiting just beyond!'

'You don't?'

'No. Because suppose I killed them or had them killed in war, well, they must know by now it was bad luck for me, as well as for them, that they happened to be just where they were, at the moment I had to do it. It's always dangerous, and generally a nuisance, to kill a man in *maquis* conditions. And if they understand this, how much more will God? In Whose existence,' he added firmly to the Rumanian, 'I am confident but not interested. So now let us have no more of it.'

He sat up again as Hebe said slowly, 'I think — mind you, I'm not sure, but I think — those men are going to cross! And in the best way for us.'

'How?'

'With sheep. It's an old trick here — I keep telling you, I know my way about this part! — You drive your beasts over the frontier and wait a bit. And then follow them. If you meet a patrol — look, your sheep strayed. There they are, ahead. Any shepherd is bound to go after his animals, to get them back. Frontier or no frontier. You lose some sheep to the patrol, of course, but that's better than being shot. And if you don't meet anyone, you go on and trade your sheep with the guerillas in the hills.'

'Unless they don't know you. Then they take the sheep, for nothing I suppose, the same as the patrol?' said the Professor.

'But anyway, all you lose is sheep,' she told him impatiently.

Hunger, and weariness, and the extra coldness of the wind on bodies already suffering from these things, were forgotten in the mounting excitement of watching the men in the valley below, making their way past point after point where they might have turned off, before they came to the lower end of a gully running up to the ridge. It was the only gully in sight which fitted in with the description given to Hebe: if they turned into it, their route would keep the rabbit's ears apart. It became more and more obvious that the men were driving their small flock according to a plan. The carrying 'Hué-hué' cry of the shepherds stopped. The men urged on the animals only by waving their sticks, and they increased the distance between themselves and their beasts as soon as the first of the sheep was hemmed in by the steep sides of the gully. For a few minutes more the little party on the edge of the trees waited, while their breathing and the sound of their hearts grew loud in their ears, and then they started in pursuit, when the last of the shepherds had been lost to sight.

'Remember to say, if we're stopped, that those are our sheep,' Hebe instructed the Rumanian as they climbed the gully. 'And the men ahead have just stolen them. They probably have too, from someone.' Mihael would be spokesman with strangers from now on, because of his fluency in Greek. But the drivers and the flock appeared to have vanished into the hillside. Listening for shouting or shots ahead, the party neared the saddle in the hills to which the gully led, but there was no warning sound. When they came out on level ground and could see down, into Greece, they stopped and waited again, watching for any movement, but there was still nothing living in view, except a few hawks. They walked on warily. It was difficult for all of them, the drifting refuse of national passions, to accept that this particular frontier, one of the danger-points of Europe, could be crossed so easily. When I have reached the Good Place, Hebe thought vehemently, relapsing into childishness, I will always have a passport so perfectly in order that if I ever use it, which is unlikely, men will incline their heads to me, as they did once to my mother, while they mark it for all to see with violet ink from rubber stamps.

For a while she kept herself awake as she walked, with the pleasure of this picture: it even helped her to forget, from time to time, the pain of uncut toe-nails.

4

THE WOMAN AT THE FARM

A T the first farm in Macedonia where they tried to ask for food, the door remained shut to their knocking although, listening, they could hear someone or something moving about very quietly inside the mud walls, listening too. It was an isolated place. The windows, barred, were set too high for them to see in. After a while Mihael gave up shouting that they were a harmless party of travellers, with an old man and a child among them, and they went on. Then came a village of sorts, a few huts, also built of sunbaked mud bricks, crowding together in extreme dilapidation as if making a deliberate show of poverty, in the hope of escaping hostile notice.

Revulsion shook Hebe, because of the extreme squalor of the place: only a frightening degree of hunger and tiredness could have driven her to approach the doors with Mihael. They had agreed that she must stand beside him: her presence might reassure those who spied on them.

People were bolder about opening their doors with neighbours about them, even though guerillas, or bandits from other localities, ransacked the villages as often as they raided the lonely farms. Save for sporadic atrocities, when political feeling was roused, everyone was safe from the lawless men of his own neighbourhood.

At the nearest door, an old man laughed at the idea of giving them anything, food or shelter, and said, 'Try the woman at the higher end of the village, Katina, who has lived through an earthquake in Turkey! If you ask her about it — we have all heard the story a hundred times and will listen no more — perhaps she will reward you with something. Who knows?' He sniggered again and went in.

The woman in the next hovel heard Mihael patiently, staring at first one and then another of them while he begged. Her dull eyes continued to shift round them, pausing for a few seconds on each face, after he had stopped and stood silent. Muttering, she went back into the dark interior, closing the door. They hoped for a while that she had gone to fetch them something to eat, but presently they glimpsed her dimly, through the one tiny window, still peering at them with the same roving, patient, beast-like regard. She would not open the door again when they knocked.

Others — some as if it were a joke, and some not — told them to ask Katina about the earthquake, gesturing towards the further side of the village. They found her house, somewhat more noisome looking than the rest, with herself, a huge sow of a woman, outside by the stream at the back, carrying water for her goats. Mihael helpfully took one crock from her, and the Professor the other, while Mihael, prompted by Jean-Paul, told an elaborate story of meeting in Italy a man who had spoken with excitement of a village in Greece — but he could not remember the name, being a little drunk — where there lived a woman who had survived an extraordinary experience. And now, what was their amazement to find that this was actually the village, where all had informed them that Katina herself was the woman! Would there be an opportunity to hear this story of the earthquake from her own mouth? Now — if they were to come into the house — for the wind blew harder on tired people? And if there might be something to eat — they would not mind what — '?

She said, 'I came out to cut a branch from that dead olive tree, after I had watered the beasts, for I have no more firewood. If you will do it for me, I will tell you the story.'

The younger men took turns with the axe she lent them, hacking and struggling angrily with the knotted wood, while the Professor excused himself as usual because of the things he carried. Hebe and Lisabet longed to enter the kitchen and sit down, even though they could see, through the door which she kept open behind her, that it was bare and unwarmed; but Katina, plunging into her tale, barred the way with her bulk.

Enjoying herself, she spun out the account with dramatic pauses and repetitions, till the firewood was cut and stacked in a neat pile.

Mihael translated the gist of it for the others, to keep up the appearance of attention; it ran that from the first she had hated everyone in the Turkish town where she had been employed — in what capacity, she did not say, and it would be difficult, thought Hebe, to imagine why anyone should give a job to a creature so fantastically grimy. But perhaps, before the earthquake, she had been cleaner. (Oh, if only the story would end. With some effort, Hebe could follow it herself in demotic Greek, unaided by Mihael, but it hardly seemed worth the trouble, except that the sooner Katina reached the earthquake, the sooner they might expect food.)

'One day I spoke to myself aloud in the street,' Katina told them, 'as one speaks when one is lonely and in a rage. "I would like to see this town flat on the ground!" I said. "And the people in it running for their lives," I added. No sooner had I spoken than there was a roar, and — it was so! Now there is an experience for you!'

' "He gave them their desire, and sent leanness withal into their souls",' the Professor quoted in English to Hebe. To Mihael and Jean-Paul, who were busily flattering the woman on her escape and her story, he said in their *patois* French: 'And after that taste of power, she will be like you two! Nothing will ever come up to it, and nothing else will seem really worth while.'

'Mind you,' said Katina, who assumed that they were discussing her marvel, 'I never for a moment believed that I caused the earthquake in Turkey by my words. Other towns felt it at the same time, and hundreds were killed against whom I had nothing. But what a thing to happen, at that very moment!'

'Yes, indeed,' they agreed eagerly, for she was gathering up her firewood and the axe, before going back into the house, shaking off Mihael's effort to help in carrying the firewood. They made to follow her, but the door was closed in their faces.

'I never promised you food,' she said through it, in answer to Jean-Paul's hammering and Mihael's protests. 'I told you, if you will cut the wood I will let you hear the story! Well, you have heard it.'

The sound of her laughter came to them as they stood staring at one another for a moment, too exhausted to take in the position at once. Then slowly, they walked on, away from the village and down the valley, until Hebe remembered that by doing so they must be converging on one of the few roads in this part of Greece. They left the main valley then, by a path which wriggled into the foothills. In this troubled region, with Government troops and guerillas both bound to use the roads if they wanted to move with speed, it was safer to keep to the small tracks as much as possible. She recognized, too, that if they still had a mind to, Mihael and Jean-Paul were more likely to work out their own route from a main road, and leave her.

And I decided we wouldn't go far today! she reflected, when they had walked another mile or so, seeing no habitations. Now I don't even want to do anything to my feet. It would be enough if I could stop and take off my shoes.

Two wolf-like sheep dogs skirmished round them, and were driven away at last by a lucky shower of stones. The attack prevented them from noticing until they were quite close to him, one of the Macedonian shepherds sitting perched on an exposed rock, looking like part of the rock itself. He was wrapped in the long, black, tent-like cloak which kept out the savage winter winds as well as the parching summer sun of this region, and gave to these weathered men an air of being a race apart, gifted with stillness, more akin to the stones of their hard land than they were to other men. He must have seen and heard them from a long way off, strangers in a place where strangers were always notable, and often dangerous, but only at the last minute, as they came up to him, his head and no other part of his body turned towards them.

'Is there a farm anywhere near here?'

With impassive black eyes he studied them for what seemed an endless moment.

'Over there.' He indicated the direction with a glance.

There was a chunk of unusually white bread lying on the rock beside him. 'Give me a little!' Hebe said, with Mihael translating. 'I have had nothing all day.' The beggar's words and the beginning of a beggar's whine came easily to her tongue, filling her with anger against the whole world — herself, her father for dying, the people with her, the shepherd — everyone who had in any way had a hand in bringing her to this. The other entry into Greece had been just as furtive, but at least there had been money to buy food. She had not been forced to beg. And the whine proved useless too, that was the worst part.

'If I gave you a little,' the shepherd said, after thinking awhile, 'I would feel obliged to give a little to all. And then there would not be enough.'

They trudged on, in the direction of his glance, although it did not look a likely place for any dwelling.

The farm they found, well hidden in a fold of ground, was not quite as smelly for yards around as Katina's, but it was of the same poverty-ridden kind; and the woman in it was a big, slovenly-looking creature too. Isolated as the place was, she did not seem afraid of them. When Mihael had spoken, as persuasively as his slowness allowed, asking for food and a chance to rest, she said, 'What are you?' in a voice that neither promised nor denied anything. It was a toneless, distant voice, as though it were hard for her to bring her thoughts to bear on what she said, or to attend fully to anything that was said to her.

'I have told you. People travelling, without money.'

'But on what side politically?'

Royalists should they be? Or *andartes*, a term which took in all the anti-Government guerilla forces? Many conflicting shades of the Left were fiercely supported along the frontier. Would it be better to try K.K.E. or E.A.M.? To guess wrong would certainly be to lose again, but Mihael was too tired to think, and had in any case little hope, the likeness to Katina was too strong.

'We have no politics,' he said, of this party of refugees of whom all, except Hebe, had become fighters or exiles for political reasons.

'You fool!' said Jean-Paul, in their own language. He could follow Mihael's Greek about as well as Hebe. 'Hereabouts you should have gone for E.L.A.S. From what I've heard, no Greek will ever believe that anyone has no politics.'

'Come in,' the woman said. 'If you are sure you have no politics? My man was killed by politics. Three months ago.' They followed her into the one big room of the house, a kitchen and bedroom combined. 'You can eat, if you want.'

There was some bread and a few dry little figs on one corner of the table. It was the same noticeably white bread which they had seen beside the shepherd. Piled high on the rest of the table lay the unmended small gear of a farm that had become too much for the hands and energies left to serve it.

'How long do you want to stay?' she said without interest. 'The child looks tired.'

Even the sound of kindness startled them now: they did not know what to make of it. Surely she did not mean that they could remain until they were ready to go on again?

'One day? Two days, perhaps?' suggested Mihael cautiously. 'We are all tired.'

The others could not believe that he had understood her correctly. 'Did you make it clear to her that we have no money?' Lisabet asked in their *patois*.

'Well, don't, until we've eaten,' Jean-Paul put in quickly.

The woman was considering them at length, much as the shepherd had done. 'I think you should rest at least three days,' she said.

They started on the bread voraciously, but after the first few mouthfuls, the pace of swallowing slowed: they had been short of food for long enough to diminish the flow of saliva: it was hard to get down as much as their hunger urged. She asked them one or two questions about their journey, but gave the impression all the time not, like the Professor, of being uninterested at heart in anything, but of thinking — and thinking passionately — of something else while she spoke.

'Where can we sleep?' Mihael asked.

'In the barn. And two in here — ' She opened the door of an

outhouse, a long, windowless cupboard leading out of the kitchen. There was straw on the floor, and among it some tumbled remnants of blanket.

'The shepherd's, do you think? Because if so — !' speaking to Mihael, Jean-Paul twisted his odd and ugly face into an amiable grin: food solved all their differences for the moment. 'Well, I've no wish to put a pair of his own rams' horns on the shepherd. I want to sleep, all night, with my back warm. You can have this place, if you like. And anything that goes with it.'

'No. For me too, the barn — though it is not that I am too tired.' The earnestness of Mihael's voice, the same which he brought to the possibility of God, showed that he had embarked on one of his laborious explanations which, unless stopped, would go on and on. 'I am never too tired for a woman. That is, if I desire her. But sometimes, as in this case, she does not seem to me desirable. I am sure, though, you can't "horn" the shepherd, as you say, unless he is married to her. It is only for married men, that. And he is not married to her, because she told us about her man being dead, through politics — ' Turning to the woman he asked, 'Why did they kill your man?' for information with which to continue exploring the self-evident.

'Because he refused to join the men who came here to get others to fight. He was on their side; he just didn't want to fight — '

'Ai, ai, ai!' said Lisabet again, vehemently, when this was translated to her, and patted the Greek woman on the arm.

'They cut his stomach open with the ragged edge of one of those big meat tins stolen from the U.N.R.R.A. people. Many such tins were brought into the country by the English and Americans, when they were sorry for us and came to help us, and their food was so easily stolen. They had no business to let it be stolen so easily.'

'Very strange they are,' the Professor observed, 'the results of being liberated and being pitied!'

'Now in the hills,' the woman told them, 'the *andartes* live on the meat and make the tins into weapons. Terrible weapons. Men held me, to make me watch while they killed him. So that the news should frighten people in other farms about here. And in the other farms, when they heard what had happened, men did join them. Some, I mean, who would not have joined them anyway: others wanted to.'

The dreary horror of the narrative silenced even Mihael for the moment. They ate on in silence, slower and slower. When they had almost finished the Professor said to her in limping Greek, 'I am not sure I have quite understood. For whom did they want your man to fight?'

'Oh, "for whom?" — it is hard to say. That has always been confused here. "Against whom," we knew. Government troops. And sometimes against men who felt some of the things he felt, but had different leaders. On every side these things are done equally. This is why I hate politics.'

'No, not quite equally,' said the Professor. 'Tell her this, Mihael: I can't yet, in Greek. A man behaves worst when his conscience justifies him in whatever he does. And the people on the Left here have the better cause, I believe. In ideals, that is. (Whether it works out better in practical government, that is something else again! Especially perhaps in Greece.) But in theory, they are nearer the truth about what men need. Shared ideals always get dragged down in practice, if they are shared by enough people. All the same, however low it has been dragged, it was a good dream we had once, on the Left — "From each according to his strength" — Good enough to persuade many consciences to foul actions. Tell her, I too was on the side of the men who killed her husband. I know evil things are done on all hands but because, with us, men believe more hotly in what they do, and aren't only struggling to keep what they've got, it is on our side that they are likely to be vilest.'

She looked at the older man with contempt, when Mihael had translated as much of this as he understood. 'You mean, if they had been Royalists who came here, they would have spilled out his stomach with something else, not a meat tin?'

'I suppose,' said the Professor humbly, 'I mean just that, no more.'

She turned abruptly from the table on which she had been leaning, and stood gazing out of the little barred window, over the gaunt hillside where the ancient bones of the earth showed through the thin soil; a pitiless landscape of rock and twisted tree and thin, wind-bitten grass, more savage-looking than usual under the bleak light of impending snow, which hurried on the dusk. But it must have seemed kindlier to her than this room, littered everywhere with memories and possessions of the man who had been killed. 'This is his blood, here on my dress,' she said. 'Rich people, like Katina — with their money they can change everything about them, if they want to. But I've rubbed and rubbed at this. It won't come out, and I've no other dress.'

They had all seen or known enough suffering to realize that the stain was no less indelible for being imaginary, or at any rate invisible. She wore the usual shapeless black clothing of the Balkan farm-woman, and it was old, covered with grease spots and smears from cooking and handling stock; no new mark could show among so many others.

She remained staring out into the fading light, away from the shared things about her, for so long that it was as if she had forgotten the people in the house. Then without being asked, she fetched them more bread, and said, 'I make the whitest bread, do you notice? He milled the flour himself, but it is partly the way I bake that makes it like that. He was much envied for my bread. And still I make it like this' — speaking wonderingly, apparently surprised that anything she did could really be the same.

'Ah, we saw what the shepherd had — a grand white crust. We said, "Now that lucky shepherd must know a fine woman to get hold of such fine bread".' Jean-Paul turned galant, to divert her attention from his nimble pocketing of some of the food: the false satiety of their condition would not last, he knew, and he was providing against the return of real hunger in the night. 'So we asked him where she lived, and he showed us — not eagerly. No, not at all eagerly! Who would want to share such fine bread, or such a fine woman?'

'He sent you here? The shepherd?' She made a sound like laughter and seemed for a moment years younger. Her teeth were superb, and when she laughed her big body shook with a semblance of jollity that must have been warm and genuine in happier times: now her amusement was as withered as her figs: it was only the lines of laughter in her face which remained pleasant. 'He must have thought you were on the Royalist side. Informers. They use people like you. Then your coming here could have been the end of me, too — that's what he must have hoped! At least the farm might be taken from me, and perhaps given to him, on your report that my man sided with the Communists, in his heart. They've sent people to the Islands for no more than that. Men and women. Just for thinking with the other side. Or killed them — I don't know. But they don't come back. Yes, that must be why he gave you the direction, eagerly or not, for here we are well hidden. Who would find this farm, undirected?'

She mused for a moment, with a look of angry satisfaction at her thoughts. 'Katina, from the next village —'

'The woman who was in the earthquake?'

'That one. She says she has seen Government-men — police — riding through the place with the heads of *andartes*, newly killed, carried as a warning. Not the bodies, just the heads, you understand. They held them by the hair. But Katina — she and her earthquake — !' She spat into the fireless hearth.

'You cannot believe Katina, or her earthquake? Ask her, Mihael.' To such travellers as these, details of official savagery in any country meant little: Jean-Paul was more interested in a human relationship.

'Oh, it happened,' she said grudgingly. 'My man was once in Salonika, and saw in a paper about the Turkish earthquake. So it happened. And it's true about the police. Others know it too. But I dare say she didn't see it herself. It's just — I don't like Katina.'

'Or the shepherd, it seems?'

'No.'

'How sad. For here was I thinking, certainly this shepherd has high regard for the woman at the farm! Why else should he show us the way so unreadily, without even being willing to point with his hand, only with his eyes? I must be careful, I thought, how I approach this maker of white bread!' Jean-Paul's pleasantries grew heavier, waiting for Mihael to repeat those words which he could not manage to convey. 'For perhaps she gives him more than bread in return. Who knows? It has been done. Where I come from, shepherds are thought to be the lucky ones. And his willingness to harm you — jealousy, no doubt. Are we not all ready to hurt where we love? But now you say you don't like him — how very sad. For him, not for me! Tell me, doesn't he really desire you greatly?'

'Yes,' she said.

'How could it be otherwise? And you speak so heartlessly. It is, after all, a poor prospect for me. Supposing I am taken that way too! Is it long that he has suffered from these pangs, the unfortunate shepherd?'

'I don't know how to say all that — we didn't find time to talk of such things during the fighting round Athens!' Mihael told him.

'More fool you. Talk like that has got me a bed, occupied or unoccupied, more times than I can remember, just when I needed it. With luck, it'll get us some extra nights here. Try.'

'He has wanted me two years, three years,' she answered in her unconcerned voice, when Mihael had succeeded. It was only when something touched her in relation to the recent, violent past and her words followed her real thoughts that she came to life for a while. Now she answered Jean-Paul's jokes without reserve, because they did not matter, and she did not know he was joking. Even to Hebe, growing sleepier again as appetite died, the dignity of the other's unawareness was plain: she resented Jean-Paul's advantage over the woman, the sniggering of civilization, though she did not know what it was that she minded, nor why. Lisabet too, was annoyed by Jean-Paul's tone, or else she broke into the conversation, suddenly changing the subject, in order to make one of the younger men take notice of her existence: her anger at being the person most often ignored by the rest of the group came out in obscure ways. Raising her voice over his, she began asking questions about the land, and the times for sowing and harvest, comparing them with customs further north, insisting that Mihael repeat every word. What she learned shocked her profoundly, particularly the local habit of eating green crops almost as soon as they appeared above ground, without waiting for their maximum growth. This could be considered unreasonable by most standards, but was fundamentally wicked by hers.

The Professor also asked questions about the land, but in the sense of its living continuity with the lovely centuries in which he would not have felt an outcast, or believed that he would not. To him, this woman from whom Jean-Paul stole bread, was less a woman than a Macedonian, the first Greek to whom he had talked in her own country, where the torch of men's delight in reason had been lit. He asked about inheritance and land-tenure: did the Macedonians still hold their farms on the complicated system of which he had read, long ago, in security, as a student in Cracow? She stood for the shining past as well as the grim present in Greece, and could not offend him by her scorn of the feeble consolation he had tried to offer her.

But here, too, her unawareness was immense, almost magnificent: she did not know that her country's history had ever been greater than the conditions of the time suggested. Jean-Paul, treating Lisabet as she treated him — as if she were inaudible when she interrupted — went on with his blandishments: what name did the shepherd murmur, when he cried beneath her window? 'What shall we call you, eh?'

'I am Dido,' she said, and because the Professor exclaimed, she asked defensively, 'What is strange in that? My father had a favourite sister, who was Dido.'

'Nothing strange,' he said deferentially, and added to the others, in French: 'A Spanish comrade told me, in a concentration camp, that half his men who died for their irreligion in the civil war fought under names like Jesu de Saluté, and Jean-Batisto, seeing nothing odd in it. And they slept, when they could, with staunch atheist girls whom they knew as Maria Immaculata, or Santa Concepcion. Tell her I am sure it is an excellent reason to be called Dido, in Greece, to have had an aunt with that name.'

'That also I'm not sure how to say in Greek,' Mihael told him, his face reassuming its puzzled, obsessional look. 'The translation of the Spanish names, I mean. Because we didn't talk of that sort of thing, either. So I didn't pick up the words.'

'It doesn't matter,' said the Professor patiently. 'I didn't expect you to repeat the Spanish part! Tell her that now I know why she has this name, very famous in far-off days, I am no longer surprised.' But he might not have spoken.

'If we had found time to think of matters of religion,' said Mihael, 'when we were on the run, by now I should perhaps have known better what to believe. As it is —'

'Tell her as best you can, then, what I said!' In his way, the Professor was more concerned to placate her than Jean-Paul. She was Helen and Antigone as well as Dido.

Mihael did what he could, and then relapsed into his own anxiety: 'I wonder now, whether this woman, after what she has gone through, can expect a time when the pain of it will be made up to her? And to her man? But how could pain in this life be compensated, in another life? Even if it is avenged, it will still have existed here, and pain can be terrible. I have seen —'

'So have we all. For once — just for once — be damned and be cheerful about it,' said Jean-Paul. 'Like everybody else.'

It was shiveringly cold in this fireless kitchen, but they were out of the wind and the snow, which was beginning to fall again. They had several nights in shelter of a sort before them, and beyond this it seemed to him fantastic that anyone in their situation should look. 'This reminds me of the times,' Jean-Paul said with enthusiasm, 'when we hid in farms together in France, during the German occupation, *l'espion anglais* and I. Did I tell you of him? Now there was also a man for you!'

'Of course you did. Many times. The one with the great moustache.' Mihael sounded surly but for the others the sense of respite and hope was contagious; their spirits were rising, following Jean-Paul's.

Lisabet said, 'But I like to hear of him. Really, it is an honour to France that he survived the war. You said everyone called him "the English spy" quite openly, because of his clothes and his face and his way of walking. Yet he survived. Whatever betrayals France made, and no doubt they were plenty, that is to the credit of the people he spied among. One feels better for knowing that they can be loyal. Ordinary people, in any country.' It was the most approving speech she had made for a long time.

'They trusted him because it was the time the Germans were using *agents provocateurs*,' Jean-Paul went on. 'They spoke beautiful French and the farmers who befriended them were shot. But *l'espion anglais* could have been nothing except an English spy, as you say, and all knew it. Even before he opened his mouth to let out that awful English accent. Our real enemy was the Allied Air Force, then. Because when we were given a rendezvous to be picked up, or to meet a drop of arms, it was always something like "Near the third haystack, north of the farm". By the time we got there, the "big birds" would have been over, and removed not only the haystacks but also the farm. So *l'espion anglais* would say — Oh, what an accent he had, right up to the last I saw of him; after two years of being dropped in the Occupied Zone, and working his way home, and then being dropped again! — *Cette fois, mon vieux, nous sommes absolument foutus*, only we never were!' Jean-Paul gave his high-pitched laugh like a woodpecker's, and launched into a story of steadfastness under terror in the early days of the *maquis*, in which his own part, not stressed at all, must have been quite as cool and determined as that of the man he took pleasure in praising. The days of full stature seemed not so irrevocably lost and gone after all, just for the time being.

They chattered, in the atmosphere of something nearing hysteria which had developed from the idea that their luck had changed: even Mihael succumbed to it eventually: they took intense momentary interest in this nameless man whom only one of them had seen, and none of them was likely to meet thereafter. Hebe alone was too much exhausted to talk. She got up from the bench by the table, craving sleep, conscious of the increased chill quick to follow a big meal on top of privation. Dido spoke with decision to the Professor, 'You will take this outhouse here, near me, you and the child, for the night. It will be warmer than in the barn,' and she laughed shortly once more, at her own thoughts. By the laugh, they were savage.

The bits of blanket were almost certainly lousy, Hebe realized, as she took off her shoes at last, in the cupboard-like recess. The snowy twilight dimly as it came through the door, showed her the grime of the floor and walls. Well, she was dirty enough, too, not to care, she reminded herself. But if you had ever been clean, alien dirt — even a lesser degree of dirt than your own — could still seem horrible. She, who had only cried once since her father's death, cried now for a little while, because the blankets were almost as far from belonging to the Good Place as she was herself. Presently, though, she found the final energy to return to the kitchen, to borrow a huge, broken pair of farm scissors, and managed to cut her nails after all, before she slept, just as she had planned.

At the further end of the long cupboard, another door led out into the walled-in yard: she and the Professor found this useful for their immediate needs, but they could discover no means of fastening it afterwards; a wooden contraption which must have served that purpose had lost its bolt, and the door stayed shut only because the hinge having sagged, the bottom of it rested on the ground. Nowhere in this district, they knew, were doors normally left unsecured at night. Dido urged them not to trouble themselves about it. 'I tell you it doesn't matter. It leads only to the yard. Beyond that is the wall.' And when the Professor asked, all the same, through Mihael, for a piece of wood with which to jam it shut, she did not hear — purposely it seemed. The main door to the house she bolted and barred herself, carefully.

Sleep, when it took them — sleep within walls, for the first time for many nights — overcame them so completely that neither Hebe nor the Professor heard the shepherd come in some time during the night, although he must almost have crawled over them to get past into the kitchen.

5

RESTING PLACE

ANGRY voices woke them: mainly the woman's, raised as if on purpose, shrill with a queer triumph and — it seemed to Hebe, listening through the crack of the door into the kitchen — much less angry than the man's low, contemptuous tone. Perhaps Dido was only pretending to be angry: people did that, the child remembered from her South American days, when her mother had made a show of resentment into a shield against all her father's accusations, in the last weeks before she disappeared. Anger which rang untrue, then, carried with it more of a feeling of insecurity than the ordinary quarrelling of the party of refugees when they were on the move, quarrelling born of simple dislike and weariness.

Hebe wriggled nearer the door, which the shepherd had pulled-to after him, and put an eye to the crack of the hinge. She could see part of the woman, who was sitting up, half dressed, in the big bed built into the opposite wall; but not the shepherd at all: he was no more than a softly menacing series of sounds. They had lit a lantern, or the shepherd had brought one in, and put it on the table. Outside it was still night.

Their talk was too fast for Hebe to follow in Greek, as yet, save a few words here and there. But several times Dido gestured towards the recess, and it was plain that the woman was using the presence of another man and a child, almost in the same room, as an excuse for refusing the shepherd what he wanted. In this part of the world, Hebe considered, that was not likely to be thought a really good reason, and there came to her, so old and experienced in some ways, the conviction that the woman was glad he had come, to be refused: dreadfully glad. Uneasiness swept over her.

Presently he went away, out by the other door in the kitchen, the main farm door through which they had come into the house. He

69

unbolted it and left it swinging open behind him: so that Dido had to get up to fasten it, and put out the lantern. Then they all slept till full day, and when they woke again, it was as if to another world, a briefly idyllic world in which the ugly little scene of the night had no place.

The snow had come down heavily, and it was much warmer. The fierce contours of the hills were rounded. No wind stirred, and the shadows of the few writhen trees were blue and restful against this sparkling freshness, an old, old landscape made breathlessly new.

The hawks no longer hunted; they flew high, and for joy alone, it appeared to Hebe when she went out into the little yard, dazed with the transformation, aware of a thin cleanness tickling the back of her nose.

Lisabet and the two men came in from the barn still as cheerful as on the previous night, but in a quieter mood. Lisabet had, after all, had her pick of the two men, and because of what Jean-Paul had said in the kitchen about preferring to sleep at once with his back warm, she was perversely pleased to have made him change his mind in the barn, enough at any rate for him to put on a show of regret, before relinquishing her to Mihael, whom he had in fact known that she would choose. The others were aware that if Jean-Paul had ever had any serious intention of competing with Mihael, he would not have been so willing to accept defeat, but as Lisabet was the one person in the party who could not realize this, she was kind and rosy with the satisfaction of her pride, and making no secret of the reason, was anxious to do whatever she could for anyone. Let all the party give her their worn out shoes, and the Professor the thread and leather he had carried so far, and they should see what she could do as a cobbler. Affection woke at once when she was allowed to look after someone and be of use again.

'These world-mothers!' said Jean-Paul out of her hearing, as he and Mihael dragged in the heavy limb of a dead tree, to start a fire in the kitchen. 'My wife was of that kind. I am often amazed, when I think that I was almost faithful to her for almost a year. You have started something!'

'No,' said Mihael seriously. 'For I am going to explain to her that I have been thinking it over, and if I am right in the ideas that have come to me lately, then it is wrong we should do this just because we are in a barn, with enough straw. It is not a good reason.'

'I would say it was! But you think she will accept your view?'

'Why not?'

'That sort isn't as easy to give up as to get.' She was, however, and remained friendly to them both. It would take time for any of them to recover their ordinary level of vitality, but for Lisabet it was another way of indulging her overwhelming need to serve, which privation had not lessened, to give in first to a man and then to his incomprehensible principles.

When the fire had driven the last of yesterday's bleakness out of the kitchen, and she was grateful for the warmth, Dido let them have more of her good white bread. All the morning they worked at mending the damaged or worn-out farm gear which had accumulated in the house: there was so much that they made little impression on the pile, but for the first time since her man was killed, Dido could feel that things were getting better, not worse.

Then someone knocked at the door, and she stiffened apprehensively: all of them held their breath, letting the person outside wait and bang again, louder. But smoke was going up from the chimney; it was useless to pretend, if either *andartes* or Government troops were outside, that there was no one in the house. Dido moved to one side of the window, and craned her head to see. 'It's Katina!' she said, and opened the door.

The two women greeted one another courteously. The refugees met a strangely different Katina — a dignified woman, still indescribably dirty, but armoured against the surprise of seeing them there by Greek good manners: she knew how to behave when paying a social visit to what passed in this region as a neighbour. Her village was nearly three miles away: because no one in it would listen to any more of her stories of triumph, she had struggled through the snow, over paths which no one travelled alone for

choice in such wild days, to find ears for her tale of how she had got
the better by cunning of a party of dangerous beggars: she was not
to be shaken from her poise by the discovery that they were before
her, and feeling, apparently, much at home. The tale of the previous
meeting would lose nothing by keeping. She ignored the fact that
there had been any such meeting, asking them, as if they were
strangers, polite questions about their journey; and taking their
tone from her, they ignored the encounter too. Hebe even warmed
to her a little: this was how a situation of the kind should be overcome, with comfortable pretence, as it might be in the house with
the dogs. Comfortable pretence was the essence of the respectability
she would one day know with or without André; but it was an unexpected quality to find in Dido's kitchen. Odd and pleasant — oh,
but it was a good day, with the crackling fire and the clean snow
and the dropping of the wind, and the memory of long sleep the
night before, from which she could banish the thought of the inter-
ruption. One asked so little of life, now. Later, it would be
different.

Katina would take no food, though Dido offered bread, and some
of the withered potatoes which Jean-Paul had managed to grub up
from the garden. No, she would come back, she said vaguely —
'another day' — implying, when these people have gone, and I can
tell my tale.

'You are so good, so soft-hearted,' she told Dido, in her best
manner. 'You feed everyone!'

'Oh, no, indeed. I am not as kind as all that.' Dido put aside the
tribute with equal politeness.

'But you are, I know. You would not refuse anything to anyone!'

'It is really you who are the kind one, to say such things!'

'After all, I have known you a long time. Always giving and
giving.' Small pig's eyes shone with malice in the fat face.

When she left, Dido stood in the doorway, watching the retreating figure and calling suggestions as to where the snow might lie
less deeply, till Jean-Paul protested by signs that cold air was com-

ing into the house. 'Tell her to let the old sow rootle her way home,' he said to Mihael, 'with her story festering inside her.'

'Are you afraid Katina will not get safely through the snow?' was Mihael's version. 'Those clouds coming up now — it looks as if more would be falling soon.'

'Afraid? No,' Dido said, bolting the door again, and taking up the hay-rake she had been re-toothing. 'I think — I am not sure, you see. It would be easier if I were sure! To hate, with a doubt — there's no comfort in that! — I think she was the one who told the guerillas, when they came through the village, where to look for a shepherd who would guide them to what they wanted — In this neighbourhood. As a warning to others! — A farmer who had Royalist sympathies. My man had no Royalist sympathies, as I told you. But — she knew she could rely on the shepherd to say that he had, if it would harm him. Yes, I think it was Katina.' The quiet voice in the quiet room made the shadows of pain and loneliness, which they conjured back, grow darker than they had seemed when she said, 'This is his blood on my dress. I have no other.'

'She could rely on the shepherd, yes, because he wanted you,' said Jean-Paul when Dido's words had been translated to them. 'But why did Katina behave as she did?' Inconsistent himself, it was always important to him to know whether other people acted on motives which struck him as adequate, and save when his imagination was caught, as by the Professor's tale of the accountant, he was puzzled, and usually aggrieved, when they did not.

'Oh, that. It's from long ago. When we were both girls. And she was a fine girl then, if you can believe it. Like a young tree.'

'You, too, no doubt!'

'Yes,' said Dido, for Mihael to translate — faithfully in this instance. 'But then that is less surprising, surely. With the shepherd, and other things.'

'It is true,' said Mihael, 'one can see better with you than with her, what used to be.'

They were both disgusting in body, these women, thought Hebe, and there was little to choose between them. Their breasts and buttocks shook as they moved. How could men put up with women? Surely André would not, or not with women like this, though even the best were coarse and clumsy about the hips, compared with a man.

'Why did you say she was rich?' asked Lisabet.

'She has fifteen golden English sovereigns safely hidden away,' said Dido, and laughed for the third time in their hearing. Anything that was stupid and frustrated, appealed to her bitterness. 'And what good do they do her? She could never buy what she really wanted — that's gone for both of us. During their war, the English dropped a quarter of a million of their gold coins to help in the fighting against the Germans, and almost all of them fell into the wrong hands! Houses in the towns have been hired ever since for so many English sovereigns a month. And they still are. My man told me. The value of the gold is safer as money, and easier to work out than thousands on thousands of drachmae. But here, if people knew where you kept it, having gold would invite *klepts* [bandits] to come and take it away.'

'Still, she could buy a new dress. Unlike you.'

'Yes. If she minded blood upon hers.'

To Hebe, alone of the party, there was no great change noticeable in Dido, no sudden slipping away of disfiguring time when the woman was stirred or angry, passionately remembering the man she had lost and the longings he had satisfied. She was saying now: 'Do you know how Katina got to Turkey, to have her earthquake? No, that she would not tell you! My man knew her long before he knew me. He took her there, the fine young tree. And left her there, too, when he was sick of her, and her boasting, and her need to get the better of someone all the time. Even of him. Even in love. Left her to rot, or die in the earthquake, or crawl home with much difficulty, as I wish she might be crawling now. She never forgave him. Nor me. Because soon after that I became his woman. And so I remained, up to the end. His real woman. Perhaps one day she will suffer like him, or like me!' To the rest of them she was transformed: they knew why the shepherd wanted her.

'These Macedonians and their hatreds!' said the Professor in their own *patois*. 'They can live on hatred — I think she does.' He spoke almost with admiration, in spite of the experience of the past with men who had also lived on hatred. But in him such strength of feeling had long been exhausted; here at least was a fire in the heart, and he missed it from his own, now that this was dead and cold, and freedom had left him with nothing, or almost nothing — an interest in the Greek scene because it touched his youth. 'It was over these hills, Hebe,' he said, 'these actual hills between us and Bulgaria, that Philip of Macedon sent back a conquered army to its own country, every tenth man leading nine others who had been blinded, while the tenth was left with one eye, to find the way, so that their people might see them come home in such a state.'

'Was it? — Let us get out of here as soon as we're rested!' Hebe said, impelled by she did not know what memory or warning, of the senses or the mind. But the others looked at her in surprise: they had found shelter and food, why should they hurry to move? and the next day she herself had forgotten the feeling of urgency, as she had forgotten the scene with the shepherd. Dido let them bar the door from the kitchen recess into the yard, after that first night.

The bright spell held, with sunshine by day between heavy falls of snow at night. The three days stretched into a week, and then on and on. A sow which had escaped the *andartes*' eye returned to farrow in the pen built on to the wall of the kitchen recess. (From long before the civil war began, or any war within living memory, it had been the custom to turn loose the farm animals, on the approach of armed bands, in the hope that they would hide: Dido had saved only this one beast, apart from the sheep which were away on the hill, before she realized that the men who came that day were not after animals. Or not as their main purpose: they had collected the goat and the chickens when they had finished with the man.) Hebe spent a frightened and wondering night, listening to strange breathings and shufflings on the other side of the partition, and found with delight in the morning seven piglets already born;

the strongest of them had found its way round to the milk before the remaining three of the litter emerged.

For the next few days she saved the lives of one or more of the little pigs at intervals, rushing to get her shoulder under some part of the big sow's bulk, and heaving and burrowing with all her strength to rescue those who were being crushed or suffocated under the weight of the mother. The sow was nervous and out of condition from a life of semi-starvation in the woods. Accustomed to space, she could not understand that her young were unable to keep out of her way in the pen, and would fling herself down at any moment, without warning. A rubbery whack of her teats on the slushy stones was the signal for Hebe to dash up and start counting, without waiting for the rising of shrill squeals which soon grew fainter and fainter. It was an interlude of enchantment: the playtime which the child in Hebe had missed: to the young woman in her, the preservation of the little pigs mattered just enough, but not too much for her satisfaction. She knew Jean-Paul and Mihael too well not to realize that when they elected to leave, anything so succulent would tend to leave with them; dead, because dead pig was easier to carry: but for the moment all that concerned her was the fun, sensible and appealing, of preventing the litter from being overlaid. When she pulled them out from under the mother, the piglets were warm and lively and easily comforted in her hands. The snow sparkled in the sun — for her pleasure, or so it felt; and for her, too, the hawks tumbled expertly about the sky, chasing one another because there was no other prey to chase. She came nearer, in that interlude, to real peace of mind than she had done since the long days spent lying alone in the bow of her father's chartered schooner, after she had warned André not to join the expedition. Or perhaps since earlier than that — when she had spent hours chivvying out of the front door the retriever who would lie dangerously at the foot of the stairs, in the house with the dogs, only to have him come creeping back through the french window. Purposeful, unexacting, good days they had been, and so were these.

Morning after morning they expected to be told to move on, but evening came and nothing had been said. Dido seemed in no hurry to be alone again with her own thoughts. She went on sharing with them whatever food she had, in return for their help, particularly Jean-Paul's ingenuity in improvising such things as a shutter-fastening from the handle of the Professor's metal cup. From the pot of medicament he made a lamp that would burn animal-fat in place of the ordinary kitchen one for which no more oil could be obtained, now that civil war was closing, more and more tightly, the supply routes from the south. Dido gave, indeed, with a carelessness that shocked Lisabet deeply. 'A feckless wife for a farmer, she must always have been! Even while he lived. One does not get this way suddenly!' But, 'What did I tell you?' demanded Hebe triumphantly. 'Didn't I say these Macedonians gave easily?' — even though she saw that Lisabet was wrong, just as she herself had been wrong — Dido was open-handed now not from real generosity, but because it was indeed possible for someone to become suddenly willing to give, when the whole purpose of keeping things had gone. Giving had become as easy as not giving, and as unimportant. Despite Katina's praise of her unchanging kindness, Dido would have been hard enough to them, in the days of her happiness, to satisfy even Lisabet's principles. Then, food had been worth conserving, because food was strength and strength was needed, for the fulness of living. What was it worth to her alone?

To get grease for the new lamp, Jean-Paul slaughtered one of Dido's own sheep, away on the hillside, pitting his wits against the shepherd's to carry off the carcass unobserved, and leave it looking as if one of the vicious vlach dogs had worried it to death. The shepherd came sullenly to report the find — the first time he had been to the farm since the night of their arrival.

If Dido suspected how the sheep had died, she was glad enough of the result, the light, not to give any sign of it. The shepherd received no encouragement for his suggestion that possibly the killer was not a dog. 'What else could it be?' she asked scornfully, with an air of dismissal, adding that in future he should keep better watch.

Feeling leapt between them. He took a stride forward. Then, holding in his anger, saying nothing because of the presence of interlopers, he gathered up his staff and cloak to go. At the door he turned, and his black eyes shifted resentfully from one to another of the people in the kitchen, resting too long and appraisingly on each for the gaze to be borne with comfort: only at Dido he did not look again before he stalked out, leaving the door swinging open behind him, once more, for someone else to close, in a gesture of insolence or contempt. He was an impressive figure, taller and gaunter than Hebe remembered from the first time she had seen him, seated on a rock as part of the landscape; she watched him with fear as he disappeared into the snowy outside world, giving still more the impression of being a man withdrawn from ordinary humanity into the company of beasts and stones. It was hard to think of him as ever sleeping between four walls.

'He will share the loss!' Dido said with satisfaction, and explained that no money passed between them now; twice a year he took an agreed proportion of her small flock for his own.

The sight of the shepherd stirred her to talk more intimately than usual: so far, the travellers had heard nothing of her man that was not wholly in his favour. 'After the killing,' she said, 'they spoke of something they thought I did not know, those two, the shepherd and Katina, when they came to me, according to custom, to pay tribute to the dead. It so happened they came at the same time. They said, and I know it was true, that when he went over the hills to market — Oh, three times a year, perhaps — sometimes he visited a certain woman in a certain house there, in the town. I had been aware of it, but not that they also knew. It was natural, you understand — he was so much a man. And I was never so excellent a woman as he was a man, even in my youth. Sometimes when I loved him most I even thought it was a pity he did not have someone finer than me in body, to match his. But I suppose she was really not better than me, just different. And he was content with me, most of the time. It was so seldom he went away from here. I told you, not more than three times a year, to buy what we needed for the farm. And of those times, there were many when he did not stop to drink *oozo* with the other men, and then think of her because she was near and he was a little drunk, but came back when he had bought the plough-shares and the salt and the casks we wanted. I am angry, though, that they thought I was ignorant of anything he did — those two. With Katina finding such clever ways of telling me and seeming not to wish to tell me — Can you see her, catching her lip between her teeth and saying "Oh, perhaps now I should not speak of it — !" But of one thing I am glad —' (Again Dido was transfigured before them, in all eyes but Hebe's.) 'How they must have felt their jealousy, those two, of him and of me, to have tried to tell me about him then, believing I did not know!' (Hebe saw only a woman, as old as sorrow and hopelessness, who could never have known any life that would have been worth while, to Hebe.)

'They are interesting things, human minds!' Jean-Paul discovered for himself, speaking in their own language.

'How can they be interesting when they are all so much the same?' Lisabet protested. 'People have minds more alike than their faces.'

'That, of course, is true,' said Mihael. 'I do not think you can rightly say that human minds are interesting. Not *human* minds. Now if we could know —'

'Yes, yes, but we can't. And supposing there is a God, maybe He still hasn't a mind. More like the inside of a dynamo, quite likely. So leave it, leave it!' Jean-Paul turned to Dido with the bantering tone which infused Hebe with anger. 'And you have still no pity for the poor shepherd in love! What cruelty!'

Dido looked at him, considering the words gravely, and said something Hebe was to remember for a long while: 'No, I've no pity for those with someone to want. For whether they get what they want or not, they're still rich — better off than those who can see nothing worth their wanting.'

The new lamp in the kitchen made it possible, now, not to go to bed in the evenings when the daylight ended. Dido sat, talking and talking, or stood arrested in the middle of some chore, as though entranced into forgetfulness by the effort she put forth to keep something of her man alive, recalling for them in smallest detail the life she had shared with him. She spoke of his ways, of a hundred insignificant things that he had done: but never again of anything so vital as the business with the woman over the hill. Strangers had killed him; while she spoke of him to other strangers, he might have some reality still in their minds, and live again in hers. But because of her desire to praise him, and only to praise, the vital acts of his life became overlaid with her assertions of his strength, his industry, which could not have been true because the farm showed signs of having been ill-worked for too long, and the impression they received was of someone so devoid of ordinary human qualities that no such man could ever have lived at all.

Moved by the unavailing strength of that love, its defeat of its own ends, the Professor talked haltingly of a side of his life of which Hebe had known nothing: he spoke of his family, not dead, or possibly not dead, but dispossessed, scattered, hopelessly lost to him in any case: yes, probably dead by now; certainly not to be searched for, because, if they lived, what could he be to them but a troublesome shadow from the past, better forgotten? And — I will not listen! the child in Hebe thought; why should I bear the sorrows of other people? There is too much sorrow!

She turned her mind away to attend to Jean-Paul and Mihael, harkening through their talk, and the two ill-fitting doors of the kitchen recess, for the thin squeals, rapidly dying away, which would send her rushing out on her self-imposed task. The two young men could still sometimes mention their war-days without bickering: the novelty of feeling secure for the time being was only just beginning to wear off. Jean-Paul reminded the other that he also had once had a wife and child, if not for long. 'A friend who wanted me to join the Resistance said, "Why don't you? Do you like your job?" Well, you know what my job was — I told you, those false teeth! "No," I said, "but there's my wife and child." "Well," he asked, "do you like your wife and child?" Believe it or not, I had never thought of that before. Many men don't. "No," I said. So I joined the Resistance.' He roared with laughter. 'Now I suppose you are going to tell me, Mihael, you got into it to prove the existence of Something Beyond?'

'I have already told you, such a possibility never occurred to me till much later. Though now you say that — ' Mihael became once more round-eyed with uncertainty ' — there was a very remarkable moment in my life. A friend of mine was much in need of money. I was, too, but not so seriously, being unmarried. I went into a bank with him — not for myself, but he asked me to come, though only as a friend. Not to do anything. A little country bank, it was, in Rumania, at the end of a market day. He knew there wouldn't be much there, even when the farmers had paid in, but it was better to try a place with only one man behind the grille. That man looked at us; he was grey with fear, although not of us, it seemed. Which was odd, because my friend was armed. My friend mentioned the sum he wanted, guessing what the bank might have. Twenty thousand *lei* I think it was. And the man went at once and got a bundle of notes to give him. He said, "Here are my life's savings, take them, what does it matter?" He handed over a little more than twenty thousand, actually. It seemed that market day was also the time when the doctor came over from the next town, once a week. The man had just heard he had only a very short time to live. Indeed, he would be lucky if he didn't live long. Because of something he had growing in his throat. Well, now, that saved a crime, for my friend would certainly have shot to prevent an outcry, if he had to. It was because of this business I moved to Italy, where it happened I went with the *partigiani* — After the man died, people might not have believed he really gave this money, like that, to a stranger, when he could easily have given the bank's money instead, saying he was forced to. Or they might not have believed that I was only with my friend as a friend. So you may be right. I wonder. . . .'

'You think God would start something to kill him, growing in an innocent man's throat, in order to keep two souls like yours from further stain?' Jean-Paul began to laugh again, and then was sobered by his own reflection: 'Well, by the priests' account, I wouldn't put it past Him!'

This was better hearing, Hebe decided. The thin, poor armour of understanding, all one had — it didn't save one much. To listen to these two was not so disquieting because their yearning for the excitement and violence of the past shut them out of her comprehension: but the talk of Dido and the older man was of experience that might come her own way in time. She too would be established with a family one day, then she too might suffer the same kind of loss. No, sometimes to understand was only to grow more vulnerable.

She held her mind as firmly closed to the weakness of sympathy as, on the Bulgarian hillside, she had held it closed to panic. One might be almost as hampering as the other in the task before her.

Lisabet, too, was pleased by Mihael's account of the bank incident: it had much of the moral quality and unexpected logic of a folk-tale. The resting-place they had found, the brief tranquillity, seemed good indeed to them all.

6

LOSS

Two piglets the sow managed to squash or smother in the night: Hebe could not remain on guard for twenty-four hours at a time. They were eaten for the main meal the next day, by the girl with as much relish as by the others, for once they were dead they were no longer her toys, and bread or potatoes with olive oil, eked out with a few gnarled beans and figs, was all that they had yet had to eat at the farm — an unsatisfactory diet, despite the goodness of the bread, for anyone except a Macedonian. (On Lisabet's insistence, the remains of the slaughtered sheep were being pickled and kept in a provident way, not at all Greek, so that the meat should be used later in the winter.)

Before the carcasses of the little pigs could be picked clean, and while appetites were still sharp, Dido said, 'I will take the rest for the shepherd,' and gathered up the bones, with scraps of meat adhering.

'But if you hate him?' Jean-Paul's eye had been on a particular piece of back, with marrow in it.

'He is still my shepherd.'

'I will take them to him if you like. I know the rock where he sits,' said Hebe, with Mihael helping her over a word or two.

'You wouldn't find the way.'

'I could see it from the corner of the wood where I dug through the snow today for acorns.'

'No, I will go.'

Either Dido thought she would finish picking the bones on the way, the girl supposed without rancour, or she had not understood. For such polyglots as these, three days with someone who spoke another tongue was enough for mastering most of the small number of words they used in ordinary talk, but the more languages they knew, as Hebe had observed, the harder it became to stick to one of them for the whole length of a sentence. She tried again, out of vague goodwill to Dido for owning the sow. That morning, with Lisabet's help, a branch had been arranged in the pen so that the remaining piglets could shelter behind it when the mother flopped down: Hebe could leave her vigil.

'It is easier for someone light to get across the snow, where it's thick,' she said.

'He may not be at the rock.'

'Well, then, I know where his hut is. We passed it on the way here.'

'You know a lot!' It was not said kindly. 'I will go.'

Dido would speak no more to anyone, but watched with a contemptuous air the badgering, by Lisabet, of one of the men who was reluctant to let her have his coat for what was bound to be an unsatisfactory, makeshift repair — for clothes, unlike shoes, they had no suitable patching material. Lisabet continued to blossom with goodwill in these days, after her success — wanting no more of any of them but that they should think their garments improved by her efforts. Her solicitude could not be kept to her own party: she had several times shown signs of trying to run the farm for Dido, which had not been welcomed.

Dido went out, carrying the excuse of the little carcass in a cloth, and also a staff — Macedonian sheep dogs were half starved and savage at all seasons, but ravenous in snowy weather.

'She is trustful!' said Lisabet wonderingly. Peasant, too, she would not have left her farm in such hands as theirs.

'Of what?' Jean-Paul laughed and looked round, and indeed, apart from the piglings, there was nothing that would repay the trouble of moving. They did not want to cook at the moment, so the sow and her family remained undisturbed, but presently they went to help themselves to more bread, and found that Dido had taken with her to the shepherd all that remained of her last baking.

For Hebe, the day dragged — the first time that this had happened since she came to the farm. It was a small triumph to have fitted up a sanctuary for the remaining piglets, but it ended her happy employment. She took the Professor out to the pen and showed him the runt of the litter, with whom she was annoyed. In the struggle for food, he had acquired as his own, through weakness at birth, the teat with the least milk in it, or possibly he had grown more weakly than the rest because it had fallen to his share: each piglet kept to his own teat. And now that there were two good teats to spare through his brothers' deaths, Hebe could not induce him to transfer himself to one of them.

'It is always so with pigs, I believe,' the Professor said, looking down at the tiny creature nuzzling and tugging in vain, while the sow lay half propped up on the bough, with her other young drinking at ease.

'It is stupid.'

'Yes, but we are all stupid, this way or some such way.' It was the last time he spoke to her on the old exacting level. Since they came to this place, with its poor semblance of safety and comfort, he seemed to have let go of whatever it was that had just enabled him to come so far. He shrivelled in spirit. 'For a little pig, you see, a sow is too big to love. There's so much of her, more than he can take in. She's like the world. He can only love a teat. His teat, good or bad. Like a man and his country.' He looked away, over the breathless white silence of the landscape around them, to the summits of the hills where the snow had begun to colour in the low sun, and added astonishingly, 'Hebe, I shall stay on here. If she will let me. And work for her.'

For a moment, because she did not want to, the girl could not believe him.

'Remain behind when we go on? Oh no. No!'

'Yes, why not? The pig that's lost its teat. This is as near to it as I'm likely to come.'

She protested angrily, 'You *must* come on. To the Coast. To get a ship.'

It was essential for her that the ship should remain in her mind, real, something that they were going to reach. If he would not come, the others might feel like delaying here still longer: and she realized suddenly how intensely she wanted to avoid this. While they stayed in this forgotten pocket of the hills the future could not come marching decorously towards her with André and *Le Bien Venu* in its train of far-off, admirable days, eventless with dignity.

She tried desperately to think of reasons why he should not give up like this, failing to find words for the idea — it was too alien to their way of thought — that for him, a man who had already endured so much, it was unworthy that his endurance should fail now, when someone as defenceless as herself had need of him.

'But it's dirty here. And one's cold. And hungry most of the time.'

'Not very cold, or very hungry.' He put out an apologetic hand and tousled still further the mouse-coloured hair, sticking out in tufts from the head which dodged away indignantly from his touch.

'But me — I must go on.' She could get no further, on that line.

'Oh yes, you must. You have great determination. You go on towards something, while I am only leaving things behind. Well, here I have left them behind. As much as I can.'

'The others may not keep me with them.'

'I think they will. Lisabet is so changed. Haven't you noticed?'

'Yes, but — '

He called her 'My dear, my dear!' as he had when her father was killed, but would not yield to the furious, frightened look of entreaty: the meanness of desire fulfilled was upon him, even though the desire was weak — for any kind of rest, any degree of comfort; and the fulfilment scanty — he had at least come to Greece, where the ground seemed to remember its greatness, though men had forgotten it.

'It's stupid,' she said again, as she had of the little pig, and turned wholly childish in her resentment that anyone should fail to want what she herself wanted so badly. 'You ought to think it's better to go on.'

His sad monkey-face puckered up in amusement at that. 'The first thing to consider about any state of affairs, Hebe,' he said, 'is not whether it's desirable, but whether it exists. And you see I don't think it's better. Not for me.'

He went back into the house. Running as fast as the soft top layer of the snow allowed, Hebe plunged down the path which Dido had taken — Dido must be persuaded not to let him stay.

What she intended to say to this end when they met, Hebe did not know: Dido would not care that his leaving the party set Hebe's particular ambitions further from fulfilment in her own mind — they would seem remote enough not to matter, even if the girl could have explained them in the scanty words they had in common; they were not desires which Dido could have felt. But perhaps the right words would come. They must come, Hebe thought as she ran. She could talk to the Professor; they shared a knowledge of a different kind of life, orderly and full of front doors: the rest of the party meant nothing to her. Old and beaten, not much of a figure of protection, he was all the same a proof that this different life really had existed — the last remaining proof, now that she had torn up its photograph.

The hawks had gone from the quivering upper air, and trembling up from the woods in the plain below, carried far in the snow-hush, the owls' hooting came to set her shivering inside. She would say how slow the Professor was in anything he did with his hands — Dido might have noticed that for herself. Yes — and an inspiration — that he had always angered the party by refusing to do his fair share of carrying, when they had anything to carry — if Dido did not believe Hebe, she could ask the others. That would matter, if he were to work for her.

A dog began baying, not far off, and she stopped in fear. The noise came nearer. Hebe looked about, wondering in near-panic if it would be possible to scrabble through the snow for stones. A stone in the hand — stones in both hands, for choice — would keep a vlach dog at bay as well as a stick, or better, while light enough remained for it to see the menacing move of an arm: these beasts were more used to being stoned without mercy than beaten: even their own shepherds kept out of reach of their teeth when punishing them. But as she had already discovered, there was a hard crust under the surface of new snow, where the first falls had melted by day and then frozen again at night. The cover of the woods was too far away to reach; there were only a few spindly bushes beside the track along which Dido's footprints had led her. As quietly as she could, aware that what she did was probably useless, she floundered through deep, blown snow into a ditch and up a bank, to stand beside a thin little tree which leant across the track. There was no defence, nowhere to hide, but it was instinctive to put something, however inadequate, between herself and the thing feared, and with this wind blowing towards her from the direction of the noise there was a chance that the wolf-like creature would not scent her. Ahead, the track with its line of footprints bent out of sight. The tumult came close; by the sound the dog was attacking something, in short snarling rushes. When she expected at any time to see it, or the thing it was harrying, she heard the shepherd's voice, raised in a shout: the noise changed to shrill yelps of pain, and then there was quiet again. The dog had gone. She waited, listening to her heart slowly ceasing to pound.

Dido appeared, but did not see her until they were abreast. The woman was crying as she walked, with her head up, her face un-moving, and water flowing from her eyes in a complete and terrible abandonment to misery. By the time she was aware of Hebe it was too late to avoid the meeting.

'You are hurt, Dido?'

'No.'

'But the dog?'

'It didn't touch me. Though it wouldn't have mattered. The shepherd drove it away.'

'Then I don't understand.'

'How should you, a child?'

'You said I knew a lot!'

'Not of this.' And again Dido said, with envy, 'How should you?'

She had not waited while Hebe scrambled down from the bank,

so that the girl was forced to run to catch up with her. Dido moved as if alone with her shamed and silent weeping, making no effort even now to restrain it. The last light of the day, red from the reflection of the sky, beating up from the snow, shone on the wet, blubbered face, which yet had some quality of dignity because of its stillness. Emotion so different from anything she had known — so dreadful because accepted — overawed Hebe, and the pleas she had come to make remained unspoken. The memory returned of Dido's voice in the kitchen on their first night at the farm, high-pitched, meant to rouse witnesses to the fact that for the moment she did not need the shepherd, and could refuse him, hating him with her mind. The world crawled, for Hebe, with passion which she would never come fully to comprehend. It made the white, cold scene about her, with its mocking air of cleanness, less real than the phantom of a man unknown, Dido's man, whose memory was too much for Dido's tormented body to bear unassuaged, and there was no one else for her but the man who had betrayed him. Hard and arrowy herself, with the strength of the single-minded, Hebe would meet defeat over and over again, but not that of the lonely spirit by the lonelier flesh.

7

YORKIM

IN silence they trudged back together through the biting twilight to the dark and apparently derelict house. (It was unwise to let light shine out at night from an isolated place, and all the shutters had been mended by Jean-Paul before the lamp had even been planned.)

Dido showed no curiosity at any time to learn why the girl had followed her, and long before they reached the farm Hebe knew that the words not spoken on meeting would never be spoken at all, for they were bound to be useless. Instinct, not real understanding, told her that Dido would be glad the old man should stay, making no demands on her, not much of a worker, but something of an ally against herself.

From then onwards the farm became, to Hebe, no longer a resting place but a prison, from which it seemed more and more impossible to escape: soon it was incredible to her that she had ever looked on it as a haven, and luck had consisted in being allowed to stay. It was like one of the autumn webs which hung in the woods where she grubbed up the sow's acorns; but not a gleaming, jewelled thing; a disgusting web, with Dido as the spider in the midst of it. Vile impulses, hers and the shepherd's, moved the strands of the web, while the creatures entangled in it lost the will to drag themselves free. Now that they had all had a breathing space, and Lisabet had repaired their gear, after a fashion, there was nothing to keep the party hanging about the place: no one but the old man had expressed any wish to remain indefinitely: they would never be fitter to struggle on; but day followed day and, hard as the life was, it made the prospect of being on the move again still harder and less inviting. Each postponement of effort weakened them all.

The snow melted, and the softer, fickle weather of the Greek autumn returned, but the piercing Vardar wind blew more and more often, between the gentle spells. And Hebe knew that in a few weeks more it would be too late to move, with real winter gripping the hills. The thought of months shut up in this farm set her skin creeping with loathing of the things which squirmed just out of her sight.

One after the other she tried the people in her party: why would they not attempt to make Salonika before the worst of the evil weather made it difficult — perhaps impossible — to hang about the docks unobtrusively, waiting for the chance of a ship? Yes, all of them agreed, really they must make up their minds to move on, quite soon. They would talk about it, tomorrow. And then lethargy took over again. Meanwhile the lines of the maps faded little by little in her mind, though this she dared not use as an argument for moving quickly, in case, if they thought her of no further use to them, they might be as ready as before to leave her behind, despite the Professor's belief in Lisabet's change of heart. It was the same with the list of contacts, in whose importance she must still pretend.

As time went on, they came to know the people of Katina's village, where they went occasionally to barter produce for Dido, exchanging olives against honey, which was used in place of sugar, or a sheepskin for curing-salt. Civil strife having paralysed long-distance trade, it was remarkable how quickly a tariff of exchange had established itself, with delicately shifting values. The one storekeeper, now the barter-master, was the old man, Zari, who had first directed them to Katina. He presided over a small permanent stock of the articles always stranded in such places by wars or alien occupation. Hebe's party had found the same kind of useless goods left in the same kind of store wherever they had been: patent medicines which had lost their labels, and children's shoes, in sizes so small that no child young enough to wear them would ever be given shoes at all in such communities — It was as though, commercially, war produced a special kind of dregs.

Zari believed unshakably that this part of Macedonia was still under the rule of the Turks, and was the only person in the place on the Royalist side: not for love of the king, or the Government, but because in his view the *andartes*, by opposing them, were distracting Greece from her proper fight with Turkey, like the German and Italian invaders before them.

They met again Nitsa, the beast-like creature who had looked and looked at them: Katina told them what was wrong with her: she had a child inside her which could not get out. Not properly grown, it had been there for years: if you put your hand on her stomach you could sometimes feel it struggling, she said, and hear it cry out suddenly at night, but it would not die: Nitsa was crazed with want of sleep because of its crying. And Katina herself they came to know well, with her continual planning to get the better of someone, in a barren longing for dominion.

Yorkim was the village butt, and would almost have missed the pitiless laughter of his neighbours if it had not followed him everywhere. A small, wizened fellow who had fits, he lived with his widowed sister, similarly afflicted, by whom he had so many children, to add to those which each of them had produced by former alliances, that the undying local joke was to pretend he did not know the full number: if he tried to count them, neither he nor they could remain still long enough to let him finish the tally — most of them had inherited the parents' trouble. When one of his own attacks was approaching, Yorkim became a malevolent little he-goat of a man, making his way in everywhere, so that no woman could feel sure at night, without searching the corners of her house, that he would not be hiding somewhere in it, crouched under a table or in a loft. He did not trouble Dido because she lived too far off and he was afraid of the shepherd. If anyone had a child unexpectedly, it was always said to be Yorkim's, and watched to see if it had fits. If so, the woman's proper man could get rid of her, should he want to, with the approval of the neighbours; though as the village had become exceedingly inbred, through many generations of isolation, and the epileptic strain was there, many more children were credited to Yorkim than those likely to be his.

There was more senseless cruelty towards the few domestic

animals, the scarred, sore-ridden, broken-eared donkeys and cringing, ribby dogs, than Hebe had learnt to accept as normal even in
Italy and Spanish America. The Macedonians were a people easily
angered, and they inflicted pain not carelessly, like Latins, but with
vindictive purpose, and a long knowledge of suffering, bred from
this ground into their bones. In their favour it could be said that
they had a high and reliable standard of personal courage, tenacity,
and an ability to glean laughter from adversity — not, however,
qualities which Hebe could admire, for she had them herself and
took them for granted: they were as necessary to life in these parts
as breathing. She could not find people worthy of respect or liking
merely for having breath in them.

When at last, gathering his courage, he asked humbly if he might
remain indefinitely on the farm, as a kind of servant, the Professor
received a curt nod of satisfaction from Dido. That day he wiled
away the evening, for himself and Hebe, by telling the girl the story
of the Lotus Eaters: it was an effort to put himself right, a little, in
her straight and unforgiving eyes. The two things coming so close
together — the request, and the old, strange tale with its personal
application — drove Hebe into a terrified resolution. Indeed this
setting of theirs was no Lotus Land, but the parallel was not to be
missed: if the others would make no effort to escape, she must try
alone. Some other means must be discovered of keeping a link with
André, if his cousin disappeared from her ken, and certainly there
was now less hope than ever that Jean-Paul would tear himself
away: he had found some meagre satisfaction with one of Yorkim's
unappetizing daughters.

Very early the next morning Hebe slipped away from the farm,
with bread from an over-night baking as sole provision for the
journey, besides the stick which Dido had carried. The loaf had to
be taken from the oven while Dido slept nearby, and was not yet
fully cooked, but it was something to clutch, something to try to
eat later: her throat was too dry with the thought of what lay
ahead, or might lie ahead, to let her eat for a long while after she
had stolen out through the yard, moving with extreme caution to

disturb no one. She did not know whether Jean-Paul and Mihael, believing in her memory, would keep her by force if they caught her, here in this obscene place, the web where the will rotted. But no one stirred in the barn as she passed.

The sensible path to take would have been the one which Dido had followed towards the shepherd's hut, leading her straight down hill towards the lower valleys — a wonderful lightening of the spirit, it would mean, she thought, to get out of these mountains! But the memory of fear lay too heavily across it; she went the other way, towards the village by a long detour. The menace from which her thoughts shrank most, as she set out, were the savage dogs rather than the savage bands of men in this region; and with good reason, even though in the time she had stayed at the farm she had become a woman, technically. This physical development was a complication more in her own mind than in any practical way; it made one of the risks of the way, rape, seem more serious to her than it had done before, although it had always been a possibility to be considered. But from undernourishment she was immature enough in body to be fairly safe from conception for several years more: besides, one of Yorkim's older daughters — the one with whom Jean-Paul had cosied down — had assured her with gruesome cheerfulness that the first three or four occasions rarely had any result. In any case, men were still men, however brutish: you always had a chance of using your wits for safety among human beings: but as she was not Orpheus, of whom the Professor had also told her yesterday, what inducement of hers could prevail against animals bred and trained and deliberately ill-treated into the utmost viciousness, in order to protect the flocks?

The village slept on satisfactorily while she approached. When she reached the first hovels a house-dog began barking persistently, but it was safely shut in. Farmers in these foothills of the Beles range lay abed even later than usual, now that for lack of markets their produce must wait upon the arrangements of people like Zari: they had never risen early, to acquire more than they needed and so invite trouble. All the same, she did not cross the bridge which spanned a much-fouled stream, and carried the path through the centre of the village: the noise had unnerved her: surely someone would let the beast out if it went on giving warning of a stranger's presence? She made her way round the outlying huts, into a gorge which promised the right direction. In this she found herself presently hemmed between the steep, shaley mountainside, and the same stream, swollen into a small torrent by other streams which joined it below the village. Soon it was clear that somehow she must get across this water if she were to go on down the gorge; it was impossible to plough far through the sliding shale. Where the stream narrowed enough to invite an attempt, the current rushed deep and fast round the boulders of its bed. It was a formidable obstacle, and she spent much time in searching for a good place to cross by jumping from boulder to boulder. In the end she was forced to wade. She worked her way over, drenched to the waist when the tug of the water made her lean against the current, using a rock as a hand-hold and the water swirled up between her body and the rock. In a few minutes she came to another stream, tumbling into the first and barring the way again, but this one was easier to negotiate. On the further side she sat down, trembling with exertion, and ate some of the wet bread before going further. Fed by the recent snows, these seasonal torrents were numbing in their coldness, but the sun shone, there was no wind and in a sheltered patch she found late-fruiting wild raspberries, as well as three not too dilapidated mushrooms which could be eaten raw. In the stillness loneliness pressed down, but she knew that she must try to keep this out of her thoughts, and went on; and the loneliness stalked behind her.

Before the sun was high two more streams faced her and were overcome; they laced the gorge, becoming minor cataracts as the tilt of the ground grew steeper. By noon, as nearly as she could judge the time by the sun, she had come down through a patch of scattered pine trees and reached open, stony country, in which it was easy to see the right general direction, but not so easy to keep to it because of the water. Beyond this lay an area of the familiar scrub-oak and chestnut woodland, common to the whole vast Struma region; it was like the setting of her father's last encampment, she thought, or the ground about the hollow where the maps were buried. Sheltered from the wind, most of the trees here had kept their leaves: small animal trails wound through the thick autumn foliage, to peter out, when she followed them, in places from which nothing was visible but the pointless glory of flame-coloured undergrowth, and remote patches of sky, ominously becoming covered with cloud. Without the sun to guide her, there was no knowing the lie of the land; the gorge had widened, there were flat places in it, and hillocks, not extensive in themselves, but hopelessly misleading when the view was restricted to a few yards by the trees, and her only hope was to keep on moving downhill. Eventually all paths, such as there were, brought her back to the streams, and the streams grew always wider and deeper.

When the Vardar wind rose again, late in the day, she was already exhausted. Much of the time in the scrubland she had been lost, and moving in unprofitable directions. Chance brought her to what seemed to be the lower end of the gorge, although by this time she was too confused to be sure. A sloping wall of scree closed it, and led up to an escarpment on which not even a goat track could be discerned. The scree proved impassable once more, sliding down and threatening to bury her when she tried to climb it. Somewhere along the way she had come, hidden by the trees, she still believed that there was probably a way out of the gorge into another valley; it might be through a water-course, or a break in the scree, but if so she had missed it. And it was no use searching for it because it might still be impracticable, or more likely she would not find it. Or — this thought came when one of Lisabet's patches on a shoe began to make itself felt — it might not be there at all. The loneliness closed in and would no longer be denied. André — thinking of André had once helped greatly, but now for some reason it would not help at all.

A sick heart recognized that she must go back, but told her, though doubtfully, that she could go on again the next day.

She took until dusk to work her way up to the pine-tree level, with discouragement dragging at her feet, and the melted snow-water tugging more vehemently as she recrossed the streams — more streams, too, there seemed to be, than on her hopeful way down. Dido's stout stick was like a much-needed additional hand, helping her against the current. Without it, tired as she was, she could hardly have got across. Before night fell she knew that she would not go on the next day. It had been dark for some hours when she saw, with a relief which was the measure of her failure, the huddled roofs of the village cutting into the stars.

Further than this she could not make a raw heel take her before morning, but she knew too much of local ways to knock, and expect any door to open after dusk. No dogs barked this time. The latch of a mule-shed, gently tried, yielded to her hand, and she went in, feeling along the wall to where there was some dry straw, on which she dropped, her head resting against a pile of harness. Presumably the mule was not there, or the door would have been securely fastened against neighbours and thieves. She rustled her body further down between two loose heaps of straw. Immediately there was another rustle and then a pause, and after that, purposeful, continuous rustling began on the other side of the shed. Rats? She thought not. By the sound, this was one creature only, and something of considerable size, moving cautiously towards her. Not a mule: this thing was creeping through the straw.

She had closed the door behind her and jammed it with a piece of wood, in case any dogs happened to be let out of the houses even earlier than she intended to wake: it was almost pitch black in the shed, to eyes accustomed to the starlight outside. The only glimmer came through a place under the eaves where a plank had sprung, at the join of the walls. Her one hope of escape from the approaching thing, whatever it was, lay in the possibility that it might not be able to see her either. On her feet in an instant, she edged her way back by the wall to where there was no more straw to rustle. As she felt ahead of her through the darkness, her hand touched, and recoiled from, and touched again, a ladder standing away from the wall; probably, she thought, it led to a loft where the fodder was stored. She held on to a rung to steady herself.

Soon the thing was also off the straw, moving still more quietly over the beaten-earth floor; but she could hear it breathing, between her and the door. She stooped, to keep her head from cutting the small aperture of sky, and letting go of the ladder moved a yard or two, obliquely nearer the breathing but also nearer the door. Somewhere here she had left Dido's stick leaning against the wall. Her fingers closed round it thankfully, after the same nervous jump-back with which they had met the ladder.

There was no sense in being afraid, she told herself: her father had been afraid, and where had it led him? She heard the thing softly approaching the place where she had been, and was immeasurably afraid.

Back by the ladder, and stretching out her arm as far as she could, she managed to scratch with the end of the stick on the wall furthest from the door: if possible she must get the thing between herself and such light as there was, as well as away from the door. She moved round to the other side of the ladder, bringing herself a little nearer the middle of the shed. Presently she sensed the thing creeping by, between herself and the wall. It could have no sense of smell, for it went on, away from her. To reach the place from which the little scrape had come, it rustled again over the straw. Quickly, while the rustling lasted, she half climbed, half drew herself up four rungs of the ladder, still holding the stick. The wood was sound enough and did not creak, but she stopped with the feeling which comes in the dark of the nearness of some obstacle. Her head came gently in contact with the underside of the loft. There had been no means of telling, as the ladder was upright, which was the right side to climb, and she had chosen wrongly. She could get no higher without clambering round again, and this, she realized, was impossible to achieve silently from where she was, half way up. Below and behind her, metal clinked faintly on metal, there was a soft, dragging sound; the harness was being moved to let the searching thing feel about more thoroughly. Only something human — more or less human — would shift the harness like that, lifting it gently. The suspicion she had known after the first rustling became certainty. Yorkim, with a caution as great as her own, was examining the place where for an instant she had rested.

That he was spending the night in this shed, instead of in his own hut, could mean only one thing: he had crawled in for shelter, feeling the onset of an attack. Yorkim as part of the life of the village was a joke — of sorts: Yorkim here, in this state, was something else. It was evident, from his caution, that either he was not yet sure who or what his quarry might be, or his dim mind believed her still unaware of his pursuit, to be come upon by stealth.

She must not move, in panic, before she was ready. She must take a few seconds to visualize, as clearly as possible, exactly at what height she had jammed the wood into the crack of the door, so that there should be no briefest hesitation by her hand, in finding and jerking it free, when she made her dash to get out of the shed. There must be no fumbling, no inch or two of misjudgment delaying her for even part of a second. With her head and neck bent, she pressed her shoulders as close as she could to the rafters of the loft, crouching on the second rung down, knees doubled under her, and her body about four feet from the floor, as she guessed; while below her this ghastly version of hide-and-seek in the gloom went on, just audibly. If he crept back to the other side of the shed, where he had been before, and towards the door, he would inevitably see her now, silhouetted against the space in the planking, but he was feeling carefully in the corner where the wall had been scratched. Over and over her mind rehearsed the detail of her tired and inattentive jamming of the door: all she knew surely was that she had done it hard, the stick would not flick out at a touch. But at what height? Level with her waist, her shoulder — the longer she thought, the more uncertain grew the memory of her action. Yorkim was not very much bigger than herself, racked and weakened by illness, but in his goatish moods, his daughters said, and half the village echoed, of formidable strength.

He was keeping still and listening now. She tried to touch with her stick the back wall of the shed, to send him fumbling once more a yard or so further away. At the moment she was nearer the door than he was, but a paralysis of doubt held her to the ladder. Suppose, when she came in, she had bent — had she? — to use her weight to push it in, why, then the wedge would be down at about knee level, and if she felt too high she would miss it altogether. For just too long, anyway.

From this position she could not reach the wall with the stick to decoy him, and the weight on her extended arm made it tremble. There was the faintest click of wood on wood, as she brought the stick back to her side. In a few seconds she knew that he was coming straight towards her.

She separated her hands as widely as the top rung allowed, took her feet off the ladder and supported her body as far from it as she could, with a bent knee pressing against each upright. Yorkim knew which was the side to climb, and crawled up, breathing rankly in her face as his head came level with the loft. His feet missed her tight-clenched fingers and soon she heard him feeling about the loft. Not silently now: he was grunting and muttering to himself, making little whining noises, seemingly aware by this time that the quarry was deliberately eluding him. She waited, with pain which she only recognized later biting into her knees, where they took her weight against the rough edges of wood: waited until she judged him to be in the furthest corner of the loft, and then dropped to the ground and made for the door. The stick half tripped her, she made a false step but recovered. He was after her in a second, chattering, whining. Her free hand felt for the lintel, found the wide crack between it and the door, felt upwards, but failed to reach the wedge. He was almost on her when she turned and jabbed with Dido's stick, lunging out at chest level, at the sound of him. She got him, jabbed quickly, higher, hoping for his face or throat, and missed; jabbed again and caught him in the body; not a powerful blow, he was too close. He went down, but brought her down with him, grabbing her ankle as he rolled over.

For a moment, or eternity, they fought confusedly on the floor, a scrabbling, flailing struggle. Then somehow she was up and free, but he grabbed at her again and she went down. There was whimpering in her ears; his, she thought, with curious detachment, not hers; and suddenly this changed to an unmistakable series of sounds which seemed to her at the moment quite inexpressibly beautiful: his grip relaxed. Excitement had done its work and Yorkim shook and gasped and choked harmlessly in the grip of a fit.

She kicked herself away from him, feeling again for the wedge while still on her knees — it was far lower down than she had thought — and locating it, pulled herself up by the edge of the open door, to stumble out into the night, this cold, weary, pitiless Greek night which smelt all the same so wonderfully of stars and solitude.

Zari had a small haystack, she remembered, in front of his house. Vlach dogs had become, for the time being, a forgotten menace, and Yorkim would be too ill to leave the shed and molest her further. The soreness of her rubbed heel re-asserted itself almost luxuriously, bringing with it into her consciousness the new discomfort of scored knees: with difficulty she limped as far as the stack, and burrowed a tunnel into the hay. Badly dried, it was fermenting a little, so warm inside that it felt as if one day it might fire itself. But not yet. The warmth was lovely.

At the house with the dogs there had been a notice on the gate saying, 'No Hawkers, No Canvassers, No Circulars.' She and André would never have any either, whatever they might be. She slept.

8

'LITTLE ECONOMIES'

THE mood of relief lasted only until the morning.

She walked back from the village to the farm with discomfort from her skinned heel increasing at every step, and about half way on this last lap of dismal retreat, her view of the future shortened from the general depression with which she had awakened, at the prospect of weeks more, months more — who could say how long? — in this foul prison. It became a very lively and immediate apprehension as to how she would be received when she returned. Dido, particularly, might well be vindictive about the theft of her bread, taken while she slept by someone whom she had sheltered for so long. But again the shadow of events proved darker than the substance — even insultingly so: no one but Jean-Paul had paid any attention to Hebe's absence.

When she stole the loaf, she must have left the fire door of the oven unfastened: the increased draught had drawn up the embers, carefully banked over-night, into a blaze by which the whole batch of bread had been burnt. Dido believed herself responsible: the catch on the oven door was one of the faulty things, long needing attention, not yet mended by Jean-Paul. It required to be closed in a special way, and Dido could not remember whether she had tried the door after shutting it, or had forgotten to give it the necessary second push when she closed up the oven for the night. With this doubt in mind, who would notice one missing lump, among a set of useless little cinder-loaves, too wizened even to be thrown to the sow?

In the disturbance of finding the kitchen full of smoke, and no bread to eat, everyone had failed to miss the girl during the early hours of the day. Later, if anyone thought of her at all, it was assumed she had gone to the village and was with Zari's family, helping to make *oozo*: autumn was the distilling season for that ferocious spirit, derived from grape-pips, after *retsina*, the gummy national wine, had been made out of the pulp: anyone bearing a hand with the work was rewarded, at the end of the day, with a meal of better food than the farm generally provided, even when the bread was good. It was the reasonable place to go, after the oven disaster, but the others, unwilling to walk so far, stayed where they were and ate the dregs from an olive-oil cask, scraped over the frosted potatoes which fed the pig. If Hebe chose to remain for the night where she had worked, that was her own concern, to all but Jean-Paul.

Suspicious, he questioned her angrily when she slipped in. She had been right, she realized: had he or Mihael guessed what she might try to do, she would not have got away so easily. From now onwards it would probably be impossible to try again, even supposing she could work up enough courage. It was queer, she thought, while she lied and lied — pretending that she had indeed been at Zari's — how they needed one another, people in their condition, and for what unlikely reasons: an imaginary list in her mind: a sick thing creeping through a dark shed.

Because she was utterly discouraged, she lied less adequately than usual, and the distraction of Katina's unexpected arrival was very welcome. Katina came bursting with news, saving Hebe when the girl was on the point of telling the truth in desperation. In the excitement of what Katina had to say, the matter of Hebe's disappearance was forgotten — there was a 'heelobowie' on the way, declared Katina! It was almost beyond belief, but it was true. Actually on the way, a heelobowie!

Dido echoed her incredulously but without interest: 'A heelobowie? No!'

'Indeed, yes!'

Despite the civil war and everything! Katina exclaimed again and again at the wonder of it. Soon the entire village, she said, would be in a state of fete. For three days at least, if the visit of the last heelobowie could be taken as a guide —

'Oh more! Nearly five days it lasted. Don't you remember?'
Suddenly Dido roused herself, it was as if she had caught the infection of the other's excitement. She interrupted as only a hostess
could, without upsetting the powerful atmosphere of decorum
which Katina always spread about her during visits. The travellers,
excluded from the conversation, could only guess among themselves
at the nature of a heelobowie. ('It is probably something to do with
the sun,' the Professor suggested.)

But the previous visit, to which Dido referred — Katina pointed
out that although this had certainly lasted for four and a half days
it must not be forgotten that it had happened during the war-before-
this-one, when conditions were easier. Naturally she remembered it.
If anyone had been drunk it was not herself — or not for much of
the time — but Dido, and her man, too, which of course was only
right for such a fine, strong, happy couple at a time of celebration.
(The war to which she referred as the war-before-this-one was the
second World War, ending for the Greeks with the lifting of the
German occupation, before their own civil war engulfed them.)
The previous war was the better one, Katina conveyed, when there
had been more invasion, it was true, but also much more *oozo*
about. She was greatly concerned by the present scarcity of *oozo*,
she told Dido. A few people might have a bottle or two of *retsina*
buried under their floors, but not many. And what would be a
heelobowie's home-coming, or the result of that home-coming,
without a proper celebration? The heelobowie might easily be dis-
appointed, and do little or nothing for the district afterwards.

Dido suggested that more *oozo* could be manufactured without
delay. *Retsina* took time to ferment, but as everyone knew about
oozo, the fresher it was, the quicker in action. How fortunate that
the news should have come in the distilling season.

Katina's lofty bearing, in what she considered society — the
company of Dido, her landed equal — continued to hold back the
others from asking the meaning of a word which they were plainly
expected to recognize, or if not, to accept in silent ignorance.

But could the heelobowie reach the village? Dido doubted it, reminding Katina that the place had no name by which anyone could ask his way to it, across those parts of Greece which he might not happen to know.

For the first time it struck the travellers that indeed the cluster of mud hovels had no name, or none which they had ever heard. It appeared on no map, so far as Hebe remembered, and its own inhabitants called it simply 'the village'. The mountains had a collective name, as a long range — the Beles — and the nearest market town, where Dido's man had gone, was known sometimes by one word and sometimes by another, in the Macedonian fashion, according to the district from which the speaker came, but at least it was called something. It was far off, however, and the *andartes* were said to hold it firmly, having re-taken it from the Government troops, depopulating the place by half between them. Hebe's gloom of the morning deepened: truly the party was lost, held up in a nameless fold of the hills!

'But even if he gets here,' Dido added musingly, 'is it likely he will get safely away again, with so many guns loose everywhere? He must be mad to think of coming, as things are.'

'Oh, they are all that, the heelobowies,' Katina agreed. 'But at least we shall have had the celebration. One cannot hope for everything.' A message had somehow reached Zari that this one had already landed at the Piraeus. 'It got through by gypsies, I suppose. Hardly anyone ever kills gypsies, because they have nothing, and give information to everyone, *andartes* and Royalists and ordinary bandits and people like Zari. They are very useful.'

'If you were really with Zari's family,' Jean-Paul demanded of Hebe, 'why didn't you know of all this?'

'I heard of it, but it wasn't worth repeating, as I couldn't make out what it was about.'

'No doubt you have never seen the return of a heelobowie,' Katina said with condescension to the girl. 'It will be specially interesting to you and the old man — if you are still here! — because you speak English. They told me in Turkey that this has many words in common with American.'

('Then it has nothing to do with "helio",' said the Professor, closing the only hopeful line of conjecture. It was Lisabet, knowing fewer languages than the rest of them, who supplied the right translation in the end. In Transylvania, too, it appeared, the name 'Hello-Boy' had become a title of honour for native sons returning, financially successful, from America: but there it was pronounced 'H'llo-bwi' which had delayed her recognition of the Macedonian version.)

'Do we know who he used to be?' Dido asked.

Someone called Ednis, Katina believed, and a cousin's cousin of Zari's, although Zari did not think the two had ever met. There was a tale hanging about in the older people's heads of a herd-boy, from a farm many miles away, who had caught the fancy of a wealthy Rumanian couple, passing by, many years ago; they had taken the lad back with them to Bucharest. There Ednis had disappeared, so far as his kin were concerned. But it was probably the same man, because there was no one else it could be, and it was the nature of heelobowies to be drawn back on no stronger line than that. Besides, why else should a message have come through to this village that he had already landed in the Piraeus?

'I will not hope!' said Hebe sternly to her own heart, while it bounded up, out of control. 'How could he help me to get away from here? Why should he? It will be by my own efforts if I reach the Good Place.' But irrepressibly her heart hoped on for a while.

Katina left, and before Dido could re-bar the door after her, Nitsa's swollen stomach and shrunken face appeared round it; she asked foolishly if the news were true, although she lived much closer than Dido to the local source of it, Zari's store. The rumour, flying round, had stirred the whole community. Several of Yorkim's family as well as their father were said to be having prolonged attacks of the shakes.

The loafers in Dido's kitchen learnt much about the ways of heelobowies, in the weeks that followed, while they crouched closer and closer to the dwindling fires which Jean-Paul described disgustedly as mere wasting diseases of the wood — but neither he nor anyone else would face the Vardar blast outside, for long enough to cut more fuel than was absolutely necessary to keep them alive. While the hard weather held, and the snow thickened, it was easier to be acutely uncomfortable doing nothing indoors.

This was the Greek tradition for those sons of poverty who had struggled away from the scenes of their youth, and, toughened by that struggle, made money on the other side of the world — To work, to save, through grinding years of self-denial, and at last amass enough, if it took a life-time, to return in glory on a visit, and become the 'Uncles' of their native villages. There, on arrival, they would pay and pay for those who had known them in their time of hardship to be drunk and gay for days on end. The bigger the celebrations, in which whole districts took part, the further these surpassed the homecomings of other heelobowies, the more rewarding the legends that would remain about the givers of such entertainment, their magnificence and power. The villages provided the liquor, the returning sons bought it at exorbitant prices, expecting and indeed wishing to be swindled, and to laugh and curse at the unchanging ways of the country, squandering their money as evidence of prosperity in a new and softer land. Then they went away again, having crowned their success, in their own eyes as well as those of their relatives. Even in peaceful times, when foreign trade was thriving, not olives and currants but 'uncles' had always been the most profitable exports of Greece.

Once they had returned as accepted heelobowies, and been honoured with a feast, they could, as a rule, be depended upon to remember their relatives with gifts from overseas, after they had left Greece once more for the places which had made them rich. But sometimes they stayed on in the motherland, instead of going back at the end of the celebration. Then of course, they no longer squandered their money but lived like anyone else; and were no good at all.

The reception of a heelobowie was an investment, on which much depended: it was well known that in some of the most dilapidated areas, whole communities were being supported indefinitely by a single individual. No one really believed that this one could reach the village safely, but it was wiser to act as if he might: in any case, preparation for his coming made it feel more probable.

In the next few weeks, everyone who could help, either by bringing in the ingredients from the farms or by working at Zari's still, made *oozo* as fast as it could be produced, while the burden of local conversation remained, 'He will not get through. How can he? A rich man!' If by some miracle the *andartes* did not hear of his coming, the troops on the other side would get to know, or belonging sometimes to one party, sometimes to the other, the bandits scattered about the hills, in the localities through which he must pass, would learn of this fine opportunity to swell their funds. People less particular in speech than Katina now used the terms for partisans or Government troops quite indiscriminately to cover as well ordinary old-fashioned bandits, properly known as *klepts*, and their choice of names in no way reflected their political views: it was recognized that it made no difference in these days into whose hands a rich man fell. There were expressive gestures, of squeezing a trigger or cutting a throat, or of other and still more unpleasant forms of extorting money. Still, there was nothing amiss in having too much *oozo*: it could always be drunk eventually, even if not at a stranger's expense, nor all on one glorious occasion.

While he fed the fire under the still, Mihael pointed out discouragingly that around Athens, the description 'Hello-Boy' carried anything but a cheering sound. During the German occupation there had been all too many of the type who had either worked for the Germans, or at best could not be relied on by the partisans: perhaps it would save disappointment if this one failed to arrive. He was snubbed by Jean-Paul's girl, Yorkim's daughter Ila, with the information that what Athens thought of anything was of no importance here. 'It was always like that,' said the Professor, dimly pleased. 'Even in the fifth century the opinion of Attica was belittled in Macedonia, if nowhere else.'

With resignation, Hebe saw that if her companions had lacked the will to move on before, there was now no chance at all of their stirring, while the possibility of an event of interest lay ahead. 'Suppose it happened, it would be a pity to miss it,' was their new excuse. They had missed so much. Not that any further excuse was needed, with the worst of the weather upon them. 'Of course, after the heelobowie — ' they said, glad of a barrier to looking forward.

The winter dragged on, as she had feared, and nothing came but icicles, and cold-sores which were due to the poverty of their blood, as much as to the shrilling wind that dried and cracked the skin, finding its way indoors through chinks which they had not enough rags to stop. The ground was too hard to provide mud which could be used as putty. Occasionally, after a prolonged bout of the Vardar rage, there would drop from the capricious sky, like a jewel, a day of still glory, so shining and irresponsible that for a few hours it would have been easy to believe in the Greek legends of lovely, young and heartless gods in charge of human fate, had she been in a mood to believe anything fanciful. But for Hebe these clear spells, too short to let them do more than get to the village and back, bartering work for a change of food, only intensified the gloom of the prevailing mountain weather, with the low light dying soon after midday behind the high peaks. And in the gloom the loathsome web of half-comprehended resentments and hungers, with Dido at its heart, shook and was still, shook and was still again, lying across her thoughts. Dido herself seemed at intervals a prey to an anxious excitement, held in check with difficulty. She was unpredictable in temper, both in her exalted and withdrawn states, which alternated with no reason that Hebe could trace. Twice more in this period of waiting the shepherd came to the farm: once he was sent away, angrily, and once it was Hebe and the old man who were curtly told to get out of the kitchen. There was nowhere to go, in the cold, but the sleeping-recess off it, with the crack beside the hinge. It was the clumsiness of the woman's body, thought Hebe, looking on, which made their acts seem wrong — how could Dido stay so heavy on so little food? — It was the sagging breasts and the blue, mottled thickness of her haunches. Even if Dido hated the shepherd, there would have seemed less evil in what they did if she had been thinner and so, to the girl, less ugly. Whispering, Hebe offered this judgment to the Professor: in former days he would at least have smiled, and possibly agreed. But now the tired monkey's eyes were less like a man's than ever, with the spirit gone from behind them.

'Ugly? Is she? Perhaps,' he murmured unheedingly. 'What does it matter?'

'If you stay here, one day the shepherd will kill you. The shepherd, or someone else. Just because you're in the way.' Softly, for the last time, Hebe renewed her entreaty that he should gather his courage again and help her to get away. 'If you won't see it's horrible to live like this, don't you see it's stupid to die?'

'Perhaps. What does it matter?' he repeated, as if it were too much trouble to think of anything else to answer.

But most of the days drifted past them unmarked by any outstanding incident, and were more deadening to the spirit because of their emptiness. Towards the end of the winter they crawled by uncounted even by Hebe.

The early liking between Dido and Lisabet, based on the loss of their men, gave way to a growing annoyance on Dido's part which was caused by Lisabet's new kindliness. More and more, wanting to do good to everyone, she attempted to reorganize the farm, such as it was, for Dido's benefit. She was distressed by the knowledge that Macedonians, like chickens, tended to pick every edible green thing as soon as it appeared above the ground, instead of waiting for it to mature. What Dido chose to do or not to do with the shepherd was Dido's own affair to Lisabet, in whom desire ran weakly, and was almost wholly maternal: but there was something fundamentally shocking in what Dido had done or not done to the onion crop. They should be eating it now, with the pickled sheep, when the olives had run out, and instead it had all gone in early summer, while figs were still plentiful. Every suggestion Lisabet made for the farm had a side of practical good sense, but the reasoning behind it was sometimes difficult to follow, for those who did not take the same beliefs for granted.

'Today we should bring nothing into the house, not even firewood, for the door is barred.'

'It is always barred. Who would be such a fool as to leave that door unfastened?'

'Two ravens flew over the house in line, closing it to us. But have you noticed, for several days the cricket behind the chimney has been quiet? It is time we turned over the good muck from the sow's pen, to let the weather get at it, ready for the spring.'

What Dido's starved land most needed was manure, but she pointed out, to irritate the better manager, that spring or no spring, she would probably never trouble to spread the stuff on the ground if they prepared it for her. Baulked in her efforts to improve the soil, Lisabet scoured in the house everything which Dido would have left dirty. Not all Jean-Paul's protests that she would get them turned out of the barn, could persuade Lisabet that the cleanness of the naturally clean might be as offensive to the naturally dirty as the sluttishness of sluts to the clean. 'It isn't right. No, no!' she said, and went on scrubbing. Dido made it plain that she would be glad, now, to be rid of the whole party, except the Professor. She had welcomed them believing that they might lessen a little her wild torment of loneliness, and they had not done so: yet gripped in the queer spell of inaction which held them all, she could not bring herself to turn them out.

The piglets grew up, beyond the stage when they could be any consolation to Hebe, or any grief in passing: one by one they were eaten, till only two remained. Hating this place and everything connected with it, she could not see with friendly eyes the one good and selfless thing which flowered here against the darkness of the short days — Ila's devotion to Jean-Paul, in the one-sided love-affair which had developed between them.

To Yorkim's daughter, who had known no gentleness at home, human contact needed to be no more than the absence of abuse and ill-treatment to be overwhelming in its effect. Ila was little older than Hebe, plain and stupid but not afflicted like most of the family. Unprepossessing himself, Jean-Paul had developed a technique of approach to women which, as he pointed out, provided him with comforts to be won by no other means. He could not be bothered to adapt the approach to the quality of the woman: therefore he called Ila pretty, by habit, in extravagant and ill-fitting compliments, praised with inattentive words whatever she did for him, and made show of an affection which transformed the world for her. He could not have woven such magic for her if he had been more fully aware of her as a person, with pathetic inadequacies of flesh and mind. She worshipped him, lay with him gratefully though without plea-sure — experience had not suggested to her that there could be pleasure — and brought him extra food, taken from her own family, and whenever she could steal them from Zari, pinches of local tobacco, for which he had appropriated the Professor's pipe. The tobacco was even harder for her to acquire unnoticed than the food, it was becoming the regular winter currency. Grown on the Beles foothills, from which it was normally exported as Turkish, it had almost replaced flour as the standard article for barter, while the depth of the snow dwindled still further the trickle of supplies coming along the roads. She accepted steadfastly, as the price of Jean-Paul's kindness, whatever punishment was meted out to her in the village or at home when the thefts were discovered. To Jean-Paul it was a more-than-usually casual course of bedding-down, but because on her side there was love, blinding and defenceless and grand, out of all proportion to the frightened little heart which held it, Ila's part of the companionship had that quality of dignity which Hebe craved from life, but the squalor of their surroundings was too great to allow Hebe to notice it. Blackness overwhelmed every-thing. It was not even possible, she found, to go on extracting pleasure from cutting one's toe-nails in security — something she had believed could never pall again. As to devotion leading no-where, it seemed merely stupid, like Ila herself — Hebe was less generous by nature than Ila.

Then on a day of glistening clarity, long after the turn of the year — when release was a half-forgotten dream, it seemed so remote — Katina banged on the farm door at noon and shouted through it, 'He's come! The heelobowie!'

Hebe was shoved roughly out of the way by Dido, hurrying to the door, charged with emotion. She stood staring at Katina, not speaking, not inviting her in as custom required, while the others clustered round to ask, what was he like, what had delayed him?

'What do you think of an "Uncle" who can only buy *oozo*, not drink it?' Katina tittered, and added with a spiteful insight beyond her ordinary intelligence, 'He knows everything about everything, except what to do with it! That's what he's like.'

Showing affront at Dido's lack of manners, she would not wait on the threshold to tell them more, but hurried back to the celebration, already in full swing, which she had only left out of courtesy. The news having been carried so far, obligation now rested on Dido, to pass it to the next outlying farm. Greek social sense, so compelling within its limits, appeared to revive in her as soon as the other woman had left. She refused the offer of a messenger, reminding Hebe disquieteningly of the former occasion — today Jean-Paul was willing to go, with Ila to guide him. 'No, I tell you. It's my concern!' She mentioned, as the farm to which she would take the message, a place Ila knew to be far away in the hills: much further than there was any need for her to go: there were nearer neighbours. Even so, she was gone for longer than they expected, although this time the track did not lead by the shepherd's hut.

Tired of waiting, they went over to the village before her return, and found the visitor, a forlorn little fat man, leaning against Zari's haystack, having trouble with his false teeth, while the party swirled round him unconcernedly, in a gradually widening circle. The celebration had begun overnight in Zari's store, and overflowed out of doors in the morning, as the news of the arrival spread. Ednis, as he turned out to be, had dropped his top plate and broken off a corner, while being sick.

'I used to be able to drink *oozo* all night when I was a lad,' he said.

'When I couldn't afford it! But maybe I was a fool to try it nowadays. Or more than a glass or two for old time's sake. That's what my wife would say anyway. Just as well she's not here, eh? Here, you have some, if you can stomach it.'

He produced from his pockets a handful of battered-looking sweets for Hebe and some of Yorkim's younger children, grimacing with pain as he explained to the young Macedonians how to eat those wrapped in silver paper — they tended to put the sweets straight into their mouths and chew stolidly through the wrappings, not having met such things before. The rough edge of the broken denture rasped his tongue at every word. 'I oughtn't to wear it. Sort of thing gives you serious trouble,' he said. 'But today I don't like not to. I used to have beautiful teeth of my own, you see. Beautiful teeth. People in the country have long memories — they might remember that.'

But no one remembered him at all, although through Zari he must have been distantly related to nearly everyone in sight. He had met his first disappointment in the homecoming already: he wanted to be 'Eddie' all round, as he was in the States, and instead people persistently called him 'Uncle', out of respect, especially after the * oozo* took hold, when they gave up even trying to say 'Eddie' occasionally, to please him, and became more and more respectful to the wealth which had brought him over half the distance from Athens in his own jeep, with neither the Government troops nor the *andartes* able to stop him.

Jean-Paul was presented ambiguously by the Professor as a man who had once made a living out of handling dentures. They all sat down against the sunny side of the haystack, and by borrowing out of the heelobowie's breast pocket a nail file which he afterwards slipped into his own, Jean-Paul managed to make the plate much more comfortable for the visitor, if less secure. There was a resemblance of features, Jean-Paul noticed at once, between the heelobowie and the Bear of Marseille; this influenced him so much that he was pleased to do something for his hero by proxy, even while fully sober. With *oozo* in him, Jean-Paul became more and more enchanted by the physical likeness, and kept breaking into the newcomer's conversation with other people every few minutes to remark on it, in French, which no one understood outside his own party. Ednis bore patiently with the interruptions, having recovered his spirits as soon as he could talk without discomfort, although with a new caution.

'False teeth are a great trouble,' the Professor sympathized with him, having long since lost, broken or sold his own set.

'Oh, no, no!' The other protested vigorously. 'There I can't agree with you. Now what's so bad about taking castor oil, for instance? Not the taste — nothing to it. Just the way it clings round the teeth. Take out the teeth, and you take out the objection!' He had a way of turning on a broad, expectant smile which compelled a response even when it was totally unconnected with the accompanying remark, as it often was.

'You suffer much, then, from constipation?' the Professor asked politely.

'No. Oh, no!' said Ednis, apparently surprised. 'Why, do you?'

He seemed delighted to find other English-speaking people in this forgotten pocket of the frontier mountains. 'That's the way things always happen to me,' he said, urging more *oozo* upon them. 'Bits of civilization cropping up where you'd least expect them.' 'Tell you, I've seen a couple of eye-baths, used to hold a still-born baby's blood for making rain magic, in an adobe hut in Venezuela! (It worked, too — well, we got rain.) And up near the Arctic circle — now here's something touches my own line: I'm in the fur trade myself, in the States — nowadays you don't find the Eskimo's wife spends all her time chewing seal skin for boots. Some chewing she still does: other times I've watched her crouching in her igloo over a home-made radio set, listening to the official fur-prices from New York and Montreal, to make sure her old man don't get gypped by the local trader! It's much harder to get skins cheap than it used to be. There's my world — all mixed up. So here I come home to talk Greek — and you talk English. Well, why not? So long as we're enjoying ourselves. And we are, aren't we? — You think they're enjoying themselves?' he asked anxiously a few minutes later as Katina, already magnificently drunk, and more dignified than usual, got up to make a speech about him, according to custom. No one listened to her, nor replied to his question.

'I've sent for more *retsina*,' he said. 'Maybe the little girl could take that?' Yorkim's children drank * oʒo* with enthusiasm, and if they crept away to be ill alone, to avoid the mockery of neighbours, they came back afterwards to drink more. But to Hebe this colourless liquid fire, which turned milky and tasted quite different when watered, was equally revolting whether she tried it plain or diluted.

'I know where there always used to be a store of *retsina*,' he said. 'In the farm where my old sweetheart still lives, they tell me. Under the bed, it was kept — Guess how I know that! I've sent for her too!' He winked, and misinterpreted the unresponsive stare of Hebe's round blue eyes — she was wondering if it were possible that a man from these parts did not realize the extraordinary rashness of wearing a gold watch where it could be seen. He had several rings on his small plump hands, too. 'I don't know why I did that,' he said apologetically, 'it's vulgar. My wife always said a wink is as bad as a pun. It's a sort of physical pun, really, isn't it?' He turned to a bystander and asked in Greek, 'Have we enough *retsina* till the next lot comes? If not, say I'll pay double for any that's found just around here. That'll fetch it out!'

'For the moment we have enough. Two bottles,' the bystander indicated them among the casks by Zari's door.

Katina stopped her address and swooped upon the bottles, ' "Enough"? I hate that word "enough"!' she said grandly, and swung the bottles round her head, to let them sail through the air and splinter against a rock, amid shouts of applause.

'That's fine! That's what I came to see!' Ednis was thoroughly happy for the moment. 'Worth all it's meant, getting here, to watch people letting themselves go because I'm back. And I can tell you, it's meant plenty!' But as he talked, relating his adventures on the way from Athens, it became plainer and plainer that he did not realize what it had really meant, in fantastic good luck, to have survived the journey and reached his old district at last, unharmed.

For many weeks after he landed, he told them, the authorities had refused to let him risk the roads to the north which were held in strength by the *andartes*. He had bought an ex-army jeep: they would not licence it. They would give him no petrol, they would issue no permits of any kind. 'They said I'd have the old can looted, and my throat cut, the first day out of Athens! — "Oh," I told them, "I've read about your war, back in the States, but I never thought it amounted to much." Well, thank heaven you can still buy everything in Athens if you know your way around. I nearly bought the Parthenon along with the authorities and the permits in the end — it couldn't have cost much more. Then I came along quicker than the news of my coming — while there were roads to come on! My, my, what roads. I'd forgotten.'

Speed had saved him, and not understanding the danger. Twice he had fallen in with armed bandits: the first time they must have supposed him to be some kind of Government decoy — a civilian driving alone, in an expensive overcoat and a wide-brimmed hat, waving enthusiastically at them a hand encrusted with gold. Men so mad did not naturally live, in these parts, beyond their first youth; and Ednis appeared middle-aged, as well as most affably alive — where, then, were the hidden troops, the trap? The guerillas had scattered and run. The second time he had lost his jeep but, strangely, not his life. Bandits surrounded the car while he was out of it, looking for food at the scrannel farms, which closed their doors on his approach. From some distance off he had seen the men with rifles in their hands waiting beside his jeep, and had turned and walked in the opposite direction, unobserved. After this he had walked and walked, just as he was, in his light, pointed shoes and tailored coat, over the hills to his native place, with his money and jewellery intact, although his suit-case and hat had been left in the jeep. 'Nice big hat,' he said, 'I could use it against this cold.' It had, he agreed, added to his difficulty in finding the way that the hamlet was known to him only as 'the village', but he remembered one of the names of the nearest town, although in fact he had never been there.

He had been improbably fortunate, too, in not meeting a hold-up until he was within fifty miles of his journey's end, but still more so in the stamina of the jeep: no other car could have survived so far the appalling bumpy road-surfaces all the way from Athens; nor, in places, the complete lack of road, where successive waves of retreating soldiers and partisans had blown the track off steep, strategic hillsides. But the only luck which struck him as worthy of the name was the chance that the sweets had happened to be in his pocket when he left the jeep. As a non-smoker he had a liking for sweets. (Not smoking had always been one of his little economies, he explained, kept up in order to return to Greece.) Yet he had managed to refrain from eating them on the long walk, in case there might be children at his homecoming — and here was Hebe, and Yorkim's brood, along with many others by now! Nearly everyone who came to the celebration had brought the whole family, down to the smallest babies: these were laid somewhere out of danger from the dancing, which was bound to start soon. They were fed by anyone, with whatever was handy, whenever they started to cry: as the afternoon wore on, most of them acquired their first taste of *ooʒo*. But for the older children, toffee was the exciting novelty.

'It's funny,' he said, 'how you can read of things, and not think, "Why, this might mean something to me. Stop me doing what I've set my heart on!" I'd been making little economies for so long, just for this, it didn't seem real, what the papers said back in the States about Greece. *Klepts* — well, we'd always had them. They didn't keep people with money from going where they wanted, in the old days. My wife would laugh at me, losing my kit and my car!' He stretched out his feet to look ruefully at his opulent, wrecked shoes, which had been chosen to impress anyone who could have known him in his barefoot days. 'Have to hire me a mule to get back!'

Politely, though they realized he would never get back — miracles did not tend to repeat themselves — people laughed at the idea of an 'uncle' on a mule.

Having come so far to see them, he spoke very little to his fellow villagers — it was easier, he found, to talk to people from the outside world, with whom he had more in common. He did not even notice the rawboned woman who stood for a while on the outskirts of the party, staring at him. In the rusty black dress and whitish head scarf worn by all the women present, she might have been any age up to the Professor's, or beyond: it was always hard to guess with a Macedonian country-woman. Hebe went over to her and asked incredulously, 'Are you the person he was asking for? His old sweetheart?'

The woman nodded. 'Was he asking for me? After all these years!' she said eagerly, and then added in a sour voice, 'Oh, it's easy for people who get money to stay young!' She gave Hebe the *retsina* she had brought and went away, the only person there who saw Ednis as he wanted to be seen.

'Tell him I'd rather he remembered me as I was,' she said, with the Greek gift of speaking simply from the heart on affairs of the heart — the strangest gift, as the Professor had once pointed out to Hebe, to find in a people who rarely spoke the simple truth on any other subject: in other parts of the world it was customary to lie first about personal feelings.

'Half a lifetime — it's a long while to care!' Ednis smiled irrelevantly when Hebe reported what the woman had said. 'Don't you let yourself get too devoted to any of us, my dear. We're not worth it.'

'Oh, I know that,' Hebe told him gravely. 'But it's not a thing I need to be careful about.' (André was a goal, a means to endurance. If, unthinkably, she failed to reach him, he could never be a crying emptiness of the heart, of the kind she had glimpsed in the woman who had gone away, and before that in Dido.)

Ednis laughed uproariously. 'You're a funny child.' He appeared amused again — smile and words as unrelated as before — when he asked her, 'What do you want to do, eh? Get away from here, as I did at your age? Lord, how I wanted it. Lord, how I regretted it, often and often, after I'd managed it!'

This was the chance of which she had day-dreamed, hour after hour, with Ednis as a nebulous figure of salvation looking sometimes like a blend of her father and the Professor, sometimes like pictures of Saint Nicolas or Santa Claus: never like a flabby, balding and over-anxious man. Still, what did the means matter: here was the chance.

He listened inattentively, while his eyes roved about the scene before him, to her passionate request for help in getting at least as far as Salonika.

The beggar's whine in her voice no longer troubled her: she spoke in very rapid English, avoiding the name of Salonika, in talking of the port she wanted to reach, so that Jean-Paul and Mihael might not be able to follow.

'Sure, sure, I'll see you that far on my way back,' he said carelessly.

If only he would, or could! Despite all the probabilities, hope soared again, for the moment. Then she considered him, while he talked to the others.

Ednis had lost interest in her, temporarily. He was asking her companions about conditions in Bulgaria and Italy. They could tell him little of the things which interested him — the cost of living, the state of employment, what shifts had there been lately in public feeling, which might affect Governments and treaties and trade agreements? He already knew from reading newspapers more than they had gathered by passing arduously through the two countries in the last few months, but nothing he had amassed in the way of information meant anything to him in terms of individual human beings. They understood nothing else, obsessed by their personal hungers and fears — Hebe realized that he could not help her, even though, just for the moment, he meant to — and even if somehow he escaped being killed quite soon — He did not belong in her world of realities.

'When will you leave here?' she asked him urgently, still trying to keep faith in the possibility of his luck holding.

'Oh, in three or four days, maybe. When the party's over. I mustn't miss any of this, must I?'

'But you do know it's dangerous, every minute you stay? The *andartes* — they'll hear. They'll know you've got money —'

'*Klepts*, you mean? Why, who'd tell them, and spoil his own fun? Everyone's having a good time, aren't they? Now little girl, don't you try spoiling mine! Or maybe I won't feel so kind when I go.'

It was no use. 'Ah, I didn't mean it!' he said, seeing Hebe's expression, and smiled disconcertingly again. 'I'll take you along — The thing I don't get, here and now, is how all you folk can have come so far and learnt so little!'

'That is the knack which distinguishes the refugee from the traveller!' said the Professor, and they discussed one of the strangest elements in the strange situation of this and a thousand similar groups of drifting human wreckage, sucked along by the huge winds of contention blowing upon the embers of war — their extreme ignorance of the forces which controlled their lives, tossed them about, pressed them forward or held them back. From closer than anyone else, too close for understanding, Hebe and her kind had seen the effects of vast economic upheavals and social disruption: they were themselves part of the results, but they were far less curious about the causes of disaster than people whose lives were not affected by the storms which buffeted them, and then passed on to topple thrones or shake whole continents. In their minds, Ednis learned from the Professor, such things meant only that in one country they could almost count on being given olive oil, while in the next it might be hard to come by the olives.

Here for once, Ednis pointed out — to turn cheerful again — they were being offered the oil, and the olives, with bread as well, all at the same time, from Zari's store. Being Ednis's nearest kinsman, Zari was bound to provide whatever food was required: but no one expected to eat much at a home-coming celebration.

This one had been going on for twenty-four hours now, and was really gathering warmth: even the shepherd shed some of his air of grim aloofness, and produced from under his cloak a reed pipe, of a pattern which had come unchanged down many centuries — such a pipe as Daphnis might have played to Chloe — and a mouth-organ, stamped as issued by the British Army Welfare Department. He drew from first one and then the other traditional airs, perhaps half as old in origin as the pipe, of which Zari said that he should be ashamed, maintaining that they were Turkish. Argument arose hotly, but he played on, the pipe for the plaintive tunes and the mouth-organ for the gay. Later, he said, he would play for the dancing, and produced still another instrument, one of the bag-pipes native to this part of Greece, the bag a whole goatskin, legs and all, with the openings tied up by strips of gut. In anticipation, the younger men began hitching up the seats of their wide, low-crutched trousers — black sacks with the legs protruding from the corners — a Turkish relic which Zari insisted was not Turkish at all because, as he said, he had always worn them himself: and had they borne in their folds any taint of the hated race, he would not be wearing them, which proved that they were not Turkish.

'That takes me back home! Same sort of argument I used to hear from my wife,' said the heelobowie, chuckling, and Hebe guessed with a flash of rare insight, like Katina's on his arrival, that although 'home' meant the States to him for the moment, while he was there, rootless and uncertain, he must always be seeing the high places of Macedonia when he spoke of it. 'She always wore a backless evening gown when she went out because she was sure, if she was really as plump as she feared she was, she wouldn't be wearing a backless evening gown. Not with her good taste. Because it'd look terrible. But she *was* wearing a backless evening gown. So she couldn't be all that fat, could she?' He tried to convince Zari that the regional dress was indeed Turkish, though the local airs were not, proving himself well-informed about music in general, not only folk-music: but the old man grew stubborn and secretive, pretending to believe and yet plainly unconvinced — This grand 'Uncle', who had at last given up trying to be 'Eddie' to anyone, might well be in league with the ancient oppressors, and repeat to them what anyone said.

'You fond of music?' Ednis asked the Professor.

'Not really. I know so little about it — Not like you, who have evidently studied it. For me is it only a bringer of moods. And a reminder of things, perhaps better forgotten. It might have meant more if there had been more opportunity —'

'And that's how it is with me! I couldn't afford to go to concerts, in my young days, and collect money for this as well. My wife, now, she liked music She'd have enjoyed the concerts, but she couldn't understand me bringing home books from the library to learn about what we weren't going to hear, except by chance on the radio. "You and your little economies!" she'd say. Well, they're paying off now!'

The last of the afternoon sun shone down benignly, the stillness of the air denying the nip in it: he had brought the false spring of the mountains with him. The party was still growing, and three more bottles of *retsina* had been discovered locally, as he hoped, to add to those his sweetheart had brought. 'Yes, they're paying off,' he repeated, as though someone had contradicted him.

Hebe found that she much preferred the wine to the spirit. *Retsina* smelt of security: the gummy tang was a reminder of the deodar tree in the garden of the house with the dogs. She drank as much as she was offered. Through an aromatic haze, which dulled her foreboding and disappointment, she heard Jean-Paul telling Ednis again what a remarkable likeness he bore to the Bear: outwardly, that was, but no doubt not inwardly; because no one but the Bear could have the heart of the bear, nor his other attributes. Inevitably there came once more the story of his getting the sister of the Gestapo chief into trouble.

Hebe translated dreamily for him into very literal English; Jean-Paul was now beyond remembering any Greek at all, even indecencies. 'That's a wonderful command you have of technicalities, my dear,' Ednis said mildly. 'Tell him, sure, I know how it is with him. I'm glad to be like a photograph of this fellow he looked up to. A man needs to find something bigger than himself in other men, that's the only good war does for him — gives him that. The proof that there's more courage than he thought possible. I've always said, God isn't enough. Not to look up to. For what's His goodness cost him?' He flashed upon Jean-Paul the detached smile which urged a reply, while Hebe turned this into French.

'*Merde*, it's true!' said Jean-Paul. 'He does know everything, except what to do with it!'

'You say, Uncle, "God is not enough!"' Mihael looked as though a new worry had come into his life.

'That's right. That's what he said!' Jean-Paul caught up the idea maliciously. Over-long inactivity had started up hostilities afresh between the young men. 'You thought, didn't you, Mihael, "If He existed, He would be altogether too much?" But supposing He is there, only not much of a thing. Solves nothing, eh?'

'You must not quarrel. You must think of now. For it's so fine, this "now"!' Understanding only the sound of disagreeable words in another tongue, Jean-Paul's girl, sitting between his thighs, pulled his ugly face down towards her, and gazing into it, upside down, saw no one knew what of unhoped-for goodness. She had noticed Dido come like a black shadow to the edge of the gathering, to stand there, where the other woman had stood, outside the scene, silently looking on.

'I wish she hadn't come!' Ila said, surprisingly, turning to Hebe, who had also noticed Dido and was watching her apprehensively. Aware of the younger girl's dislike for her, and all her tangled family, Yorkim's daughter rarely spoke to Hebe. She twisted her head sideways, as it rested on Jean-Paul's knee, to keep Dido in sight. There was indeed something arresting about Dido's appearance: even through a mist of *retsina* this was noticeable, although nothing had changed outwardly. Above the familiar dress with the stain on it — the stain which no one could see but herself — Dido's face wore the exalted look which had startled the travellers on their first evening at the farm, but she had looked like that so often lately that they were accustomed to this expression.

Katina observed her at the same time, and stopped her loud

boasting to Lisabet of the golden sovereigns hidden cunningly in her roof, where no one could ever find them. She grew soft-voiced and uneasy, aware that something had happened or was about to happen, but was much too drunk to make a move. Mellow, but nothing like as tipsy as the other, Lisabet bustled over to Dido: 'Now it is not right at all that you should have missed so much of the celebration! A lucky celebration, too: did you see the magpies? You should have let Ila and Jean-Paul take the message for you. They're younger, it's only reasonable — '

Without looking at Lisabet, her glance darting between the shepherd and Katina, Dido put her hand on the other's chest and pushed Lisabet aside. She stalked across to the haystack and sat down beside the Professor. 'Get me some,' she said, indicating the *oozo*, as if she would make known to whoever was there that henceforward he was her serf. He got up obediently and fetched her a crock, avoiding Hebe's eyes, and Dido drank with an air of triumph. To Hebe's bemused stare, Dido seemed to be, not part of the scene of rejoicing, but something that belonged only to the earth under it, sad and terrible and Macedonian.

The dancing had started: a line of men, each with a hand on his neighbour's shoulder, were stamping through a set figure between two rows of women whose turn was due to come later, when the men tired; they clapped softly to mark the beat of the tune played by the shepherd. It needed accentuating; he was by now, like most of the guests, nearly as far gone in drink as Katina: Dido had timed her arrival well: the prey saw the trap closing upon them soon enough to dash for safety, but could take no action. At intervals the younger dancers put in an incongruous step from the Charleston, which by 1947 had scaled the northern fastnesses of Greece. Ednis recognized it with applause: 'What did I tell you? Civilization, you never know when it'll meet you! Not that I mean civilization by this step. Just the transport it's taken to get here. All the convoys of the American army, rolling over Europe! That jiggle's certainly chosen a long way round from Africa!'

A woman in the crowd, still unaware of the growing tension,

put the shepherd's big black hat on the head of her two-year-old child, screaming with laughter at the effect, and the child, pleased at first with the attention, sensed that it was being laughed at, after a moment, and screamed with rage, increasing the laughter. 'Mothers — they're the same everywhere,' said Ednis. 'How they hate the dignity of their children. Always destroy it if they can. Because why? Because having dignity of their own is a way for the children to escape from them, and they don't want that — You got a mother?' he asked Hebe. 'No, nor've I. So we don't have to act they're wonderful.' Again the meaningless, inviting smile broke loose from the acuteness of the observation.

'But you have children yourself?' it drew from the Professor.

'Not now. My wife took them with her. A pity eh? You can see I like them. Keeping those candies all those miles, just in case.'

'Your wife — ?'

'She left me. Some time ago, really,' said the little man who had come home, looking with naked, quivering distress round the gathering which had so much to atone for. What was going wrong with it? Nearly all the people present were as richly drunk as they ought to be, but the few who were not, were whispering urgently together. 'She didn't like my little economies.'

Helped considerably by *retsina*, there rose in Hebe the realization of small, bleak tragedy without any possible redress. 'It's been a very nice celebration, though,' she said, astonishing herself, and stood up. 'We shall remember it.' No one else would think of repaying him with thanks for the party.

'Go — now — quickly!' Ila was urging upon Jean-Paul. 'Those two men standing near Dido, they aren't from these parts! Nor that one. Nor that!' But he was too merry to understand, and insisted on trying to tell the heelobowie more about the Bear.

Ila looked imploringly at Hebe, 'Make him go,' she said, her lips scarcely moving. 'Those are *klepts*, come down from the hills —'

'I know.'

9

A MOMENT OF SEEING

THE mist of *retsina* dispersed rapidly from Hebe's mind, before the cold breath of danger.

First she would warn Mihael. He was likely to be less fuddled than the rest of the party, and could act promptly — it was part of his belated puritanism not to drink much, even when the rare opportunity offered.

'I'll come back, in a minute. If I can,' Hebe said softly to Ila. 'Go on trying to make Jean-Paul understand.' Mihael and Lisabet were sitting on the other side of the haystack, watching the dancers. On her way to them, walking casually, as if to fetch more drink, Hebe passed close to Dido, who had called over to her one of the strangers. She was pointing out Katina to him, and telling him of the golden sovereigns. Presently other people, to save their own skins, would say what they had learnt from Katina's boasting — that the horde was hidden in her roof, where she believed no one else could find it. Katina would be loth to part with it, but even if she gave all the gold to them at once, the bandits would not feel sure that there might not be more, which could be extracted under pressure . . . Dido was making certain that Katina should not die too quickly. Nor, doubtless, would the shepherd; not quicker than Dido's own man had died. That could easily be secured by an imaginary tale of the shepherd's possessions, or of information he had laid against other *klepts*. Though it was for the heelobowie's money that the strangers had come, on Dido's summons, little hauls on the side never came amiss during a raid.

The last fumes blew away from Hebe's wits . . . 'These Macedonians, they live on their hatreds —'

The Professor was near enough to the other two to hear what Hebe said to them in smiling French. 'Move. Not too quickly. Bandits still gathering — not many here yet. But they'll attack if they see people starting to run.' She did not look at the Professor. He had chosen his part. Probably he would not be killed — yet — as he was Dido's property, and the men from the hills owed her some return for her information. In any case he was not Hebe's concern now, no longer one of her father's party, whom she would get to Salonika if she could. Whether or not he took in what she had just said, he made no movement.

Mihael rose, stretching, pretending well, alert in an instant, but Lisabet was hopelessly sodden. 'Nonsense,' she called amiably after Hebe, who had strolled on, circling the haystack to return to Jean-Paul. 'I tell you, I saw three magpies on our way. Everything is favourable for everybody.'

Hebe hesitated and looked round at them. Lisabet burrowed her back comfortably into the stack; even through the wonderful still-ness of the rare, fine day, the chill of the evening came creeping at last along the ground. 'They flew towards the morning sun,' she assured Mihael. 'In Transylvania too, in the old times, after the harvests, celebrations often used to last several days. It is the right time.' Mihael nodded at her, in curt farewell, and moved with an aimless air towards the shed in which Yorkim had crawled. It was the nearest cover except for Zari's house and store, which would certainly be searched when the slaughter started.

Ila had made no progress, Hebe found, in getting through to Jean-Paul's intelligence. She herself tried once more, also in vain. She dared not raise her voice, even in their own *patois*, for fear of appearing to give a warning. From the edges of the gathering too many local people were already melting away: the bandits were growing restless.

'But it is formidable, I tell you, that likeness! Hebe, translate. We must tell him about the day the Bear got the *Polizei* to light our beacon for the arms' drop — '

Hebe's eyes met Ila's, and Ila's were bright with fear but steady. 'Go, now, Hebe. They're watching you foreigners. Leave him to me.' It had never crossed Ila's humble mind to hope that when her god went away, as he must, sooner or later, he might take her with him. At any costs she would stay now, to give him a better chance of escape.

For a moment, as she turned and began to saunter in Mihael's tracks, Hebe believed the killing was upon them, when a woman gave a stifled cry, and a stranger's hand leapt to his belt: but the woman's husband, or brother, or a friend, flung an arm round her neck, fooling with her roughly, silencing her, acting the lover, and dragged her outside the drunken crowd, where the shepherd was still piping.

A diversion delayed Hebe for precious seconds as Yorkim and Nitsa, moved by the general excitement, attempted to join the dancers, hopping about opposite each other; he fell, suddenly overcome, clutching at the queer, misshapen creature, dragging her with him almost into the bonfire which the children had lit. Neighbours pulled them back by the legs, out of the heat of the flames, while he twitched and yammered. Hebe jumped aside to avoid his threshing arms, and a briar from the pile waiting to be burnt tore at her ankle. For her, it was an instant of balance between panic and control, and the swift, unguarded moment of escape from Yorkim's reach made the desire to run almost irresistible, but the briar entangled her foot. Despite the menace of the moment, there flooded through her being, in a brief fusing of time, the feeling of the dawn after her father had died. Then she had gone on, with the hands of the wood reaching out to detain her: now, too, nothing should stop her. Deliberately she stooped, and freed herself, and wandered on, unhurried, between the watchful strangers who glanced at one another questioningly, and then moved apart to let her pass.

Out of sight, at the back of the mule-shed, she found waiting for her a Mihael transformed by the return of *maquis* fighting conditions, which he understood, into someone she had not met before, brave and competent and dependable. Here was peril that could be countered by cunning and action: there was a grim cheerfulness about him.

He had worked at the rotten wood round the loose plank under the eaves, making a space big enough to boost her through, and when she had dropped down on to the straw inside, he followed her. The wretched mule, a mass of goad-sores on back and flanks, was tethered to the ladder under the fodder-loft: it lashed out at human approach. Mihael chose his time, closed in and freed it, driving it into a corner, safeguarding Hebe from its heels, while she climbed up to the loft. There he made her lie flat against the wall. Outside, terrible screaming started while he carried up armfuls of dirty litter with which to cover her. 'It's all so old, it looks as if it hadn't been disturbed at all,' he said reassuringly as he piled it over her. 'And you're so small and flat, you don't make any bulge!' He wrenched the ladder free of its fastening, and kicked it away. 'With the mule loose and the door fastened outside, even if they come in, they won't think anyone's up here. Not if I go.'

'What will you do?'

'Get out by whichever way they don't come in — the door or the hole! You've no need to worry about me!' But he made no move to leave her, only loosened his belt-knife, when they heard scrabbling below them, and looking between the planks of the loft, saw a man's arm and then his body coming through the hole. Light, dimming outside, was dimmer still in the shed, but their eyes were accustomed to what there was. Relief was wonderful as Hebe recognized Jean-Paul, and called to him over the noise outside which rose and fell in waves. Mihael knelt to give him a hand up to the loft. Jean-Paul was still partly drunk, but shaken into caution. No one ever learnt how Ila prevailed upon him to stagger away in time: he himself remembered nothing of the last few minutes of the celebration.

'Anyone see you get in here?'

'No.' When the screaming rose loudest they had to cup their mouths with their hands to make themselves heard without shouting.

'Where's Ila?'

'How do I know? The *andartes* have got them surrounded, where they want them, between the houses.'

Mihael stood up. 'You look after Hebe,' he said, and dropped to the floor.

'Where are you going?'

'To get Lisabet out if I can.'

'Don't be a fool! What for?'

'Oh, you know, when one's been *copains* — '

Surprise sobered Jean-Paul still further, bringing back some recent memories. 'Still cadging favour with *ce Bon Dieu*? Who, after all, mayn't be much of a thing!'

Mihael stood for a second or two, grave without the sullen look of the past few months, considering the question if only because he must consider something while he took off the tattered coat which might hamper him in fighting: the light from the fire found its way through a chink on to his uplifted face. Directly below Hebe, he was framed for her between the edges of the two planks on which she lay, looking down. Long afterwards she remembered him as he appeared just then, even to seeing with her mind's eye the rough sides of the wood cutting into her vision of him; and knew with certainty that she would never be witness again of such splendour of face and body, a young man's magnificence, something to take the breath away: for this was one of the moments of seeing, which come to quite ordinary people, when the veils between them and some other reality shiver and lift a little. But while it lasted she was aware beyond everything else of her own terror, scarcely of seeing him at all: the sound of shooting came at intervals, now, through the ceaseless screaming. The *klepts*, who had used only their knives in the rounding up stage, were ready to finish the job.

'*Enfin, je m'enfous du Bon Dieu!*' Mihael called up to them, and there was the white flash of his teeth in the gloom as he moved out of the light, and then he was gone, and that was the last they saw of him.

The noise moved further away, and later broke out again, near by. The *klepts* were searching among the hovels to make sure that they left as few witnesses as possible. Not much bigger than Hebe, Jean-Paul wriggled his way under the straw, too, and lay beside her against the wall. A man came into the shed, but seeing the un-tethered beast, and with no ladder leading his eye to the fodder-loft, he looked no further, driving the animal out before him when he left.

For a long while the two in the shed stayed where they were, after the ring of spades in the stony ground had ceased to break the renewed quiet, when the shouting was over. Full dark fell before they heard the few donkeys and mules left to the village from previous raids being rounded up and taken away. The creatures brayed, and it sounded like wild laughter at the fate of those who had viciously misused them: but in the new hands they were not likely to fare better: the patter of their hooves and the voices of the men died away into the night.

'All clear,' Jean-Paul said at last. 'We'll get out now.'

'Away from this place? Right away? You mean we'll go on?' It was hard to believe that the time of release had come in this fashion.

'Of course. We're the last people they'd want left alive, able to identify them one day, maybe. They'll come here again. To-morrow or sometime. To see who's crept back into the huts.'

'And the others — Mihael and Lisabet?'

'Oh, by now, *tu sais*! We're not waiting for them. Well, you heard the digging, didn't you?'

'Some people did escape. The ones who got out early. You were too drunk to notice.'

'Maybe. Greeks. The *andartes* or whoever they were won't trouble much about them. What Greek would take evidence from a Greek against another lot of Greeks? But we're foreigners. Get your feet over the edge, and I'll swing you down.'

He went out first, reconnoitring, and came back with the shepherd's cloak, wrapping it round her several times, tucking the ends in warmly at the back of her neck — she was shivering violently. 'Lucky he took it off to play — you see I wasn't so drunk. I remembered that. And the fools forgot it.'

They went softly towards the bridge over the stream which ran through the village, and listened awhile, but there was nothing stirring, even the dogs had been disposed of or driven away. 'It's a pity about those two little pigs, back at the farm,' he said. 'I always meant to have them with us when the time came. But this will be the quickest way out of the mountains. Down this gulley.'

'No,' she said. 'You get caught in a closed valley that way. No pass. Just a wall of scree at the other end.'

'How do you know? How far have you been?'

'About five hours' walking.'

'Then you did try to make it alone that time! And to leave us in the lurch without the names of contacts at Salonika! — By God, Hebe,' he said, cackling in reaction from the evening's horror, 'you have almost as much of *them* as the Bear!' He clumped her behind in friendly style through the thicknesses of the cloak. 'Well, we'll go back, then, and down by the hut where the shepherd used to live.'

Suddenly, on the path along which Hebe had followed Dido, he stopped and said, 'But how stupid to leave those little pigs! After all the care they needed to help them grow up. You stay here,' and disappeared into the darkness.

Whether he would come back, she did not know, and soon, could not greatly care, when the drowsiness of exhaustion took charge: she crept under an overhanging bank, not far from the place where she had waited for Dido. The cold half-roused her from sleep at intervals, but the vast, stout cloak made it possible to endure. And when she awakened fully, with the first streaks of dawn in the sky, he was there once more, offering her kindly a few raisins which had been in a tobacco pouch for an unknown time — since Ila stole them for him — but were still recognizably raisins, after a few seconds' sucking.

' "Greece is the country where one grows more and more thankful, counting smaller and smaller blessings!" ' He quoted the Professor in one of their happier moments, and cackled again. 'No pigs for us! The *andartes* have been there and cleared the place. Taken Dido back to the hills with them — otherwise anyone who survived in the village would kill her, of course, for what she's done. Taken the old man, too, I suppose. Anyway, he's not there. Still, I found these. With my old groundsheet-cape — that'll be useful to us! Under the straw in the barn. Another thing the fools didn't see. I always had to hide anything Ila brought, if I didn't want to use it right away, or she wouldn't bring me any more till I'd finished. That's why these raisins were in the pouch — the Professor never knew he'd lost it.'

'Ila — ' said Hebe, and could not go on. ('And when they had eaten they grieved for their companions.') What a long time it was since she had first heard that: more than a quarter of a year ago: she had been quite a child.

Jean-Paul was shaking his head, like a man coming out of a dream. 'You know, we got soft at that farm! Not carrying everything we had about with us. They've got your U.N.R.R.A. shirt: I looked for it specially. We stayed there too long! I wonder why?'

Hebe did not answer that, and they went on, past the shepherd's empty hut, towards the lower foothills. Following her own train of thought, Hebe said: 'Now Dido will be able to get herself a new dress, won't she? With Katina's money, maybe.'

'Katina's or the heelobowie's. The *andartes* will let her share some of the spoils. That should make her laugh! And will, no doubt. You remember her laugh? I never liked it.'

'All the same, a new dress without blood on it — that is funny, in a way, when you think what she did for it. No, not funny, but — ' She could not find the words.

'Yes, it is funny. There are quite a lot of things funny about what's happened,' he said. 'If you look at them the right way. Mihael's doubts — well, now he knows, if there's anything to know. For me, it seems altogether too odd to think that a lump of meat buried in a trench, with a lot of other lumps, can be all that's left of him and his doubts and his crossness with the book he read — remember that? Still, that's what the Professor thought, or thinks, wherever he is, and he's a clever man, if he was only a schoolmaster, really. Lisabet — she was so sure we were all going to be lucky because the right omens took us along to the heelobowie — now that *is* funny! And the heelobowie being so like the Bear. I wish I had told him about the Bear working right under the nose of the Gestapo, but I was too drunk.'

'You told him, all right,' Hebe said, thinking not of him nor the Bear nor the heelobowie but of the Professor: so Dido would keep her unsuitable slave, someone who had shared the beliefs of the killers of her man — had even spent years in prison for those beliefs — someone on whom she could visit an untiring revenge.

'Did I? Good,' said Jean-Paul on a note of finality, and after this they did not talk any more of the others, or, if their names were mentioned accidentally, spoke as if these were people known a long while ago, almost in another life, like Jean-Paul's *l'espion anglais*. It seemed unchancy to recall them more clearly: Hebe was not alone in believing that ghosts were unhelpful while the living pressed forward.

They had friendlier relations, all through the next part of the trip, than at any time since the first few days at the farm. 'You know, it is just as if you were my daughter,' he said, when they camped that night, many miles further down the mountains. 'You must be about her age, too. It is just as well you are also a plain child: at least while your hair is so ragged and you could do with a wash. Or several. I am interested to realize I have not the least concern with you except as a daughter.'

'You deserted her, didn't you? Just as you meant to desert me. You and Mihael. Till I destroyed the maps.'

'Now how did you know that?' he exclaimed, surprised but not ashamed.

'I understand a little Dutch. You should have guessed that. My father was from Holland; he used to talk Dutch when he had taken too much *aguardiente*, in South America. It was safer: because then no one else knew what he was talking about. He had a special pair of Dutch *clompen* he used to throw at the rats he saw then.'

'But they weren't real rats!'

'Well, they weren't real *clompen*! He had them made in Brazil because he was homesick for Holland.' They both laughed as though this were truly very funny. They were lying under the

tent-like cloak, with the French army cape below them as a ground-
sheet, in the ruins of a disused hut. Something comparable with
what had happened in the village above must also have happened
here; there were several deserted hovels around them showing
signs of recent habitation.

For once, they were fully fed. During the morning it had occurred to Jean-Paul, still bemoaning the loss of the piglets, that with
the shepherd out of the way there was nothing except his dogs to
protect the scattered sheep, which the bandits had not attempted to
round up during the night. Presumably they would come and get
them later. Evading the dogs, he had caught and killed two of the
lambs; these they had carried across streams and through scrub, to
cook at leisure in the evening. They were traversing much the
same sort of country through which Hebe had struggled, but now
valley led into valley, she had some protection from the vlach
dogs, and help across the streams, the meat meant sustaining meals
when they halted, and time, by comparison with aimless days at the
farm, was once more full of purpose. Their new friendship was
cemented by the shared discovery that each had tried and failed to
get the better of the other.

She took the lead again in deciding which way they should go,
as soon as they were free of this sharply-folded part of the Beles,
and could more or less choose their direction.

'You are sure you remember the maps?'

'Quite sure.'

'That was not only a *blague*, then, after you learnt what we meant
to do?'

'Haven't I proved that? When have I taken you wrong? In the
general direction, I mean. Not just in choosing between this path
and that path, guessing which would be easier.'

'You went wrong when you were on your own. Choosing a
valley where there was no way out!'

'That was chance. I've told you, of course I don't know every
detail of the ground. But the lie of the country, yes.'

'Well enough to avoid the main roads where the *andartes* or

Government troops might travel? Where are they, for instance, from here, those main roads?'

'It would only confuse the picture in my mind to explain,' she said. 'While I am concentrating so hard on avoiding them, you understand!'

'And the contacts at Salonika? You have not forgotten them!'

'Not one,' said Hebe, smiling.

'All the same it would relieve my anxiety if you would run through them aloud, to make certain,' he said, smiling as ingratiatingly as the calamities among his teeth allowed. 'You've had so long to forget. Indeed, it would be a marvel if you hadn't, a bit.'

'No doubt,' said Hebe, laughing heartily. 'And you must remember what I also said before — I am getting tired of repeating myself — I shall only lie and lie if you try to get anything out of me!' Still firmer set their amiability in accepting that neither of them would ever trust the other at all, if it could possibly be avoided.

Towards the end of a week's walking, they came upon an old lady digging. A heavy onset of rain, which had held off since they started, set them looking for more shelter than scraggy olive trees provided on an otherwise bare and stony hillside. 'We got soft at that farm,' Jean-Paul grumbled again. This had become a recurrent theme with him on the move, taking the place of the bickering with Mihael whenever the Professor slowly harnessed himself: it gave some feeling of continuity to their life to have at least one topic of complaint unchanged, day after day. 'We used to travel, whatever the weather. I don't know why we don't now. I can't think how we stayed so long at that place. Well, there's some sort of ruin over there. It looks older than the last lot.' It turned out, according to the old lady who had encamped herself there before them, to be about two thousand years older.

They saw her first from back view, bent double, shovelling into a deep hole in the ground a pile of the golden, crumbling stone which took the place of earth in this region. Her heavy black skirts, bunched up under a leather belt, suggested the usual peasant figure, but there was something alien and bird-like in her gestures, she moved too quickly, going on with her toil in the deluge as though she worked against time.

'I've found nothing and I've got nothing,' she said over her shoulder without looking round, speaking a worse Greek than theirs. 'So it's no use your bothering me.'

Under an open umbrella, by the side of old excavations, lay a pile of the huge U.N.R.R.A. meat-tins of which Dido had spoken. 'We'll get some of those!' Jean-Paul told Hebe, in French. 'You talk to her, here, and I'll go round the other side — '

'What's that? I'm too deaf now to understand French,' she said in English, turning on them an aloof, incurious gaze, her voice exhaling an atmosphere of settled beginnings which was most prepossessing to Hebe. In these unmistakable tones people had spoken in the house with the dogs, though less compactly; but her words, too, made sense to Hebe: naturally a half-forgotten language needed concentration, and the catching of key-sounds, which might become harder as one grew older — economy, whether of explanation, effort or goods, was closely knit in Hebe's mind with respectability, possibly because André had thought well of it. (How they would save everything, she and André, in due course, at *Le Bien-Venu*.)

'Not a thing are we going to take from this person,' she said fiercely to Jean-Paul, 'unless it's offered!' And to the old lady, loudly, in English, she explained. 'We're not *klepts*, nor *andartes*, but just travellers.'

'Oh, I thought, till I saw you, that you were another Government patrol coming to be a nuisance. One never wants to let them have anything. That's why I always try to put them off. Tell them I've found nothing. Actually, my son and I found a good deal. Here and elsewhere, before he died. He was very well known as an archaeologist. But what do these people care about that? Now, wait while I throw my tongue over a biscuit. Then we'll get under the lee of that wall.' She shouted for someone, but there was no reply. 'Well, we can all have something later, when my boy's servant returns. You had better wait here till the rain stops.' She dropped her spade and with surprising strength — she appeared so fleshless, the colour of weathered marble, she was like the pieces of delicate broken columns lying about — she put a heavy, fallen stone over the hole at which she was working. 'It's safe enough here at this season, and at any time, of course, in the wet.'

'Safe from what?' Hebe asked, astonished, but the old lady did not hear as she led the way to where, in a gap in that part of a temple colonnade which was still standing — all that remained of an ancient glory — shepherds of a later date had built a pen for their beasts out of the rubble. She pointed out that it was her son who had added a coping, which made it possible for them to keep dry if they crouched in a line against the wall. Most of the roof he had contrived for the pen had fallen in, during the last rains, but the old lady did not seem to mind. She had an encampment under a tarpaulin in the soundest corner, and seen from close to, appeared no longer to be of marble but of spirit alone, beyond reach of weather.

'What are we safe from here, just now?' Hebe repeated. It was extraordinary that the old lady could survive at all, with her stores, in this needy, warring landscape: as unlikely as the heelobowie's journey.

'Malaria. So few people know that one in four cases is fatal, in this particular area of Greece. We didn't know. He had several bouts here. And I thought nothing of it because I have never been seriously affected by it, anywhere. And then he died. About four months ago.'

Even Jean-Paul was charmed beyond the idea of stealing, when she explained what she was doing on the site of the diggings — reburying, in various places, all the treasures which her son had recovered. There were fragments of statues, amphorae and inscribed stones, taken not only from this temple but from other excavations where they had worked together. 'Well, these Greeks, with their Troubles — really, it's just as it used to be in Ireland when

I was young. Each side spiting the other! — they won't let me take the things out of the country. And why should they have them? We found them, and they can't appreciate anything so good nowadays. What a Government! Not that there really is one in Greece today.' She turned to Hebe as to a worldly equal. 'Absurd, isn't it, how one always says that, and assumes there is! Lord Elgin was quite right in what he wrote, you remember, when he took the frieze. Barbarians. Not fit to look after it.' She peered out with wrinkled mischief, through the curtains of falling water, towards the spot where she had been at work. 'The difficulty there'll be for other archaeologists, later on! Everything jumbled up here, and so much of it from elsewhere, and, of course, from quite different periods. No clues left. Either to time or place, in most cases. They'll dig it all up again some day — perhaps. And then label it wrong: that's certain.'

She put Jean-Paul in mind of the Professor's accountant-friend whom he had so greatly admired, and they stayed two relatively pleasant days in the diggings, while the skies poured. At night they shared her drier corner of the pen. A tottering old man, speaking Albanian, which none of them understood easily, appeared as dark fell on the first evening, and opened for them one of the big meat tins: Hebe glanced at it sideways, realizing what a ghastly weapon it must have made. One of the labourers who had dug for her son, the Albanian had stayed on to look after the old lady, she told them, when the archaeologist died, because he had nowhere else to go, with the *andartes* based on his village just across the frontier: it was he who had begged from the U.N.R.R.A distributors the supplies on which she lived. She treated him with gracious formality, as though he were a family butler, and was amused at herself for doing this: she explained about butlers to Hebe, who had not met any but liked the sound of them, especially those in the vanished world of the great Irish country houses, from which the old lady had come. It seemed a pity that it would plainly be unsuitable to have one in a café in provincial France.

'But I always make him wash my underclothes,' said the old lady, 'in case I fall ill,' and she added casually the formidable statement, 'I've always been as ready to meet my doctor as I am to meet my God.' Hebe delighted in her, and opened her heart somewhat.

'You and I have courage,' the old lady said, having heard most of her story as they squatted by the wall, watching the savage rain-clouds swirling past. 'This is a quality people always expect to find joined to some excellent purpose. Just because it's beautiful they think it ought to be useful. Nonsense. It generally isn't. Neither your purpose nor mine is really worth while. Bourgeois stagnation, and confounding one's successors! But it takes just as much courage to pursue, as if it were. Courage of just as good quality, too.'

In the first bright, dripping dawn after the rain stopped, she awakened them briskly. 'Well, I must be about my work, and you about your journey. It's been very nice — I'm going north, after this. There's another cache we made. I'll finish here as quickly as I can. Because one never knows how long one's got, in these days.' She gave them half an open meat tin to take away, about five pounds of concentrated food, a regal gift, and closed the umbrella over the pile that remained.

'Tell her,' said Jean-Paul with real concern, 'to put that lot properly out of sight of anyone going by.' He remained devoted in memory to the old lady, and always referred to her afterwards with respect as *La Méchante*. 'Get her to understand — she thinks malaria's the danger round here — there are plenty worse things than mosquitoes.'

'Oh, I don't think so,' she said, unconcerned, making them feel in turn the weight of her umbrella handle. 'You see, I'm not wholly unprepared. This was specially made for me — lead. Not that I've ever had to use it.'

'How the Bear would have loved her — !' commented Jean-Paul, in Marseille-terms which he could rely on her not understanding, even if she caught the words. 'A deaf old crone defying Greece with a loaded umbrella handle! That's better than Mihael's woman with a mouth like a wound. Tell her she reminds me of my mother.

Not that I remember my old girl very clearly, but I hope she was made of the same sort of leather.'

'Come with us!' Hebe urged upon the old lady.

'Dear, no. What to? All chi-chi at home nowadays. Impossible people on unbelievable mounts, knocking down what used to be my lovely dry-piled walls.' She ended her refusal with a remark over which Hebe pondered for hours along the way: 'You're too young to realize that to people of my generation, lipstick looks terrible on a horse.'

Just as they set out she called them back. 'Go to the Quakers at Edhessa, if you want help, and kindness — given for their sake, not yours, you know. That's if they're still at Edhessa. Probably. Wonderful people. They kept me alive for three months. After my son died, and I'd an idea of going too. Sat up talking to me, night after night. Persuading me into living. Because *they* think it's wrong to take life, even one's own. Though there's nothing to live for. And now I doubt if they'd remember my name! Yes, go to them, and learn the cold of good works. Dear, the cold!'

10

'THE COLD OF GOOD WORKS'

'WE may as well see what they'll do for us, these people?' said Hebe, as they walked away from the diggings. They started off towards the rising sun, over a glistening path of sun-coloured stones which flung back to them the almost unbelievable light of early Greek spring, so that they moved in radiance, a private rainbow round each foot. 'Since the worst that can happen is nothing,' she persisted, when he grunted instead of replying.

She hoped that he would not guess her reason for wanting to follow up the old lady's suggestion. At the moment her remarkable sense of direction was entirely at fault: the movements of fighting columns across their path had turned and turned them, till she was not even certain that they were still to the north of Salonika: it might lie due east. Unfortunately the old lady, consulted in a moment of privacy, had not known either, but she had indicated the general direction of Edhessa. At Edhessa, Hebe would have a chance to re-orientate herself.

'Nothing?' he said. 'Oh, no, it isn't! You're as bad as *La Méchante* on malaria. It's a detour, it must be, and if we don't run into more troops on the way, the Quakers can still try to put us in a D.P. camp.'

'It wouldn't be to their advantage.'

'No money. No papers. Responsible people always want to. As if you didn't know that! Is it by any chance — '

'We've got to choose our risks when we can,' she said quickly. 'Fighting men kill you. The police send you back where you've come from. Busybodies put you among the D.P.s, because they're sure it's better for you. We'll watch those Quakers, and move on quickly if they start looking troublesome.' Her spirits were heavy at leaving the admirable old lady. Why was it that when no effort seemed worth-while for the moment, even for respectability's sake, one always had to pretend the hardest?

'Is it by any chance that you don't know where we are, this sudden keenness for Quakers?' Jean-Paul returned to the charge.

'Listen,' said Hebe. 'I just happened to remember, Edhessa isn't far out of our way.'

'All right,' he agreed mildly, to her surprise. 'I daresay relief workers round here hardly see anyone who hasn't lost everything. So if this lot started their job with the usual itch to label everybody "Dispossessed Person", they'll have had enough of it by now and not bother about us. Which way's Edhessa?'

'East with a bit of south in it. There ought to be a road in the next valley.'

'Well, get us on to it as soon as you can, and stick to roads in future. We'll be more noticeable off them than on, where there are more villages.'

Nightingales were to be heard by day now: what was it the Professor had once quoted, 'Oh, the apple tree, the singing and the gold' — ? A pair of tortoises scuttled across their way: it was pleasant that these need not be eaten, because of the old lady's present. Hebe's spirits rose to the point where it was well worth pretending again, when necessary. 'I wasn't specially learning the way to Edhessa when I studied the maps,' she said. To open one's heart to anyone, as she had to the old lady, was an indulgence that must be paid for by added caution. 'So I can't work out a route ahead. It's on the edge of the ground I know. I've a much clearer idea of the roads on from there, to Salonika.'

'Oh, well, I wouldn't hold it against you if you were all mixed up,' Jean-Paul said, surprising her again. 'Frankly, I'm lost. I never was any good in the country at finding my way. In a town it'd be different. But I'd sooner have you with me than not, as things are. Apart from the contacts in Salonika, I mean.'

This was disarming. Among such confusion of feeling, Hebe thought, it became more and more important to hold to the single purpose of getting back to all that André meant. One must not be distracted from this by kindness, any more than by fear, though here was Jean-Paul growing gentler and gentler, apparently because Ila, Mihael and Lisabet had died so horribly.

'You'll see,' she said at a venture. 'There'll be no difficulty whatever about the next part of the way,' and found later in the day that she had been telling the truth by accident. They fell in with a temporarily retired bandit from Mesimeri, the famous *klept* village four miles from the town of Edhessa. As he told them with pride, over three quarters of the population of Mesimeri had been in the bandit business for generations, irrespective of civil or any other wars. Mesimeri's reputation had spread far beyond the confines of Macedonia: he seemed slightly hurt that they did not know of it. All the same, he suggested that they should make their way there together.

He was loud in complaint against the troops attached to the British Military Mission, not for what they were doing in Greece at all, which angered the guerilla forces, but for what they had just ceased to do locally — they had removed their Medical Post from Edhessa. Only women and children normally lived in Mesimeri: no fit man between the ages of sixteen and sixty, he explained, cared to be seen in the place by day, lest it should be asked why he was not in the hills. Nor could any likely-looking woman of marriageable age afford to be long there either, for the question would arise why, if she could get one, was she not following her bandit lad to the hills? In either case, prestige rather than safety was at stake in keeping away from the place: Mesimeri was left alone by all the conflicting parties in Greece: it was convenient to let the old and young remain together, where they could be supported by their own relatives, rather than by the State or any other authority. But before the British forces were withdrawn, because of the encroachment of the guerillas with whom they were no longer officially at war, the Medical Officer at Edhessa had supplied a great need — the Mesimeri man laughed heartily, with the excellent detachment of Greek humour, as he described to Hebe and Jean-

Paul the sheepish queues of fellow-bandits who had lined up day after day with minor injuries outside the British post, to ask for sticking plaster. This they had received free, and applied spectacularly not to cuts and abrasions but to their faces, or wherever it would show to advantage, suggesting serious hurts, as an excuse for returning to the village on reasonable occasions, such as the calving of a cow or a visit to a sick mother. For him, nowadays, he said, going home would be more difficult to cover, but he must risk the consequences in order to impress on his children that they should not leave the village on any account, to prevent them from being moved by the *andartes*, along with thousands of others, over the borders into Jugoslavia or Bulgaria. He could not say whether the Quaker women had remained in Edhessa, after the military moved back towards their base at Salonika, but thought it likely enough: relief workers were hard to dislodge.

Hebe was free in his company not only from any anxiety about the way, but still further from fear of the vlach dogs. It was a hundred times pleasanter to be two than one when they attacked, as they threatened to do several times while he was with them, but far nicer still to be three: he had known the brutes all his life and was an adept stone-thrower. And his presence brought them safely through an unexpected encounter with an armed patrol, whether Government or guerilla they did not discover, in which the leader fortunately turned out to be an old Mesimeri neighbour of his.

From Mesimeri they went on without him, but with his instructions about the way, to Edhessa: here they found that everything which could be shifted, not only soldiers, had been evacuated to Voiaia: then on to Voiaia, to find again that the place was almost empty. The *andartes* were gathering strength, their activities increasing with the lengthening days: it became more and more difficult to avoid them. There were significant tales in this district of local men returning from the north in Russian uniform, with only the buttons cut off, and of one, from a notably lazy family, keeping the buttons in place, because, he said, it was wasteful to remove them while his wife had plenty to do without sewing them on again, should they be needed in a hurry. Hebe and Jean-Paul had cares enough of their own to think about without brooding over the importance of this, or taking in fully that where they walked, the fate of the world boiled and bubbled again in the ancient Greek cauldron: open intervention from Russia meant war at once, they knew; war without confines. But Hebe was having trouble with her shoes once more, her toe-nails were starting to hurt against the broken toe-caps. Beside this discomfort, the extreme danger in which all civilization stood at the moment seemed too irrelevant to grasp: Jean-Paul had lost the heelobowie's nail file.

Many sore miles further on, at a small place forgotten by all the military, but just within the area protected by Government troops, they found the two women who had come out from England to distribute the Friends' relief stores, as part of the United Nations Rehabilitation and Relief Administration.

Jean-Paul and Hebe saw them standing in a stationary truck, cheerfully doling out tins of condensed milk to a crowd of clamouring women on the ground.

'The milk scheme!' exclaimed Jean-Paul. 'What a pity no one would take you for under two. Or that you're not a bit fatter, when at least they might believe you were pregnant!' Even international wanderers, for whom the larger political issues could be obscured by the smallest blister, knew all about the U.N.R.R.A. mothers' milk ration: it appealed so much to the sardonic Greek sense of humour that for the last few days, jokes had been made about it by everyone in this area from whom Hebe and Jean-Paul had begged when they could not pilfer. (Hebe was now as shameless in begging, if not in stealing, as the man.) 'Tell U.N.R.R.A. you need the free milk!' they were advised, by those who refused them. Two tins a day could be claimed by each woman from the full nine months before a birth until her child reached the age of two, in all parts of Greece where the German destruction of the railways, during the occupation, was believed by the Allies to have caused particular hardship. In fact, the areas of distribution were decided, on the spot, less by the amount of hardship they contained than by their accessibility to the distributors: this part of Macedonia was far better off than the northern region; the houses, though poor, were no longer hovels, the farms occasionally had live-stock which was not hidden away.

'Not mothers, either of you? Well, that's a change!' observed the older of the two Quakers, speaking a fluent, idiomatic Greek, when Jean-Paul and Hebe had jostled their way to the tail of the truck. 'Mind you, we wouldn't have been surprised if you'd both said you were. We get odder claims to the milk than that! — Oh, you're English, are you?' — Hebe, grinning, had replied in that language — 'Well, climb in here till this farce is over, if you like, and then we'll see what we can do for you.'

'It isn't really a farce and you know it, Lesley,' said the younger woman, turning round, her eyes gleaming belligerently through her glasses. 'Not this part of the job. Not like the giving out of grain, I mean. Because if only one tin of milk in ten is of use, I — Oh, well!' She returned her attention to the gesticulating women.

In a moment Lesley sat down with Hebe and Jean-Paul, giving them a damaged tin to finish, with biscuits spared from the tiny meal the Quakers had brought for themselves. She was a handsome woman, thirty-seven years old, as she mentioned almost immediately. She discussed the milk situation with them while the remaining supplies were given out by Miss Hutchinson — not more than twenty-two, plain, and obviously worried about her dignity, whereas Lesley was worried about her age. Miss Hutchinson insisted on being addressed as Miss Hutchinson by everyone except Lesley, who did not care what anyone called her, so long as they made demands on her practical kindness.

'Of course this is a farce,' she said. 'No woman in Greece has ever *not* fed her child herself, I gather. If she couldn't, I suppose she'd give it olive oil and soaked bread. Anyway, not condensed milk. The tins are just currency round here. Worth about a tenth of what they were bought for, by charitable people at home.'

'They don't look pregnant, most of these women,' Hebe remarked, drawing a deprecating glance from Miss Hutchinson.

'They aren't,' said Lesley. 'Or not more of them than you'd expect anyway, among this number of Greek women. But how are we supposed to tell? No doctor's certificate — No doctors.'

'Of course, that's the funny side of our job,' put in Miss Hutchinson, in a lull in the distribution caused by two of the claimants breaking into violent argument. 'We have to take everybody's word for everything. But I don't care! I feel, how dreadful if one of them really needed it and didn't get it. I suppose I'm just silly about Greeks.'

'Yielding to none in my admiration for your character — except perhaps to you, Claire! — Yes,' said Lesley, and intervened to appease an elderly woman who had already received her two tins but was outraged by another's plea for four, on the strength of an absent daughter, also officially pregnant.

'They're so brave!' said Miss Hutchinson. 'And they've endured so much.'

Lesley announced firmly above the hubbub that only those who came personally for their allowance would receive it. 'You'd like us to put you up for a day or two perhaps?' she said, turning back to the newcomers. 'We must find you some other shoes. You can't go much further in those. There's a bale of second-hand clothing just come. When the truck's empty, we'll give you a lift back to where we're staying. You'll be able to sleep on the floor somewhere. Though I can't think where, for the moment. It's pretty full.'

Beyond the fact that they had in view some definite goal, Salonika, now only fifty miles away, she seemed uninterested to learn any details about them. 'Yes ... Yes ... Well, you were lucky, if others weren't,' she said, sympathetic but not concerned, when they spoke of the *klepts*' descent on the nameless village in the north. It was as if she had seen so much suffering that she limited her thoughts strictly to the wants of people who had somehow survived misfortune, and could be helped to reach an objective. The dead were dead: there was nothing to be done for them. She talked French with enjoyment to Jean-Paul, when she heard him speak it to Hebe, and proved an acquaintance with the slang of Paris and Marseille at least half as intimate as his own. Miss Hutchinson's French was of the English schoolgirls' variety, admired by Hebe alone for its purely formal quality.

'You've been around!' Jean-Paul said, admiringly, when Lesley had deftly made it impossible for him to offer her the kind of gross flattery which he found suitable for any woman older than Hebe, but younger than *La Méchante*.

'Oh, yes, I've been around,' she said, and laughed. 'The blow-fly of chaos! Wherever there's destitution, there I am, I and my kind. We can't resist it. And wherever we come there's more destitution, because we teach people not to depend on themselves.'

'Just as well I can't follow half you're saying!' Miss Hutchinson smiled pleasantly over her shoulder, 'Because I'm sure I wouldn't agree with it!'

Lesley talked with brisk self-mockery of the relief-service she had seen, during the last few years, in Poland and Bulgaria, stressing the inadequacy and frustration of the efforts made to repair the enormous human dislocation of the time. They did not know how to take this belittling manner of hers, and let her tell them of a hopeless battle against starvation and typhoid in Bulgaria, without at first disclosing that they themselves had passed through the district at about the same time, struggling across the frightened tide of refugees which flowed north and west while they were making south. Then Hebe said something showing that she knew the nightmare place which was being described, with brittle brilliance, in unfeeling words. Lesley stopped and grimaced: 'The real onset of middle age!' she said. 'Much more significant than the first grey hair. The moment of discovering that youth no longer bothers to tell you it knows as much about something as you do. Or more!'

'All finished,' said Miss Hutchinson, spreading empty hands in the sight of the remaining women. 'No more now. More to-morrow.' Even in Greek, which she spoke with difficulty, she managed to recall to Hebe the admiring authority exercised over the dogs in the house near Bristol, where they mattered so much more than anything else.

'It's easy to tell that your friend is an Englishwoman, though not that you are,' said Jean-Paul to Lesley, while the women who had quarrelled were being persuaded into the truck by Miss Hutchinson, to be given a lift to their village, in the hope that they might become reconciled on the way. 'She talks to all these people as if they were animals. The sort one is kind to.'

'No, indeed I don't,' Miss Hutchinson turned pink with distress when this was passed on to her, appreciatively, by Lesley. 'They're the most heroic people I've ever met, the Greeks. Look what they did against the Italians. It's not their fault they're not really starving hereabouts, and we were told in London they were. Of course I'm thankful they're not, even if we look silly, being taken in about it the way we were. I'm proud to do anything I can for them. As if I could think of *Greeks* like — '

'But I am sure she thinks — tell her — very well of animals? Say, horses? Then why should she not think the same about Greeks? It was a compliment I meant.'

'But I don't think of anyone — '

'For goodness sake, Claire, just start up the truck and get moving. Never mind what you think about anything, if you don't want all our throats cut by your heroic friends. We've ten miles to go, and it'll be dark before we get in, at this rate.'

Flushing still more deeply, Miss Hutchinson climbed from the back into the cab in front and drove off, picking the way skilfully between the pot-holes of an appalling track. Resolute against taking offence, she found her revenge on Lesley's irritable nerves by growing sweeter and sweeter in response to sharpness. She chatted with animation to Hebe, explaining that they chose a different distribution-point every few days in an area of about twenty miles round their isolated depot. 'We're supposed to have a driver, you know. A local man. But he's disappeared. Probably in jail, we're afraid. Or sent to the islands. In that case we shan't hear what's happened to him for years, if at all. It's disquieting the way people just vanish around here. Whatever party they belong to. But it nearly always happens when they're alone. So it's nice to have company along the road. We pick up someone whenever we can.' A little later she called back to Lesley, whose battered handbag lay beside her, on an empty milk-crate next to the two Greek women, 'Look after your bag, won't you? I daren't take my eyes off this road for a second.'

'That's all right. There's no money in it,' Lesley answered.

'I didn't mean it that way! It may slide off when we bounce.'

'Well, stop bouncing for a moment. That truck coming — it's Douglas driving, I think. He's in for a grain-raid, by the look of those goats. Pull right off the track, will you, so that he can get by as fast as he dares.' Lesley smiled reassuringly at Hebe and Jean-Paul. 'Not the sort of raid you've known. This is just entertainment. Watch.'

They were on the outskirts of a village: two goats lay side by side in the middle of the twisting track ahead, apparently asleep. Approaching them from the opposite direction came a heavier truck than the women's, one of the low-slung U.N.R.R.A. grain-carriers. It rounded a sharp corner, into sight of the animals, too close to them to be able to back away in time. The driver slowed down to a crawl, with his horn blaring. The fantastic state of the road surface made it impossible to drive at more than ten miles an hour in any case, and this gave the inhabitants of the village time to prepare for the truck's approach. Before the goats, tightly hobbled, had struggled up and hopped out of the way, from the mud huts alongside the track emerged the black figures of several old women, armed with their formidable broad-bladed cooking knives. These they jabbed vigorously into the sacks, trotting alongside the truck when it re-started, to jab again, ignoring the helpless threats of the driver, who grinned and waved to his fellow-workers as he lurched by them, accelerating hard at the risk of his springs to shake off pursuit. A second wave of old women, from huts standing further back, followed the knife-carriers with pans and whisks, brushing up the spilled grain from the road. 'The absurd part is, they don't even eat it themselves,' said Miss Hutchinson, manœuvring carefully past the sweepers after she had regained the track, in order not to scatter the grain still more and make it harder for them to pick up. 'Unmilled like that, it's only good for seed-corn, which is what we import it for, of course. They feed their chickens with it.'

The amusement of the Greek passengers in the milk-truck was even greater than that of the English Quakers, but they drew their head-shawls courteously across their faces, to hide at least some of their laughter at the ways of these strangers who were trying to bring back prosperity to their land. 'Of course what they can't understand,' Miss Hutchinson went on, 'is why the U.N.R.R.A. drivers don't simply run over the goats. Really it's rather clever of them to guess we wouldn't. That's why I said, perhaps the grain distribution is rather a farce. Still, it's an example.'

'Oh, rubbish!' said Lesley. 'It's funny, that's all, Claire! Can't you see how exasperating it must be, if you've any pride, to have people like us coming into your country and doing good to you, uninvited? We're not an example, we're just natural prey. Who are we, anyway, to decide that they really ought to plant the seed-corn they didn't ask to be given, if they happen to prefer throwing it to fowls?'

'You're so unfair, Lesley, I didn't say they oughtn't — ' But Lesley had turned to Jean-Paul, as to a fellow-cosmopolitan, and Miss Hutchinson could not finish her protest.

'Being smug and — though you mightn't think it — being stingy,' Lesley told him. 'That's always been our trouble as Quakers.'

'What makes you do this job?' he asked curiously.

'You mean, when surely I would rather live in my own country with a husband and four children? — As a matter of fact, I would, too,' she said lightly. 'Ah, if you could get me to tell you that, I should sound just like Claire here — Miss Hutchinson!'

'The love of God?' Hebe suggested.

'That does extraordinary things to people,' Jean-Paul agreed, as Lesley shook her head. 'Both when it gets hold of them and when it lets them go. A man we knew, Hebe and I, he was like that, I can tell you! — At least, I suppose one could call Mihael's worrying about Him, the love of God? — Anyway, it gave him a reason for acting in a way you'd never have expected of him, if you'd known him long.'

'Well, my reason for behaving quite out of character would be much more embarrassing to admit. Oddly, one could — or I could — own to the love of God as a motive without undue discomfort, although in my case it doesn't apply — '

'Lesley, what on earth are you talking about?' Miss Hutchinson asked in English.

'Literally, nothing on earth!'

'I can recognize *l'amour de Dieu*! You of all people. Always saying you don't know where to look if I even see the good in someone!'

'You see it so very, very relentlessly,' said Lesley, without dropping the thread of her conversation with Jean-Paul. '— But there are other explanations of unlikely conduct, you know, much more surprising. More surprising to oneself about one's own behaviour, that is, than the love of God would be. It's possible to do something, and know why one does it, and think it an improbable reason for doing anything, but still go on doing it. Well, that's how it is with me. I'd rather have a husband and four children, which in fact I haven't got, and if I'm not careful will never get, yet I don't go in search of them in suitable places. Let's not go into why.'

The Greek women broke in, wishing to take their leave, with a gentle murmur of apology for stopping the truck again so soon.

'But this isn't your village, surely? We'll be coming to it in a minute.'

True, they said, chuckling, but they had friends at this place, and would take the opportunity of visiting them. 'They will be so astonished to see us coming by car!' Each in turn made a dignified little speech of thanks for the milk, the ride, and pleasant society on the road.

When they had gone, Lesley discovered that a stub of lipstick and a battered powder-compact had disappeared from her bag, despite Miss Hutchinson's warning. The missing articles were too well-used to be sold, neither could possibly have been wanted for personal use by the women themselves. They must have been taken during the distraction of the grain-raid, when Jean-Paul and Hebe had not been within reach of the bag, so that no suspicion could fall upon them. 'Oh, well, I suppose the old girls just like to keep their hands in,' said Lesley tolerantly. 'Heaven knows when I can get any more.' The incident put things right between her and Miss Hutchinson. It was something for them to laugh at together: Miss Hutchinson had done her best, and Lesley had lost the props for her vanity all the same. The only bond that united them — but it was strong — was their amusement at every aspect of the situation in which they found themselves in Macedonia.

Hebe learnt more of this later in the day at their billet, a requisitioned house formerly owned by one of the *andartes'* leaders who had been caught and executed. Its four small rooms were crowded with an assortment of people who for one reason or another had nowhere else to sleep. 'But that's all that's the matter with most of them,' Miss Hutchinson said, over a shared meal of thin porridge, made thinner to include the newcomers, and eked out with some baked beans, much fewer because of their arrival. 'Most of our guests live better than we do, by day — More resources! So the joke's definitely on us. When you think of the stories we swallowed at home about destitution everywhere in the Balkans! I know I was moved to tears. But then I always am, much too easily, as Lesley says. It seemed so awful, in London, to think of these people being hungry when they'd been so gallant.'

'If you'd been taken in by your better nature more often,' said Lesley, 'you'd know it's being gallant that makes people hungry.'

'Then we got here with supplies and they weren't. Hungry, I mean. Not really.'

'Of course we know there is starvation in Greece, in patches,' said Lesley, 'where there's no means of transport. Not because there isn't food in the country. So we also know that wherever we might be able to do something useful, we can't go. Can't get our supplies up. And if we could go, it'd mean the need for us wasn't there — they'd be able to get other supplies, just as easily. It's peculiar to the Balkans, I think, for army after army to roll backwards and forwards over a country, and not cut down one single bearing olive tree. Official, or otherwise, troops are all the same here about that. It must be the only inhibition Balkan soldiers know. Every other house for miles around has casks of oil stored up. There's nowhere for them to sell it. And we, of course, can't afford to buy it. Not for our own use.'

'The way it was further north, where we were,' Hebe told her, 'the *andartes* held the roads, and people were very hungry. At least, they held most of the roads, most of the time,' she added, remembering the heelobowie. In this relatively civilized atmosphere it became more and more satisfactory to think that she had managed to thank him for the party, in spite of all the *retsina* she had drunk.

'But I'm glad we volunteered! Although I suppose we mightn't if we'd known more.' Miss Hutchinson's eyes took on the dedicated shine which tended to exasperate Lesley. 'We can do something for the people round here just as important as feeding them, I find. We can make them feel somebody cares what happens to them, and that's the big thing! Whether they're in want or not.'

For once, Lesley was too much interested in her subject to mind the other's approach. 'Just round here,' she said, 'they're a particularly gaunt lot, which misled us when we first arrived. But it's a gauntness of several hundred years' inheritance. They've always lived on the edge of hardship. Nothing to do with any present shortages. Well, it serves us right, being stuck in this place for another three months — we've done three already, but we had to agree to take over a district for six, before they'd let us into the country at all — We ought to have foreseen that the transport trouble would be responsible for everything. Or I ought to, because I've been had this way before. As that charming old Turk in the next room says, "I hope I will let this be a lesson to me".'

'By the way, I think there's some trouble between him and the ex-Armenian family,' reported Miss Hutchinson. 'I told him,

"Well, you're all Turks now. Since the last treaty. So you must just make the best of it." But I don't think he understood. He doesn't talk much Greek, and of course I can't talk Turkish.'

'Just as well. It must be about the most explosive sentence you've ever devised, telling a Turk that because of an annexation-treaty he must now love the Armenians as his brothers. Don't let them sleep anywhere near each other. Those ex-Armenians are expansive dreamers, they roll about. I could hear them through our wall last night. I don't know what "tempting providence" means, but I should think it's something like letting a sleeping Turk who was born an Armenian, encroach on a sleeping Turk who was born a Turk. We'll put you in between,' said Lesley to Jean-Paul. 'Non-Balkan insulation. That'll be all right. I hope.'

'I'll arrange it for you if you'll be fair to all of us for once, Lesley,' said Miss Hutchinson. 'Including yourself! Admit that no one but Quakers would find it so funny to be let in for what we've got!'

'Oh yes, yes,' Lesley said distastefully. 'That's all part of our essential smugness.'

'If you've been here three months,' Hebe calculated, 'it must have been just after you came that you saved someone we call *La Méchante*.' She had wanted to mention the old lady before, when the theft of the lipstick put her in mind of the puzzling remark about its use on a horse. The interesting picture this conjured up still recurred to her at intervals. She would have liked to ask for an explanation from Lesley, who knew about lipstick, but she was afraid of being laughed at: Lesley, despite her benevolence, seemed a formidable person.

'Saved? Who?'

They told her of finding the old lady at work in the diggings. 'She looks for things from the past. Well, she did. Now she re-buries them. An old, old lady, like marble. She didn't tell us her name, and we didn't tell her ours, either, because there was no one else there, except a servant we couldn't talk to, and when it's like that you don't need names. It's just "you". She thought a loaded umbrella would keep off the Government troops, or the *andartes*.'

'We get so many old people coming through. Of all nationalities. Wanting something or other. It's very easy to get them muddled —'

Plainly, they had forgotten the enchanting old lady. 'What was the matter with her?' asked Lesley. After a little while, that was all she could recall of the people she helped — not their personalities, only their needs and sorrows.

'Her son died, and she didn't want to live.'

'Oh, yes!' said Miss Hutchinson. 'There was someone like that! I remember. We talked. How is she?'

But they did not really want to know, Hebe felt. The old lady had passed on her way, and they could do her no more good. How little human beings could mean to one another! Almost safe, almost warm, almost not hungry for once, Hebe shivered a little. Cold indeed.

11

THE BEEHIVE

ALMOST unbelievable it seemed, after so much striving towards this goal, that Salonika lay within five days' walking distance.

The intervening ground was said to be full of fighting patrols from both sides: Jean-Paul proposed staying where they were until they could get a lift in a truck: once a week the young Quaker called Douglas took his life in his hands and drove through with stores.

The nearness of the port forced another crisis of decision on Hebe. To have brought even one of her father's party so far was a feat of which she felt reasonably proud, however big a part luck had played in her efforts: but because there were no reliable contacts ahead, shipowners ready to take refugees without passports or money — none at least of which she knew for certain, to back up her vaunted list — she and Jean-Paul must part soon, and this time finally. It would be pleasanter to make this happen before he found her out, beyond any possible doubt. It would also be safer: one should not rely on a change of heart in someone so erratic. He was quite capable of taking the discovery badly.

She had another three days before Douglas was due. Carefully, without rousing Jean-Paul's suspicions, Hebe set herself to extract from him the names and whereabouts of his closest relatives in France. It was disappointing not to be able to see this part of her venture quite through to its proper close, but if she could not know where Jean-Paul settled, as a means of tracing André later on, others of his family must be available instead. It was not enough that André's parents owned the café in Lille: they might die before she had finished with the good school stage, or the place could change hands. Where possible, nothing should ever be left to chance.

' — And your Aunt Marie, the tobacconist? I bet she laughed when she heard about the false teeth and the police? No? She was too straight-laced?' (Good. This was an aunt to have. She and André would look her up, in due course.) 'Perhaps that's because she's not from Marseille, you said? They're stricter, aren't they, about family life in other parts of the midi? Oh, from Carcassonne! And her brother, Joseph? He also — '

Outside the small, bare house, cleaner than Dido's but more crowded, kingfishers flashed in the strengthening sunshine: real halcyon days made plain why all the loveliest legends of spring had risen from Greek soil. Here was another period of brief satisfaction for Hebe, snatched from adversity, like the interlude of the little pigs. Miss Hutchinson lent her scissors and washed her hair for her, cutting it in a bell shape: she was no longer lousy. She took stock of herself, and was not discouraged: it was a long time since she had studied herself in a glass. If she were still much too thin and angular, not really pretty, as Jean-Paul had said, at least her shiny, light brown hair looked passable now, and her striking, fierce blue eyes even better. She must remember to stay sunburnt if she could, in the days when her looks might matter: the darkness of her skin went well with fair natural colouring.

At night she lay squeezed against a partition wall because the ex-Armenian family took up more and more room, refusing to be separated by anyone from the born-Turk, with whom they argued skilfully and dangerously on the rights and wrongs of annexation. But the lack of space had its compensations: through the wall could be heard everything said by the two Quaker women in the minute room they had elected to share, with complete disregard for their own comfort, in order to make more room for stranded people.

'That girl — Hebe — she knows much too much for her age.'

Quite right, thought Hebe, recognizing Miss Hutchinson's voice. But could she not realize that it would be all the more of a luxury to forget?

'I daresay.' Lesley sounded sleepy and uninterested.

'Noticing at once those women weren't pregnant! You know, they're not father and daughter, those two!'

'Come to think of it, probably not. Or they'd talk the same languages. He knows no English. Still, does it matter?'

'The child may come to serious harm.'

'For once — just once! — do face realities, Claire — What chance has she got, with things as they are out here, of coming to anything else?'

'They ought to be in the hands of the refugee people. Much safer for her. Couldn't we get a message through to the D.P. organizers at Salonika? That's where they're going, isn't it, that pair? They could be watched for there.'

'They could, but somehow I can't feel it's our job to see that they are. We're here to feed people, whether they need it or not. We're not here to control their lives, even when it looks as if that's what they need a lot more.'

Hebe decided not to repeat all this to Jean-Paul in the morning: he would say he had warned her, and want to move on without delay, whatever lay ahead. She was the one more willing to stay where she was, for once. It was good to rest a little in the sun, among the nightingales: for the moment, happiness lay in just not being lousy. And after all, Lesley had not accepted Miss Hutchinson's suggestion.

The second-hand shoes, much too big for Hebe's narrow feet, were being gently broken in. There were several English books to be borrowed, too; none of them of the kind Hebe most enjoyed, but one in particular, belonging to Miss Hutchinson, she found absorbing as far as she had gone. This was a biography of Robert Louis Stevenson, and at the beginning it described a child with whom she could easily identify herself, because their ages were the same: but he was often ill, and afraid of the dark — How wonderful to dare to be ill, and afraid of no more than empty blackness! — the book was a rich fantasy of indulgence for Hebe: she had known only two days' sickness since her father died, and these, luckily, were at Dido's farm, where the others could not leave her behind, as she had always known they would if she failed to keep up with them on the move: all but the Professor. But more than for these reasons, she wanted to stay on to listen again to the voices coming through the wall in the night.

The thought recurred to her that only by knowing why people did things could she make them give her whatever it was she wanted: but she had gone a long way, in body and spirit, since that discovery first came to her. Now, there seemed to be more point to the understanding of other minds than the gain it might bring. She would have given a great deal, had she possessed it, to know why the two Quaker women chose to endure their comfortless existence, laughing at the poor results of their ability to be deceived. Both had homes to go to: Lesley's, judging by something she let slip, was a pleasant one with money in it.

Discussion between the Turkish factions, new and old, was so prolonged and noisy the next night that she could not hear what went on next door, and for this was forced to wait until the following evening, which promised at first to be much quieter. A Cretan, who had just escaped from one of the Greek Government prison-islands, arrived after dark to ask for shelter. Compared with the conditions from which he had come, everything in the Quakers' little house struck him favourably, including the congestion on the floor. A mild-mannered little man, he smiled continually with nervous pleasure. Gun-metal caps on his front teeth gave his smile such peculiar ferocity, seen for the first time by lamp light, that even the ex-Armenians were awed by it into temporary silence.

The two women next door seemed to have no realization of the thinness of the partition; even the breathy earnestness of Miss Hutchinson's tone came through, shy but persistent: 'You know I think you're marvellous, Lesley. And it isn't just a schoolgirl crush, whatever you say! Only I do think you oughtn't to talk to me the way you do in front of people. How can the Greeks respect me if you don't seem to?'

'I don't suppose they respect either of us. Why should they? We're a couple of fools to be here. You know that. So do they.'

'It makes things so difficult.'

'As a matter of fact, I do respect you — One of the few people who live according to their conscience.'

'You always make out I'm such a prig.'

'I'm sorry. I suppose — ' Lesley seemed softened for the moment, but Miss Hutchinson broke in again, unfortunately, with 'It's not fair!' said in a pouting-schoolgirl voice, and then the biting edge came back into Lesley's tone.

'Can't you understand that one of the queerest things about human goodness is that in action — in real life — it's the most moving thing in the world? But put into words it's nearly always boring and embarrassing? You have a knack of making it articulate which I've never known equalled! Hasn't it ever struck you, in books for instance, that genius and goodness are the two things that simply can't be conveyed? They're only overwhelming when you meet them in the flesh. And then they mustn't be explicit about themselves. To be bearable, virtue must be either dumb or unconscious.'

'I don't see why,' said Miss Hutchinson.

'No. I know.'

'And I'm sure the Greeks feel — '

'Oh, Claire! — That "A little practical help is worth a deal of sympathy"?'

'I wasn't going to say that! Though why you should mind me saying it when you're actually living it all the time, I still don't see. I don't suppose I ever will. I was going to say, I also wish you wouldn't talk in public about wanting a husband and four children. I'm sure the Greeks don't understand what you really mean when you say that.'

'If there's one thing they understand admirably — ! I don't share your feeling for them, as you know. I don't think they're a pleasant race, on the whole. Too brave and too cruel for my liking. But they're quite clear what women are for. And quite right about it, too.'

'Then they won't take what you say as a joke.'

'Naturally not. I'm nearly forty. For a woman of these parts, that's old age.'

'Well, it embarrasses me when you say that sort of thing. I mean, except to me.'

'How easily we embarrass each other. Just by telling the truth. Different kinds of truth. It's a pity — '

Renewed argument, followed by uproar, broke out on Hebe's side of the partition; the ex-Armenians had got the better of the Turk once too often: knives were produced. Even the gun-metal smile, a nervous *tic* now, could not get them sheathed. Time after time, both sides were pacified by the two Quakers, who seemed completely fearless in dealing with armed men. They enlisted the help of others in the room, but time after time, trouble started again. Racial habit made it impossible for the ex-Armenians to believe that to be right in an argument was not necessarily to be persuasive. When peace seemed imminent they thought of a new reason to support their view of annexation and struggled back to shout it, over the heads of the pacifiers, at the murderously angry Turk.

Threat and counter-threat led to barricades between the rooms: it was dawn before the situation subsided into the occasional insult, yelled without likelihood of reprisal.

Too keyed up to sleep, after hours of strain, Lesley went out into the courtyard round which the house was built, and Hebe joined her. They stood silently together, while the first light of the new day drew from vague blurs into rounded shapes the four bee-skeps of plaited straw which bordered one wall.

'I noticed the bees flying yesterday, for the first time this year,' said Lesley.

'I know something about bees. We kept them in South America. I'm one of the people they don't sting. Are you?' It seemed good at this hour to talk about such homelike things.

'I shouldn't think so. I'm afraid of them. And wasps.'

'I didn't think you could be afraid of anything!' Enviously, Hebe had watched her walk between the knives, and the shouting men, curtly telling people to behave themselves, in the maternal voice to which grown men, tired of shouting, were slightly more likely than not to listen: it had been a gamble, and Lesley had won.

'I? Oh, yes. Of time. Of almost everything.' She laughed a little at Hebe's puzzled face, peering up at her through the half-light. 'If you can enjoy things a great deal — and I can, you see. That must sound odd, considering where I am now! —The civilized things. Good companionship most of all — Well, if you're like that, you'll find you're always afraid of having the means to enjoy them taken away from you. Or, if you're still more like me, you'll be afraid of yourself. In case you deprive yourself of them until it's too late for enjoyment. In case you're stupid, and throw your life away, to no good purpose.'

This woman, thought Hebe, was like the alarming saint of whom the Professor had spoken, the one who valued highly the quality which Hebe herself possessed, or so he had fancied: intelligence. But if intelligence counted with Lesley, it became still more incomprehensible that she should come by her own choice into these lawless places. In this moment Hebe longed, almost with passion, to know what moved Lesley to choose hardship and boredom and danger, she for whom the ways of escape were always open: money, a passport. But no sharp-tongued saint could safely be questioned twice on a subject which plainly she had not welcomed when Jean-Paul broached it. Instead of what was in her mind, 'Shall I look into the hives for you?' Hebe asked. 'To see if anything needs doing? The bees are easiest to handle at this time.'

'Will you? The owner took so much trouble over them, I'd like to keep them going. You see the way the midden's built up to shelter the entrances — I'm told he was settling his bees for the winter when they took him away to be shot. It seems more pointless than most killings, to execute a man attending to his bees.'

Hebe took up the skeps one after another, and a soft sleepy buzzing arose, but the morning air was too raw for the bees to fly. Only one colony had died out during the unusually long, severe winter. Chilled brood lay sealed in the comb, the dark patches just distinguishable from the paleness of uncapped cells. Lesley borrowed a knife from the still-muttering Turk, and with their faces close above it, while Lesley held the skep for her, Hebe began cutting out the spoiled comb, to make a safe housing for a later swarm. There was no honey left in this one skep: the bees, dead of starvation, fell out in great, feather-light clusters: but the blade sliced through the pollen-cells, built close round the brood to feed it, and these were full, the young having failed to hatch. Out into the cold spring dawn poured, in almost unbelievable strength, the hot and living smell of a dead summer: it came as a sudden battering of scent against the nerves, calling on their separate memories and responses — heady and evocative beyond all other appeals to the senses. A cloud of fertile dust hung invisibly in the still air about them, not with one fragrance only in it, but a hundred — the gathered essence of all the flowers of a past year: time out of reach returned.

Hebe straightened herself sharply, the knife idle in her hand. She had not actually been in the company of André while those flowers were in bloom, but the overpowering smell of sunshine, of white afternoons, brought back the time when she had saved him from the immigrant trap by the act which had lost him to her. She caught her breath to speak, but was forestalled.

'I was in England last summer. I thought I could stay there,' Lesley said. 'Make some sort of life for myself — this isn't a life. For three months it was all I'd hoped. And then another call came. To take over here. I said, "Of course, when?" like a girl accepting a proposal she's been waiting for!'

She stopped and said, 'Go on, child, finish that job!' as if trying to prevent herself from saying more, but they were both exhausted, Lesley especially, off-balance after the turmoil of the night, and the sudden magic was irresistible. Hebe said urgently. 'Tell me why you do this?' She stooped over the comb again, releasing fresh waves of lily and hyacinth and sweet-plumed grass.

'It's more difficult to explain than the love of God, the love of human beings just because they're human. The pity for them, that makes it essential to try and help, even if the help doesn't accomplish much, or anything — Oh, not the pity of mild contempt which people like Claire Hutchinson feel, for those who don't enjoy being good as much as they do themselves. So that they have to find excuses for whoever it is they serve. Like exceptional courage among the Greeks — The pity of respect, I mean, because men have always been so ill-served by their gods, and so much finer than any god they've ever devised. "Faithful unto death" is something no god can be, but ordinary, frightened men are, all the time. In every unnecessary war. In peace, too. They go on hoping for stray bits of happiness in such awful circumstances. With so little chance against the forces waiting to defeat them — bad luck and sickness and sorrow. It's because humanity's weak and afraid it's touching in its occasional greatness. And lovable always. Not often as individuals: in general. Beside that sort of love for one's own kind, the love of God has always seemed to me so pale. So much easier a burden to bear, too. You can content a god with worship, but what can you do for man? I don't know how much of this you can understand. You can't imagine what it's like to be driven to do something which you know is almost always useless. The need to try and lessen the hurts of the world. Of course, that's beyond anyone's strength. You do what you can, and it's still too little. But once you've begun to love people in that way, and are bound to help them, if you're able, unfortunately nothing else seems worth doing by comparison.'

'And yet you do resent missing so much, because of it?'

'Bitterly. You do understand something of it! There's no way to do this work except with an empty heart. If you gave a bit of yourself all the time, to everyone you met, soon there'd be nothing left to give. It doesn't lessen the sum of human agonies to ache over them one by one. And it's the emptiness of heart that becomes frightening at last.'

'Perhaps the love of God is more satisfying?' Hebe suggested, once more old beyond her age or experience.

'So they say. People talk as if you could choose what you'd prefer to love!' She drew the girl to her and kissed her casually on the cheek. It was the first kiss Hebe had been given since her father died. She stood rigid.

'Have you done with the hives now? Let's go in, and sleep, and forget as much of this as possible. That smell — "It's not fair," as Claire's always saying — taking it for granted that some time, somewhere, something must be! How lucky she is to be able to believe that. She's naturally a much better person than I am. I expect I'm jealous, that's why I'm so nasty to her. It must be wonderful to have giving come easy to you. And I'm for ever telling her there are no indecencies like those in words! — I shall be horrified by all this, Hebe, when we meet again in the morning!'

But they did not meet again. It was quiet indoors, except for the restlessness of the sleepers on the floor, when Hebe crawled to her place beside the partition: Miss Hutchinson's voice, high, clear, going on and on with a gentle urgency, became audible through it at once. Lesley must be just getting into bed, Hebe thought; she could hear the irritable creak of the springs as Lesley turned about under the soft persistence of the other. 'You must see that, after tonight! I mean, we've no right to let a child face . . . well, scarcely more than a child, anyway . . . And that man she's with — Dreadful!'

'How unlike you, Claire. So downright and unqualified!' This was Lesley's mocking, controlled voice again, not the unguarded tones of the courtyard. 'Generally you say you're afraid I'll think you're *rather* awful, but you somehow can't *entirely* like — somebody no one else can stand at any price! Specially dreadful, is he? Why?' But Miss Hutchinson was not to be diverted from Hebe's welfare.

' . . . when the D.P. people would at least look after her properly . . . We might feel we'd really accomplished something . . .' followed by Lesley's 'Are you sure that isn't the reason? Just to feel we'd accomplished something? Anyway, talk of it in the morning, Claire. Let me sleep now, can't you?'

It was a struggle for Hebe, too, to remain awake, to hear Miss Hutchinson out: 'But this *is* the morning. I know you're tired. Goodness knows, Lesley, so am I. But . . . duty . . . least we can do ... Douglas comes early with the stores ... In about three hours now. You could ask him to try the military line to Salonika ... suggested before ... No business to be wandering about the roads.' And Lesley's weary, final capitulation: 'I suppose you're right, really. We ought to do something.'

Hebe unwound herself from the shepherd's cloak, collecting in it the few things she had been given, the spare shoes and a comb. It was a pity to leave the book unfinished, but it had only been lent to her, and this still counted, except on the road, in the matter of food. Perhaps she would find another copy somewhere, and read the end. She propped it up against the partition and left it there.

Another small, hard fact she had gained, to add to the armour of the mind; people, even the kindest, were likely to betray you immediately after they had betrayed themselves to you, however innocently. This was something to take on with her. But it was sour learning.

Moving softly between the close-packed human cocoons, of whom only the man with the metal teeth seemed still awake, she found Jean-Paul in another small room and knelt beside him, shaking his arm, repeating in a whisper what she had heard: but sleep affected him now as drink had done before the massacre. 'No hurry,' he muttered, 'they can't do anything in a moment.'

'They can and they will. That Miss Hutchinson! She said, "When the man comes with the truck —"'

If she could persuade him to an instant decision, to abandon the idea of Salonika altogether, well and good, they would go on together for a little while more. If not —

'Oh, her!' he said. 'No need to bother what she says. You know what's wrong with her? I had a try at her, while you and Lesley were outside!'

'You fool! You couldn't have wanted her. Not that one!' (Any more than he had wanted Lisabet, she thought, nor, very often, Ila, except for the things she brought.)

'Just wanted to see how she'd take it. And *merde*, was that funny!' Action for its own sake, Hebe remembered, heartening herself for what she must do, had always been his weakness, threatening their relationship. Now it had hurried on the parting of their ways. 'Danger's supposed to make them easy,' he said, closing his eyes again. 'It does too, sometimes. You know what I always say of women who won't fall for my line?'

'Yes,' said Hebe with resignation. It was no use. ' "Do 'em good to be raped by gorillas." ' She had heard this over and over again in anecdotes. 'Well, why couldn't you let her wait for a gorilla?' She got up from her knees.

'Because it wouldn't help. Not with that one,' he said chuckling, before sinking back into sleep. 'She'd be worrying all the time if it was doing any good to the gorilla. Now go away, there's a good girl. And when I wake up, I'll think out what tale we'll spin the man with the truck about where we're really going. Say, anywhere but Salonika, of course. Then we'll get there all right after all.'

It was good, she thought, as she picked up the bundle she had left outside the door, and walked out of the house alone, that in the end they parted with a grin on both sides: there had been so much between them, of treachery and kindliness.

She took the road leading away from Salonika. If it had been hard to believe, before this, that they were actually quite close to it, now, as soon as she turned her back on that goal there was no longer any such difficulty. All that was hard was to be debarred from it, when it had cost so much to approach; and to feel herself alone again. Alone. Alone — her feet padded the sound in the dust. But if the authorities there were to be told to look out for her, with or without the complication of Jean-Paul demanding contacts in the port, they should not find her.

Alone again, alone. Her luck had held, though, she reminded herself. This was really the first occasion, since the day of the burnt bread, on which a good chance of getting away unobserved had presented itself to her. It was entirely due to the Turks, those ex-Armenians, who had wearied everyone so thoroughly that they slept late. She tried thinking kindly thoughts of people she had known from Armenia, but this proved impossible. Alone, belonging to no one. Yet once more the shadow of events was blacker than the reality. The moment she had dreaded since her first failure had come again, and there could be no going back. Her heart thudded in time with her feet, along the empty, dusty road. But it was free dust still, and from the bushes on either side a host of nightingales filled the world with beguiling promises.

12

'THEMBIRAZI'

P RESENTLY the fugitive from the islands, the man with the frightful smile, caught up with her and asked, as she was going in the same direction, if she, like himself, happened to be bound for Corinth?

It lay on the route to Athens, she learned, and to reach it they must soon turn off this road. She agreed at once to make first of all for Corinth: the wise course was certainly to get off this road as soon as possible, in case Jean-Paul thought of following her: and though her mind could not switch over hopefully in a moment towards a different goal — and one so much further away than Salonika — since Athens, too, was a big port, Athens, she thought, would do. The enormous persistence of her nature drove her on.

He showed no surprise at finding that she was travelling alone, apparently without object, but began immediately to talk about himself. Imprisonment had drained from his mind all interest except in this one subject. Confiding by nature, he wanted no more than a pair of ears into which he could pour details of his experiences and opinions, his likes and dislikes, while he journeyed; and at no time did he ask anything more of her than to listen, although, This is where I meet trouble! Hebe had thought glumly, when he over-hauled her on the road. She agreed to go with him only because you had to choose your risks when you could, as she had said before to Jean-Paul, and the vlach dogs seemed the one most to be feared in the circumstances. But the metal smile proved wonderfully mis-leading. 'Ha, they haven't reckoned with me!' he said several times, of the enemies who had sent him to the islands: and it became plain, after only a few minutes' conversation, that no one had ever needed to, or indeed ever would. Timid and ineffectual, he must have been gathered up with political undesirables by mistake.

Now, as he told her over and over again, he was a marked man. In a way this appeared to please him, it gave another aspect to his personality. But it also meant that if he were caught he would be returned indefinitely as a prisoner to the horror of the islands. He hoped, therefore, that at Corinth his brother, who was a blacksmith, would kindly knock out his front teeth for him: they were much too recognizable. Then with a beard in place of his present moustaches, which were fiercely curling and just as deceptive as his smile, he expected to be able to live safely under another name. His concern was that with his startling teeth he might lose all his individuality: 'my special character,' he called it wistfully. 'I will tell you something,' he said. 'I envy you. Yes, I, who am so complex and have lived through so much! At your age I always longed to be a little girl. This is naturally rare in boys, but then I was in many ways an exceptional child. I wanted to play without shame with dolls.'

'I don't remember ever playing with dolls,' Hebe told him. 'I don't think I ever had time.'

'Poor child. What you have missed. I used to get hold of my sisters' dolls when I could. I liked undressing them. Since I have been a man I have of course undressed women. But it's not the same.'

Hebe agreed that no doubt it could not be, and wondered what would happen if they met any of the Macedonian sheep-dogs. He turned out to be as nervous of them as she was: they made vast detours round every farm and village, and managed to avoid all encounter with the brutes: the price was living for a while on edible roots and birds' eggs, which luckily he was clever at finding, and the time of the year made plentiful.

Soon they were entirely outside the area she had memorized from the maps. It was an extraordinary relief, even though it meant being dependent on someone as feeble as this, not to have to bear in mind any more the lie of the land, nor to pretend that she did when her memory failed. It had not served her badly, she reflected, that immense effort backed up by bluff.

One of their detours, started at the sight of a flock of sheep which might or might not be guarded by dogs, took them on to a road where they were picked up by Government troops who swooped upon them too suddenly for Metal Teeth to attempt an escape.

In terror, he grimaced ingratiatingly at the soldiers, looking impressive at once, and was mistaken by them for a local *klept* of exceptionally brutal reputation who was expected to meet the patrol somewhere along the road: the sergeant in charge had been ordered to pay him a reward for betraying the gathering place of an *andartes* band, to which several of the *klept's* own family had belonged. Hebe's companion, frightened into silent nodding at everything the sergeant said, received from him three golden sovereigns of the reliable English sky-money which Katina had hoarded, and he and Hebe were given a ten-mile lift on their way in an army truck, passing in the road a shouting, dishevelled figure at whom the troops fired a warning burst to make him get out of the way. They missed, and did not stop to investigate who he was — The usual Judas-payment was five sovereigns, and the sergeant, issued with this sum and finding the recipient glad to take three, was eager to have done with the transaction. The travellers were not questioned at all before being set down.

They made their way rapidly across country for a while after this, to avoid a possible meeting with the *klept*, or with any *andartes* who might have escaped the ambush and also mistaken Metal Teeth for the informer, or with Government troops who had discovered their error.

A fisherman they could now afford to bribe took them across the Gulf of Corinth to Patras. The blood-money sovereigns enabled them to eat royally as they travelled the long, beautiful road leading from Patras towards Corinth. There were no flocks in this region, and consequently no sheep-dogs: they could safely bargain for whatever they fancied when they came on human habitations. They travelled so royally indeed that Hebe could see the road as beautiful, one of the most beautiful in the world, winding between golden hills flecked with pine trees, and the dark, purple-shadowed sea — When the mind was free of the body's cravings for a space it was much easier to approach, at least, that quivering awareness of another kind of reality, which could only be fully accepted in a few heart-lifting moments.

On one occasion they feasted upon chicken, bought and not stolen as it had always been with Jean-Paul — the height of reputable luxury to Hebe. Tiresome to a really remarkable degree, her self-absorbed companion remained a generous sharer of everything to the end of their time together, a journey of six weeks. He even offered to carry the shepherd's cloak across his shoulders for her, on the hot stretches: no one with whom she had travelled had given her this kind of consideration before. Frequent satisfaction of stomach made it possible for her, watching the reflections of the hills in the water, to attend at times only to what she saw, and shut out of her ears some of his inexhaustible flow of information about the most trivial episodes of his life, but whenever she became hungry again, or over-tired, she heard it all. Never was she to know any other individual quite so thoroughly, against her will.

At Corinth, before starting on the grim transformation of the fugitive, the blacksmith passed Hebe on to a friend from Kalamaki who owned a sailing caique, trading with Athens, and she parted thankfully from the man with the doomed teeth to go aboard this craft. She had come to believe that his escape from the islands, which he constantly attributed to a miracle, must have been a conspiracy between his jailers and fellow prisoners, who could not help liking him for his good nature but could not endure his company any longer.

In the caique, by contrast, she was left strictly to herself, cooking and mending in return for her passage: the boy who normally did this work had refused to sail at the last minute because, he said, he felt left out of everything, an explanation which only became clear to her during the voyage. The skipper and mate, the sole crew — two magnificent looking young men — were engrossed in a passionate love-quarrel about a scarf which one had given to the other, and the other had passed on to a lock-keeper on the Corinth canal.

Trouble over this lasted all the way to the Piraeus; they had no attention to spare for her beyond issuing her with stores from which she produced hazardous meals, compounded over a brazier surrounded by a highly inflammable cargo of resin. Her luck, which had seemed exceptionally good of late, was mounting at an almost alarming rate, she felt, when the craft neither caught fire nor was wrecked by the negligence of her crew during a bout of rough weather — How long could it hold at this level?

In the land which had first smiled on male sex relationships, and garlanded female love with song, these partnerships had become so rare, in the twentieth century, that the crew could not afford to break with one another, despite the bitterness of the dispute which several times threatened fighting between them in the course of the voyage, and made co-operation over the navigation an intermittent matter. She had embarked on the caique wondering once more whether this was where she would lose her virginity, and ended the trip walking off the boat thankfully at the Piraeus, disregarded by both men but resentful of the object-lesson which each had made of her in discussing with the other the ungainliness of women's bodies, in the moments when they approached a reconciliation. Remembering Dido, she agreed on the whole with what they had said, but her immaturity made her still passable in her own eyes.

And in Athens, her luck lasted over the first day, while she wandered about and wondered how she could possibly continue to exist in this jungle of streets, until she had decided on the next move. She came upon two elderly women tourists in distress, and was able to put them under an obligation to her. Their agitated voices, speaking in English, caught her attention as the prospect of the night and the morrow was beginning to look bleak indeed. During the day it had been easy enough for her to eat, because she had arrived in the town on Easter Sunday, when strangers in Greece exchange hard-boiled eggs in the streets, assuring one another in conversational tones that Christ has risen: for someone young there was no real difficulty in acquiring a few eggs without giving any in return, but where to find shelter and sleep seemed an insoluble problem.

The caique was out of reach in the closed and guarded docks: she could not go back there when dark fell.

The two tourists were an Englishwoman and an American who had been under the impression that the Athenian crowds were apologizing for jostling them. They replied graciously with almost the only word of demotic Greek they knew — 'thembirazi': it doesn't matter in the least — to the salutation that Christ has risen. This was ill-received, especially by a fanatical looking old man with a ragged white beard, who denounced them loudly to passers-by, attracting an unfriendly audience. They made matters worse by waving aside the proffered eggs as a vendor's trick. Misunderstanding had reached an uncomfortable state of tension when Hebe stepped in, with explanations in English and Greek. Quickly-swayed, the Athenian crowd started to laugh at the old man, with whom they had at first sided against the blasphemous foreigners: the two ladies fastened thankfully upon Hebe, taking her back with them to their modest hotel. She was equally welcome to them as a saviour, and as an obviously undernourished child whom they could question in their own language.

On behalf of a small weekly paper, edited by the American's husband, they were carrying out an inquiry into malnutrition among children in Southern Europe as a result of the war. 'And it's been disappointing for us so far in Greece,' the Englishwoman explained. 'My friend and I, we'd always planned to do a little tour together some day — Oh, ever since we were girls in the same school in Belgium — you know Belgium?'

'No,' said Hebe, thinking over what she should tell them of her own background. (Thereafter the ladies laboriously spoke French together whenever they discussed something they did not wish her to understand, such as whether they should take her down to the dining-room with them for dinner. They decided against this, her hair and her clothes were too unkempt; a tray in the room would be better.)

'Well, we know there are plenty of hungry children in Belgium, of course,' said the American. 'But life has kept us apart so long, we felt we'd rather go somewhere fresh once we got together again. And when Mr. Loftus said, "Why not an inquiry — " '

'In these days it seems wrong to enjoy spending money just on yourself,' put in the Englishwoman. 'Even when you've saved up for it for years. So we've been combining the report we're writing with a cruise. People talked to us in Italy, and in Malta, but in Greece the parents seem too frightened to talk, or too proud, or something.' They poured out their troubles to Hebe, sitting by the window of one of their adjoining bedrooms, which overlooked the flat roof of the house next door. Here, goats and chickens and a lusty Greek family lived, mainly in the open and inextricably mingled, it appeared.

Practically every child in Athens looked ill-fed, they insisted, but no one would admit poverty to strangers, speaking through an interpreter. They understood well enough that too many children had already been spirited away, some by the *andartes*, some by the Government, each side saving them from the other, for families to take any chances with foreigners who were trying to meddle too, but all the same it was galling for the ladies, who had hankered and planned for this trip so long, to be put off on all sides with what they knew to be lies.

Hebe was asked innumerable questions, but they talked as much as they listened, and she gave them far less of her experiences than she had to the old lady at the diggings: they were not to think her lacking in suitable background. She dealt vaguely with her father's activities: a seafaring man, she conveyed. It dimmed the pleasure of these unexpectedly good surroundings a little to know that they considered her unfit to be seen in the dining-room; but she had no doubt at all that they were right. It took determination, however, to suppress the comment, 'If you knew how that to me was equal!' — proving that French could be picked up outside Belgium — when they conferred together in that language about closing the shutter of the window overlooking the flat roof and the Greek family. ' — Before anything else happens!' said the Englishwoman. 'Like yesterday, dear! But it makes the room so dark, doesn't it?'

Next door, the handsome young mother had begun suckling her baby, while her husband's hand caressed her bare brown shoulder, straying sometimes over the other tight little round breast: they were both so young, parenthood looked like a joke between them.

Hebe brought her eyes back into the hotel room: it was urgently important to keep the ladies' goodwill. Perhaps, if she were skilful enough, they could be induced to support her all the time she needed to stay in Athens. Finding that she had nowhere to sleep, they had already offered to let her remain with them for the night.

They rang for the old houseman. But the hotel was full, he said, surveying Hebe with distaste. No other room was available. By tipping, they managed to get a couch put up for her in one of their own rooms, not without grumbling on his part. Hebe heard what he said, despite the ladies' kindly attempt to cover with raised voices his warning of the dangers of taking in people from the street. Pilfering, vermin, he said. One day, oh, one day — ! Now she must look on things this way: she and André would not take in uncouth people either. If to be looked down upon was the price of help, she was prepared to pay it — at present. She gazed fixedly out of the window again, keeping her face expressionless. On the crowded roof a small child had crawled up to the family group and was using the other breast.

In the hotel, too, it was dinner time: a bell rang. The two ladies freshened themselves by changing out of their sight-seeing clothes: one took off her dusty shoes and stockings, the other her blouse.

'Those people — !' Passing close by Hebe to fetch clean stockings, the American followed the girl's eyes with her own to the tangled figures on the roof, but she kept her hand from the shutter and said with an effort of tolerance, 'It must be terribly difficult for mothers out here, you know. I mean, breast-feeding all the time, they can't have any idea of the weight of the baby's intake!' Firmly she recalled Hebe's attention: 'Now, dear, tell us an average midday meal in that Struma part you know. Not necessarily what you had. What other families ate.'

Hebe returned her eyes dutifully to the room once more: she

thought the lean, vigorous Greek family very pleasant to watch, the man especially; like one of the magnificent looking pair in the caique, except that this man was very much interested in a woman: he had pushed the toddling child away, to put his arm right round his wife while she nursed. But this query was more important: what could be called an average when there were no averages — because, so often, no midday meal? Would that in itself do for an average, and satisfy the ladies? If only she could keep their curiosity going. She described the meal they had eaten when they first arrived at Dido's farm, figs and bread, the very white bread which could not be typical; but then, what was? She looked anxiously at the two tourists to see if this would be acceptable, and her eyes fled in disgust out of the window again. How well justified they had been, the men in the caique, in the things they had said about full-grown-women's bodies and the comparisons they had made, to her annoyance at the time —

Thick thighs, the skin dead-coloured between the network of little veins, and dimpling where the slack muscles tweaked at it, glimpsed above stocking-tops, while the owner of the room modestly groped for her suspenders — And the other, caught as she slipped on her fresh blouse, adjusting a ribbon-strap above breasts where the flesh oozed out shapelessly on either side of constricting material — Here, suddenly, was Dido, glimpsed in supreme ugliness from the sleeping recess. Only with Dido it had been the shepherd's hands, sinewy and somehow less repulsive than swollen bags of material, which pressed into the over-softness of the flesh. Something in Hebe's necessarily unfastidious mind retched at the innocent spectacle of middle-aged ladies getting ready to go down to their dinner. Outside on the roof the baby had drunk his fill and been put down, among the livestock, and the young man was beginning to make love to his wife more actively, while she laughed and pushed him away. Hebe had never before happened to see a comely young man and woman playing together with intimacy; while the strained and abnormal atmosphere of the caique was so fresh in her mind they seemed to her particularly happy and acceptable, but one of the tourists, stepping swiftly to the window as laughter drifted in, closed the shutters with the suggestion that this would keep the room free of mosquitoes and flies at night, which was possibly true. Hebe's tray of food was brought in at this point and they left her to it, having unobtrusively gathered up their valuables. They were very tactful and careful of her feelings, as well-intentioned in their own way as the Quakers.

'I don't think the child could have seen — ?' Her sharp ears caught the English voice as they went down the corridor.

In the morning they gave Hebe a small sum of money and some underclothing, which hung oddly upon her, and a recommendation to the British Consul which she knew too much to follow up — he, far more than Lesley or Miss Hutchinson, would be inclined to think well of the official way of dealing with refugee problems. But they did not suggest, as she had passionately hoped they would, that she might come back again the following night, or any other night. Plainly they did not think the view suitable.

Her fantastic run of luck broke then. Eked out as best she could manage, the money dwindled fast, in a town as expensive as Athens: some of it was stolen in the crypt of a church, used as a charitable sleeping-place for the homeless, to which she was directed by a priest when she appealed to him, emboldened by the long hair done up in a bun at the back of his head, in the Orthodox style. This chignon made him look so like an English schoolmistress in the illustrations to the best books that she unwisely supposed the people in the refuge he advised would be more than human or less than Greek. She slept with the larger notes safely on her person, among the folds of a vast new vest, but even a few shillingsworth of drachmae meant a bundle of many thousands, and the smaller notes were left in the pocket of the black cloak rolled up as a pillow. By some sleight of hand they were abstracted before morning with the cloak still under her head. She did not try for a roof again, but spent two fairly warm nights in Constitution Square, where many of the city poor dozed on benches. For someone of her age, work — even the washing up which she had done before, in Colombo — was not to be come by in Athens, where there was much adult unemployment.

Discouraged, she drifted to the Piraeus. Any ships in the port which might have been bound for England were out of her reach, beyond the guarded gates of the deep-water quay: she could not get near enough to have a look at them, which would have seemed a little comforting. The caique had gone.

A group of seamen, talking eagerly together, their crews' passes in their hands ready to show, hurried towards the docks from the land side of the big gate, where she stood disconsolate. One of them glanced at her casually, looked again, puzzled, like a man reminded of something unimportant from the past, troubling only while it remains unplaced. Then he nodded and waved as he went through the gate, and disappeared at a run with his companions. It was André.

13

THE MANAREZS

S HE remained for a long time staring after him, aghast. Whether or not he had really recognized her, she could not tell: it might be that in his concern with getting back to his ship he had merely seen a face which was vaguely familiar. But the world fell to pieces for her, on a bright spring morning. With her mind she had always accepted the possibility that he would not know her again — might have wholly forgotten what she had done for him — yet only with her mind. By now she had borne so much, if not for his sake, at least with the thought of a linked future to help her, that this no longer seemed possible.

He and his friends did not return. Other men were streaming through into the docks. Eventually she asked the guard on the gate, whom she had already questioned about ships for England, whether there was a French ship at the quays, to which these men were returning as crew. No, he said, they were from a Portuguese ship, warping out on the afternoon tide. She described André to him. He thought he recognized the man: if so, yes, that was one of the hands. Did she want to send him a message? There would still be time for that.

She shook her head — what message was there to send? — and walked away, forgetting to thank him, so that with Greek good manners outraged, he shouted reprovingly after her.

Naturally it could not be a French vessel for André. Not yet. She found a spot near the docks which commanded the harbour mouth and sat on a bench there, waiting for a steamer with a Portuguese flag to pass. It came into sight several hours later, cleared the entrance and grew smaller and smaller at last, as it headed into the spaces of the sea, a grey shape sinking inexorably into the haze on the horizon. A mood of unreality held her. It could not have happened, that she had actually met André again and lost him.

For some while an old man with one eye had occupied the bench with her, mumbling foolishly to himself. Once he spoke aloud, as though they had been communing together and he knew all about her: 'There is no sight more terrible to the heart, is there, than a ship leaving with all one's thoughts on board? I too have been in exile.' He used a Greek which she could recognize, by this time, as being very pure and unlike the ordinary demotic of the streets. He retired again into his mumbling, and wandered away: came back and presented her with the remains of the meal he had been spinning out for hours — grapes and sausage — and wandered away again. The feeling of unreality prevented her from being surprised at his voicing her thoughts. She had a curious fancy that he was the ghost of the Professor, although so far as she knew the Professor was alive somewhere. He was almost certainly a professor of some sort: civil strife pressed hard on such people.

There was unreality, too, about the child, a few minutes later, who ran out into the road, under a car, to avoid a slap from a weary mother dragging by with a fruit barrow harnessed to her back: unreality about the crash of the car overturning the barrow, about the hubbub, and the oranges rolling, dappled with blood, towards her own feet. Then an excited crowd of people were round her and the car, helping up the woman, who was unhurt, shaking their fists and yelling with rage at the car which had killed the child.

'Get the police. For God's sake get the police,' a woman's voice wailed from inside the car. 'They'll keep us here hours. Nicholas ought to be in bed.'

A big, florid man in the driving seat was trying to pacify those who were supporting the woman in the road, and lifting up the dead child to show its injuries. 'Is there anyone here who speaks English? We couldn't help it, I tell you. We weren't going fast. Get the police. *Police. Polizei.*'

There was a boy of a little more than Hebe's age, lying on a built-in bed at the back of the car, with his face fixedly turned away from the shouting. A woman from the swelling crowd ran round to the rear window of the car, furiously trying to show him a piece of the child's torn and sodden clothing, but he only shifted his still face slightly and stared straight upwards.

The attitude brought back a memory, jolting Hebe out of her sense of not belonging to the scene. 'I speak English,' she said, reluctantly. 'And I saw what happened. It wasn't your fault.'

'Thank heaven for that. Get the police, can you? There mustn't be violence. My boy's ill, you see.'

She edged her way out of the press, and with a dignity that reproached him for shouting at her previously, told the guard on the dock gates that a foreign car was in trouble up the road. He could call the police or not as he liked: she was tired of helping English-speaking travellers, it did not seem to lead anywhere. She drifted back to the car, to see what happened.

Men were leaning in from the running board, shouting threateningly at the driver, at the boy's averted head, at the woman who sat beside him, one hand straying about her mouth, the other stroking his arm in fear; but when the police arrived to take charge the thin skin of restraint on the Athenian crowd was still unbroken, although it could not have lasted much longer. There had been no violence.

'I shall want you as a witness tomorrow,' the owner of the car called curtly to Hebe, over the heads of the other onlookers. 'You'd better get in here with us while we find our hotel, so that you'll know where to come. Where do you live?'

'Nowhere.'

'Oh, tomorrow!' The boy had caught the one word, and raised his voice shrilly. 'You know I want to see the Parthenon tomorrow. Have we got to spend the whole of our first day here fussing because something puts itself under our wheels? Have we? What was it? Is it badly hurt? I won't look.'

'Hush, Nickie. A child. Dead.'

'Well, we were crawling, as usual. Make this girl tell them. I still want to see the Parthenon!'

'Another day —'

'You know there aren't enough other days!' he protested sullenly.

The sick boy's father — Mr. Manarez from Trinidad — was afraid of losing sight of his witness as soon as he heard that Hebe had no fixed dwelling in Athens. He preferred to keep her at hand. For the second time, Hebe was put up in a hotel in the town, but this time in luxury, in the dressing-room of a suite in the Grande Bretagne on Constitution Square, and if there were adverse comments from the staff, they were no longer audible — Mr. Manarez gave an impression of impatient wealth and power much more effective than the kindly, worried air of the two tourist ladies. He did not ask if Hebe would like to remain with them over the emergency, he immediately arranged it: he was a man who expected to have everything his own way, except in the matter of his son, who was dying.

None of the Manarez family pretended any longer that this was not so: time was too short, and Nickie himself too intelligent for acting to be of use. Hebe had not imagined that love could be so concentrated, in its insecurity, as the devotion of both these parents to the boy for whom they had undertaken a world tour, in order that he should see and do whatever he had a whim to, or whatever he could, in the months or weeks that might remain to him. It seemed to preclude any personal feeling between them, this helpless love which shone through everything they did — through the woman's habitual gesture of anxiety, her fingers straying about her mouth, through the man's abruptness and overbearing manner of speaking. Whatever they had once felt for one another had been swallowed up in the long, corroding fear for their child: they were fellow-ministers to him and nothing more. It always surprised Hebe when they made chance references to the days when they had both been something more — when he had been working his way up as a successful merchant and she had been the wife of a sugar planter, defying local society to leave her husband for him. She was of all-white blood, but in him, to eyes trained by South American standards, there were traces of colour. 'My parents' runaway match was the scandal of Port of Spain,' said Nicholas, when he and Hebe were left alone for a few moments. 'Very hard place to scandalize, Port of Spain, what with one thing and another. And now, who would have thought it? I'm what remains!'

Despite money poured out wherever it might be expected to help, Mr. Manarez and Hebe were kept hanging about for two days, moving between the hotel, police headquarters and the scene of the accident. They drove from one to the other in the Rolls Royce, adapted to the needs of Nicholas, which crept when he was aboard, to avoid jolting his back, but without him, to Hebe's satisfaction, swept through the streets of Athens even faster than the other, wild-moving traffic. In the end, the visitors were exonerated from all blame. As soon as the case was settled, Mr. Manarez increased his pace of driving still further, remarking grimly on the way back to the hotel that this was the only town he knew where the number of exceptionally reckless motorists appeared to have made little impression so far on the number of exceptionally reckless walkers. Elsewhere in the world they could be trusted to eliminate one another, but not in Athens. The boy remained with his mother on the hotel balcony, for the whole of the two days of police inquiry, demanding at intervals the probable time of Hebe's return. He had taken a sick fancy to her company; alone of those around him, she did not seem sorry for him. It was a long time since he had known freedom from pity: not since infantile paralysis had left behind a degenerating condition of the spinal nerves, and that was over two years ago. Hebe was asked to stay on, for the three days which the Manarezs intended to remain in Athens: a decent dress had necessarily been bought for her, to make her testimony more telling with the police; she might just as well be used further, to help in entertaining Nicholas.

At first, for her, the magnificence of her new setting remained slightly clouded by the unreal feeling of having been so close to André, for such a little while. Then the sturdy single-mindedness which was her greatest possession took charge again. Here were front doors of an exceptional kind, through which she was not only admitted, they were opened for her. Decorous lights shone down upon varied food procured without effort. If the chance meeting with André meant nothing to him, at least he was not further away from her for having crossed her path once more: the road home was longer than she supposed she must secretly have hoped, that was all. In any case, she had never imagined it short. She settled down to enjoy every meal at the Grande Bretagne, but above all, the service that went with it — such things could not last.

In the evenings she sat by the boy's couch, watching what she had not troubled to notice before, the miracle of the sinking sun tinting the marble of the Acropolis as it brooded above the city, from pale amber through brown to warmest rose. The Manarezs' balcony overlooked the upper part of Constitution Square garden, full of shrubs and seats: she could see the place where she had spent two restless nights: someone else, of the Athens poor, was stretched out on that bench when she craned over to look.

'We'll go up to the Acropolis tomorrow,' Nicholas said, when Hebe returned from the court. 'My father'll get men to carry me up the steps. We can take the car to the foot of it. And then I can lie and look at the Parthenon. You've often been there?'

'I've never bothered to go,' she said. 'Why should I?'

The boy gave the bubbling giggle that reminded her of the laughter of the South American peons, and made him seem much less white than he was by blood. His skin had been bleached by illness till the slight hint of darker blood became more evident in the shape of his features because of their unsuitable pallor.

'And we came all the way here from the West Indies because I wanted to see it! Oh, well, to see that, and also Mount Hilarion in Cyprus. We're going there next. And then on to Egypt. You must come up with us to the Parthenon tomorrow.'

When she answered doubtfully that she thought of going down to the Piraeus the next day while he was out (a Portuguese ship was reported in: suppose it were the same one, putting back for some reason?) he grew excited, and appealed to his mother, for ever hovering within call.

'Tell her she can't. She must come with us. I want that.' It was typical of him, like his cry of 'I won't see', in the car, that he grew angry if anyone's long-term interests crossed his short-term ones:

but he was grateful for any casual services he received, and very courteous to the hotel servants. With his parents, who fussed, especially his mother, it was hard for him to be patient.

Mrs. Manarez took Hebe aside. 'We should be glad to pay you, of course, if he would like you to go with him. Please do whatever he wants.'

Aware that this was a wise move, Hebe said, 'You needn't pay me. I don't mind going.' And it was true; because of his weakness and his age, he was a continuation of the book she had not been able to finish near Salonika: it was interesting to be with him, since she was not harrowed by his condition: almost as interesting as eating and sleeping grandly for once. Firmly her common sense told her that of course it was not the same Portuguese vessel, whatever her hopes said.

On the Acropolis the next day, she and Nicholas talked of Greece as she had seen it. This was a Greece more fascinating to him, in its remoteness from anything he could experience, even by imagination, than the classical Greece of which he had learnt in an expensive school before he became ill — a school in Switzerland, where that faint suggestion of colour was not likely to be recognized. Money had been plentiful all his life — 'You mean you moved about without any? Without any money at all, sometimes?' he asked, in one form of words or another, over and over again. It was the aspect of her travels which most amazed him, for whom money cushioned, however ineffectively, every moment of the painful day. They were children together, each with an insight into a different world of desperate realities.

Near them his parents talked of a demand from the woman who had been pulling the fruit barrow at the time of the accident. 'I agreed from the first we'd pay for the funeral,' said Mr. Manarez. 'But now she's just trying to get something out of us — she and the lawyer who's put her up to the idea of new black clothes for the whole family.'

'Oh, but after all, it was her child who was killed. Even if it wasn't our fault that — ' Nicholas's mother had a habit of not finishing sentences, as though she dared bring nothing to an end.

'That's right, side with them! And with everyone who's on the make when we're around.'

'No, no, dear. I wasn't. Only it was her child —'

'She's got plenty more. Like most of these people.'

'Yes, but perhaps this one —'

'They wear black anyway, for their working clothes. I've paid for the funeral, haven't I, though I didn't need to. And compensation. More than they could have expected if we'd been responsible. She already has a black dress — that's what gets me. These people, egged on by slim lawyers, trying to make something more out of it. New clothes for about six of them.'

'You hear them? That's to let them worry less about me,' the boy said with cold understanding. 'Bothering about things that don't matter to either of them. So's not to think of what they can't buy.'

Talking to Hebe, he noticed little of what he had come so far to see. The carrying chair he used whenever he left the car had been set down, at his wish, outside the small, superb temple of Nikki — 'My temple,' he called it, amused — rather than in the Parthenon, because Nikki was less familiar to him from photographs and description. But the exquisite building meant nothing to her: splendour of line, not of movement or colour, was a beauty she was not prepared to perceive. And because she was unaware of them, save as stones, the ancient stones were scarcely more than stones to him. He made her tell him in detail about the night of her father's death — 'And when they had eaten, they grieved for their companions' — he recognized the line from Homer, but for the moment the journeys of the ancient Greeks were schoolroom stuff, dull compared with the stratagems forced on a living and present child, two years younger than himself.

Her long pretence about the maps and the list of agents captured his attention more than the story of the *klept* raid: violence was so far from his world. She quoted to him what the old lady who re-buried treasures, and trusted in a loaded umbrella, had said about lipstick on a horse; and made him laugh a little — made him explain to her what the old lady must have meant, and then they both laughed. At the sound, his mother looked towards them with astonishment, and the beginnings of resentment.

'I'd like to stay on a whole week longer than we'd planned,' he said to her casually, when the porters hired for the occasion lifted his chair, to carry it down the steps of the Acropolis to the waiting car. 'And of course I'll want Hebe around till we go. She props me up much better than you do. More firmly — Though you know perfectly well it's more comfortable when you do it firmly!' he added, to punish his mother for the gesture which exasperated him, the hand straying to the mouth because he was being moved. Her love for him could never prevent her from doing the things he disliked, not only betraying anxiety but hesitating when she performed any physical service for him, lest she should hurt him — with the result that often she did hurt him. 'All the same, arrange for me to come up here again tomorrow, will you, alone with the porters,' he said. 'I can't take in the Acropolis and Hebe's Greece at the same time.'

For ten days more the Manarez family stayed in Athens, Hebe remaining with them. Three times, in his better spells, the boy was taken up to the Acropolis without her, but in the evenings, if he were not too tired, he clung to her society. Though both of them had been forced into precocity, it was Hebe's childishness alongside the precocity, answering the frightened, protesting childishness which came out sometimes in him, that he gripped on to ruthlessly. Father and son were much alike, she found, in their highhandedness. She could entertain him, and sometimes make him forget pain, but refreshing beyond everything, to him, was the relief of being with someone who did not in the least mind his dying.

He had a costly microscope as a toy — he had wanted to be a doctor — and while he rested Hebe went out and collected slugs for him on Lycabetus, so that they could examine together the extraordinarily swift-moving parasites which glide about their shiny bodies: from the same expedition she brought back in a paper bag, slipped skilfully over the flowers they visited, several of the bees responsible for the famous Hymettus honey, for the sake of their wings and leg-joints, marvellous in detail.

'I wish my old nurse could see this — Old Amy, who's in Jamaica now,' he said. 'She'd think this was magic all right!'

'That horrible old black thing!' said Mrs. Manarez. 'I believe she was an Obeah woman.'

'Of course she was, and I loved her,' Nickie said, and at the time the subject dropped.

After the fourth day at the Grande Bretagne, Hebe decided not to go out again by herself in Athens: Jean-Paul was there.

She saw him from the car, in which she was driving with Nicholas, soon after she had bowed from the waist, in gracious imitation of her mother, towards the two ladies who had worried on her behalf about the scene outside their window. Hot, dusty and on foot, they looked into her eyes from the distance of about a yard, as the Rolls paused for a second or two at a road-crossing. Their expressions when they recognized her, neatly dressed and in such a vehicle, were balm for any disappointment she had suffered in their hotel. Jean-Paul's surprise seemed as great or greater, a few hundred yards further on, where the car was slowed down again by a sudden unconcerned rush of people across the road, but the look on his face was not so wholly pleasurable to see. Possibly the scowl she got was a trick of the sun, and he bore no malice for the way she had let him down about the contacts — it was not a chance, she thought, that she would care to take.

'Someone else seems to know you. Want to stop and speak?' asked Mr. Manarez, ready to accelerate.

'No, thank you.' The car slid away smoothly, leaving Jean-Paul staring after it, with his face still screwed up in a way that might mean anything or nothing.

'Oh, Hebe's the friend of half Athens,' Nicholas said irritably. He was growing as jealous of her, in his own way, as his mother. 'We'd never get anywhere if we started being sociable. Who was that queer-looking man, anyway?'

'Never mind.'

'What?'

'I said, never mind!' Hebe answered.

'You're not here to be rude to Nicholas!' Mrs. Manarez told her sharply.

'But I didn't —'

'Nor to answer me back!'

Nicholas turned his head and shot Hebe a glance of amiable complicity as she subsided into silence. He came back earlier than usual from the Acropolis that afternoon, and invented an errand to get his mother out of earshot of the hotel balcony for a while.

'Now, who was that man? I believe — wasn't it the person you deceived about the maps? What was his name?'

'Jean-Paul. Yes.'

'Oh, this is really exciting! He'll have a grudge against you! He must know by now just how you took him in. I expect he realized for certain as soon as he found you'd skipped off, so near Salonika. But I'd give anything to know if he went on there by himself and then couldn't find the contacts. Oh, anything!'

'Would you? I wouldn't. I'd just rather he wasn't in Athens,' said Hebe practically. For several hours, skulking about the corridors while waiting for Nicholas to return, she had been considering with growing dislike the prospect of being left alone in the town, as things were, when the Manarez family moved on.

Nicholas, however, was delighted by the intrusion of drama and someone else's risk into the dully dangerous life he led as an invalid. 'I wish Old Amy was here. She'd kill him for you! — She could, really. At least, if he believed in black magic. She's the person my mother dislikes more than she does you. Same reason. Me. Only she's frightened of Old Amy too. Why didn't you want us to know who that man was?'

'Habit. When you've had to keep things to yourself a lot, you get in the way of feeling it's safer.'

'If only we could find out if he went to Salonika! But I don't see how we can. I think he must have. They wouldn't bother to warn what you call "the D.P. people", those Quakers, once you were out of the way, would they? And isn't it interesting, Hebe, what faith does? — D'you see, he couldn't find a ship, because he was discouraged, once he knew how you'd been lying. If he could somehow have gone on believing in your list of agents he might — ' He broke off, seeing the glumness of her face. 'What d'you think he'd do to you if he caught you?'

'I don't know. You can't ever tell about anything, with Jean-Paul.'

'Oh, well, you'd better come on with us to Cyprus,' said Nicholas. 'He isn't likely to turn up there. You know I can always make my people agree to anything if I say I really want it.'

'I know.' She took a deep breath to steady herself: this was what she had been waiting and hoping for, from a few moments after she had recognized Jean-Paul. Here, as with the heelobowie, was opportunity; unpleasant, but not to be let slip. She had used the hours alone in the hotel stiffening herself to take it if it arose. 'I'll come,' she said, 'if your parents promise to pay my passage to England when I leave you. Not back to Greece, but all the way to where I want to go. Near Bristol, in England.'

'What? Don't be silly, Hebe!' He was astounded. Someone was not doing exactly as he wished.

'I mean that. I won't come without. I'll stay and take my chance here. Dodge Jean-Paul if I can.'

'You can't do that. He might do anything, with a grudge against you. You said so yourself.'

'That's my affair.'

'Why won't you come?'

'Without the promise of a passage, you mean? I'll come all right if you get it for me, and thankful! It's because I want to be back in England. I've told you, that's part of my plan.'

'You'd be no further from England in Cyprus than here.'

'That's right,' said Hebe frankly. 'But don't you see, this is my best chance of getting a passage. Maybe the only one. If you want it — because you don't like my being left behind in Athens with an enemy around the streets?'

'This is — well, it's a sort of blackmail, if you know what that means!' said Nicholas furiously.

'That's right,' Hebe agreed once more, and stuck to her decision with frightened obstinacy.

It was one of the hardest things she had done. At intervals through the next two days, whenever they were alone for a moment, the sick boy begged and stormed.

'You're ungrateful!'

'I'm sorry, Nickie!'

'Just because you know I could make my people take you along to Cyprus, for my sake, you think there's no limit to what you can ask.' Often she heard his father speaking through him. 'But why on earth should they promise you this? When my mother doesn't like you anyway. You saw this morning, she's jealous.'

'I know.'

'Anyway, England wouldn't let you in. You haven't got a passport. You couldn't get one, because you can't give an address, or say how you got here, or where you're from, or anything.'

'I can. I'm Laura Klee — Laura, not Hebe — from Rose Lodge, Avonmouth, near Bristol' (the house with the dogs). 'You'll see, your people can buy me a passport if they want to.'

'Serve you right to be left behind here, with that man.'

'I daresay. But you wouldn't be happy in Cyprus, thinking about it, would you?'

In the end they did not go to Cyprus. Nicholas's illness took a sudden decisive turn for the worse. There was no point in continuing the tour: the Manarez family sailed for the West Indies, Nickie having expressed a wish to be at home and see his old nurse again. And Hebe went with them: she had extracted her promise.

'If you behave yourself as long as he wants you,' Mrs. Manarez said, with loathing in her voice, 'we'll give you what you're after. Send you back to England when it's all over.' 'When it's all over' needed no amplifying: the moment which she had watched approaching for two years was almost upon her: she found some outlet in her biting contempt for Hebe's ability to take advantage of the situation. 'But mind you, only if you do exactly what we want of you!' She never spoke willingly to the girl again, although they ministered to the boy together.

14

THE UNEXPECTED

No direct voyage to Trinidad was possible immediately. Air travel did not suit Nicholas, whose breathing was affected by altitude. The best that could be done for him was to book a passage from Athens to Madeira, change ships there for Jamaica, and wait to arrange the final stage of the journey from Kingston. 'Good, then I'll see Old Amy as soon as we get to Kingston,' he said, when this was explained to him before they left the Grande Bretagne. 'She could do something for me. I know she could. Send her word to meet us.'

'But my darling, I don't know where she is in Jamaica,' Mrs. Manarez objected. 'When we get there, we'll inquire.'

'A cable to "Old Amy, Accompong" would reach her,' he persisted. 'She's a descendant of the Maroons, you know. They're still around Accompong in the Cockpit Country. Someone there would know how to find her.'

'But if you're sure she's as well known as that, Nickie dear, why not wait till we're in Kingston and then your father can do it all by telephone, very quickly?'

'It doesn't matter,' he said wearily. 'She'll find out I'm coming.'

Strange indeed, to Hebe, was the feeling of heading again for the West Indies. Apart from the comfort on board ship, which in the First Class was on the scale of the Grande Bretagne, she found the voyage little pleasanter than it had been in the crowded emigrant ship with her father, for here, too, was an all-enveloping atmosphere of fear.

During the first part of the trip, as far as Madeira, Nickie was too weak to talk to her much: Mrs. Manarez would only speak to her, curtly, if forced to: Mr. Manarez scarcely ever stopped. Needing to talk to someone not torn by his own dread, he explained to her by the hour his manifold business projects, revealing a side of himself which she had not suspected: Mr. Manarez was that rare, almost unthinkable combination, a sensitive bore. Business was his world, he knew his limitations and hardly ever ventured a comment on any other kind of human activity. Aware that fellow-passengers sidled away from his endless accounts of sugar-deals and complaints about labour conditions, he could not stop himself following them forcefully to finish the long anecdote, in the hope that somehow, something before the end would have made the preamble seem worth while, after all. He took to conversation, in his anxiety, as other men might have taken to drink, but had not the advantage of Metal Teeth in remaining indifferent to the listener's interest, or total lack of it. More and more he fell back on Hebe's society, when Nickie's impatience with the deep yearning in his father's voice, and the man's helpless realization of it, drove him out of the boy's cabin for all but a few minutes a day, night and morning. Having paid for her passage, he felt that he had a right to her attention, and unlike his wife, he had no ill-feeling for someone who could drive a hard bargain, in any circumstances.

Hebe listened to him with a fair show of interest. For all she knew, this might be included in the condition of 'behaving herself' — it was difficult to be sure what the words would cover.

'When I was young,' he told her, 'I was working too hard making money to have time for anything else — oh, except Mrs. Manarez. Now I've got leisure to talk, nobody seems to have time to listen. Women!' He shook his head, making one of his rare excursions away from finance. 'They've changed so. Used to be so sporting. Why, the W.A.A.C.S. in my war — World War One. Long before your time, of course — you never could tell what they'd be up to next. They knew a thing or two! Pretty well everything, pretty well all of them. But where've they gone? Must be still around somewhere. They're my age, wherever they are. Can't all have died. And they simply can't have turned into these crumpled looking spinsters you see everywhere, and the dreary mothers of families who've obviously never had a bit of fun in their lives, and wouldn't approve if anyone else did. But what's happened to them — the jolly ones everybody knew?'

Hebe could only agree that certainly they did not seem to be on board this ship — the one between Athens and Madeira. Nor did they appear in the next: there were only four passengers besides the Manarez family with whom she exchanged half a dozen words throughout the voyage to Jamaica. Three of these were the two sons and the wife of her stateroom steward, all travelling steerage on one ticket: the lads, identical twins, took it in turn to appear at meals, while the wife depended on food smuggled into their crowded cabin-for-two by her husband. There was also, in the First Class like Hebe, an amiable, wealthy but decrepit American whose sheer age astonished Hebe. She had always understood that the United States was a young country: it seemed extraordinary that someone who claimed to have been born a citizen should have had time to grow so old. He travelled incessantly, on a patent-medicine fortune, for ever chasing the health and vigour that would now for ever elude him.

The steward's family she came to know through happening upon the man juggling expertly with Nickie's oranges in her stateroom. To explain why he had taken them from the boy's cabin, and in hopes of ensuring her silence, he confided to her the family ambition, to her immediate interest. It was to get work together as a circus troupe in Kingston, his wife having been a slack-wire artist. To that end the boys were diligently practising fire-eating and sword-swallowing, with lighted candles and table-knives. Here was exactly the kind of dauntless and limited aim which Hebe could appreciate: she promised to say nothing, and supply more oranges. Whenever she could escape from Mr. Manarez, she slipped away forward to form an encouraging audience for them in their cramped quarters. One boy had his mouth badly burned; the other, holding his gullet open with ever-wider and longer slips of wood, as he graduated from the small knife stage, had occasionally to break off his efforts in order to be sick, but both returned with assiduity to their practising as soon as this could possibly be done: she left them each time with reluctance to return to the Manarez atmosphere.

Every day they progressed a little towards their desire, which was more than could be said for her other acquaintance on board. He, however, believed by the habit of years that just ahead of him on every voyage waited the perfect climate, the infallible new doctor, or hypnotist, mud-bath or mineral spring which would work a miracle and give him back his prime. This habit of hope, together with a modest form of snobbery, made him a cheering companion for her in those moments of leisure which were long enough to allow her on deck, away from the sickbed tension around Nickie, but too short to let her pay another surreptitious visit to the steerage. He had no wish to mingle with the notable, nor to be recognized by them, but only to talk of them.

Hebe consulted him about schools in England, where he spent a month every summer, and he was delighted to advise her, assuming that all the very evident Manarez money lay behind the inquiry. From him she learnt of the unexpected obstacle of entrance examinations, but he reassured her, these could be avoided: there were schools and schools. Although the English public school had much in its favour, there were places less rigid, and yet more especially designed for the *élite*. She was thinking of a really high-toned establishment, was she not? Well, then, that would be all right. 'I expect your formal education has been a good deal interrupted by travel?' he said.

'It has. Oh, yes, very much.'

'Mind you, I'd say that wasn't a bad thing at all. Knowing the world is more important than book-learning. And at the sort of school I'd recommend for you, they'd think so too.'

'Is my accent all right?'

He seemed a little taken aback by such directness. 'Well, I wouldn't know about that. It struck me as — as cosmopolitan. And of course that can be an advantage, too. Now at the very lovely place in Hampshire where my sister's niece is — my sister's niece by marriage, that is; she married into the Doddingtons, of Buckingham

— why, they've got girls of nice families from all over. You hear Norwegian accents, English accents, American accents. There's a Polish countess who's got to be one of my niece's best friends, and an Italian Contessa she hasn't taken to so well, though they share a bedroom. I'd say they don't talk half such good English as you, either of those two. So I wouldn't worry about that.'

'I wouldn't worry, but I thought they might,' said Hebe, relieved. Although English had been her first language, her voice had become so coloured by long periods of talking South American Spanish, refugee-French *patois*, and Macedonian Greek that in her mother-tongue her accent was classless, unplaceable and, as he had noticed, slightly foreign. Whatever she spoke nowadays, the words had a way of sounding as if they were being translated.

All he told her of his niece's school might have come straight from one of the books over which she had pored. She took down the address of this haven for the academically neglected daughters of the aristocracy and the very rich. If her desires were given to her at all, they were bound to be satisfied on a considerable scale: she would be able to pay.

He mentioned with pleasure the names of old girls who had reached a gilded international status, as deposed queens or heiresses.

'Will you be going there to see your niece when you're in England?' she asked.

'Sure will! Take her and her friends out to tea. Don't know which of us gets more fun out of that.'

'Will you put my name down to go to that school too? You know the place, it'll come better from you. For the autumn term of next year. I'll be nearly sixteen then.'

'But don't you have to consult your father?'

'My father?'

'Your uncle, then, is it?'

'Oh, him. No. Mr. Manarez isn't concerned in my education. I manage my own affairs.'

'You do? Well, that's enterprise, and I certainly like enterprise. Anything you ask, young lady! Looks as if I'll soon be taking you out to tea, too! When this fellow I'm going to see in Florida has patched me up.'

'That will be very nice,' said Hebe. (The white blouse, and the gym tunic, or were they not worn with visitors for tea? She would be very cautious, and observe. She would put no foot wrong.) 'Laura Klee, the name is.' Casually she showed it to him on her new passport, which she carried with her whenever she went on deck, not imagining that it impressed people who had long had their own, but like a bride with a wedding ring she has almost despaired of acquiring, she felt happier for being seen with it, even if no one noticed. This was what money could do: as she had expected, the Manarezs had met with no difficulty in getting it for her, when at last Nickie insisted that she must travel with them.

'You won't forget, will you?' she said. 'Look, you write down where I'm going in England — ' She gave again the address of the house with the dogs: it made the plan feel quite close to realization, for a few seconds.

' "Near Bristol".' He paused, thoughtfully. Mrs. Manarez called her name loudly, nervously, angrily along the deck, and the grim present engulfed her again. Nicholas had rallied a little and was asking for her. She did not see the American again for long enough to do more than exchange greetings, but she had a comforting conviction that he would remember.

For several days Nicholas would scarcely let her out of his sight, clinging to her unemotional company in fear of what lay close ahead, excluding his parents from the stateroom save for brief visits, because now he could not bear any more of his father's resentment and his mother's uncontrolled misery. He wanted to talk half the night, to talk or to listen to tales of a world where a bed was a luxury, until suddenly exhausted he would fall asleep.

From these sessions Hebe stumbled away heavy-eyed in the dawn, always to find Mrs. Manarez standing white and hostile outside the door, in case he called, or needed anything. 'Don't think you could have looked after him as well as we have, all this time!' she said once. 'You're nothing but an ignorant, silly little girl.'

In fact, the degree to which this was true, the measure of her deficiencies, was the measure of her value to the boy just then. Hebe had very little sense of humour: detachment, self-criticism, a taste for incongruity — none of these was compatible with the kind of force which drove her, and this lack Nicholas found more diverting than anything else about her. She could still make him laugh occasionally, even now, as she did with the solemnity of her account of entering herself for school.

'The things you're going to have to unlearn!' he said, 'among all those nice young girls from nice old families! I wish I could be there to hear when you forget to forget sometimes.'

'I shan't,' said Hebe placidly.

He knew something of a world of art that was closed to her, but into her conversation came quickeningly snatches of what the Professor had said, without the self-consciousness of most borrowed wisdom: to her, the old man's easily recalled phrases were not wisdom, hard-garnered, sifted and compressed by much pondering: they were self-evident truths, she repeated them only because Nicholas found them interesting. They discussed St. Theresa of Avila, wrangling amiably because Hebe quoted what had been said about her own brains when she first heard of the saint, on the Bulgarian frontier, and Nickie questioned whether she could possibly have any brains at all, setting her aim so low, bearing so much for so little, as he put it.

'Extraordinary creature, you!' he said. 'You don't seem to want the things other people will do nearly anything to get.'

'Well, what do other people want, that I don't?'

'More than anything else, I suppose, to stand out from their fellows, one way or another. Wealth — fame — men have always been ready to die for the chance of being kings, haven't they? And women have been after power of other sorts. Over people. Or holiness. Or love. But not you! All you hanker for is safe mediocrity! Provincial mediocrity at that. The kind of thing that nine out of ten of the people who have it would give their souls to escape.'

'Not if they haven't always had it, Nickie.'

Of her ambitions, she had told him only the desire for respectability, the way of life that went with a small family business. Something prompted her to leave out all mention of André. She was defending herself as best she could when he said suddenly, 'You can marry me if you want to? You could make sure of quite a lot of money that way. To buy what you want.'

'No,' she said. He was coloured, a little. He did not fit into her plan. 'Thank you, though.'

'You'd better, you know. My people have always put odd sums in my name to save tax. As my widow — '

'No, I say. I won't.'

'Oh, all right. It wouldn't mean anything, except the money. But we could marry, in Jamaica, because I'm over sixteen, and that's the legal age. You know, eighty-two per cent of children in Kingston are illegitimate, so the Law says to the Church, "Catch 'em young — if you can!" ' He gave his moving, bubbling laugh. 'Oh, Hebe, how long now before we get there?'

'Five days, I was told. I saw the first flying fish today. It was wonderful, because — well, it was.'

'Four days, *they* said! They lie to me all the time. I want so much to see Old Amy again. I do! You know, I believe she could let me sleep and not dream whenever I wanted to, without drugs. I believe she could keep me alive a bit longer!'

'I daresay your parents weren't lying. Four days — five days — no one's sure just when we arrive.'

'All right, they weren't. But you'll have to help me to see Old Amy in Jamaica. They won't want that, they'll want me to go into a nursing home. Even though it isn't any good, and they know it. But they'll want it so that they'll be able to feel afterwards that they did all the right things. Old Amy wouldn't be allowed with me there. Except visiting hours. "Dirty old black thing" — she is, too! Now play chess with me.'

Something unexpected happened to Hebe then, the waking of compassion: not in a moment, but over a period of a few days. She who had not had enough leisure of heart to pity anything, felt at last with more than her mind or her imagination for the frightened boy. Their relationship was not affected: she knew her particular value to him too well by now to show sympathy.

They landed before his brief flicker of strength was over. For one day and one night only she saw the other Kingston, into which they disembarked; the gay, pleasant white man's town of the Myrtle Bank Hotel and the good shops, lying alongside the raucous, over-crowded black man's town where she had stayed before. At dawn — Jamaica's pearl coloured, most wonderful hour — she looked out of Nickie's window in the hotel towards the sound of singing coming from the sea. Dark figures were diving into the misty water from a jetty just outside the Myrtle Bank garden, young native workmen enjoying themselves before starting on the day's jobs: they were transformed by the dawn light into majestic and other-worldly creatures. Becalmed, one of the big trading schooners which plied between the islands drifted by on the tide, towards the harbour mouth, with her sails shivering. It had seemed an endless night, Nickie had been exhausted and yet unable to rest, refusing to take sleeping tablets, saying they made him dream and feel worse on waking, refusing also to let her doze a little. He was holding on to her endurance, as though if she slept, the thin cord by which he clung to life might snap. An altercation with his parents in the evening had upset him: they had begun urging on him the excellence of St. Joseph's Sanatorium, the best nursing home in the island. It was a relief to Hebe to watch the day break, and the swimmers, and to try to describe to him what she saw. Then her eyes fell on a nearer figure, a tall native woman standing very still, close to one of the king-palms in the garden, where she had no business to be, staring up fixedly at the windows.

'I think your Old Amy is here.' A feeling of apprehension ran through Hebe at the sight of her.

'Oh, that's marvellous.' He was immediately transformed by excitement, and looked for the moment quite happy. 'They put off sending for her. I knew they would. "Wait till you come out of the nursing home, darling!" And yet she's come.'

'She must have seen a passenger list.'

'Perhaps. And perhaps not. You don't know what an Obeah woman can do. Smuggle her in, Hebe, quickly. Go on. Quickly. I'll be all right, while she's here.'

There was no one about in the corridor. For once, worn out, Mrs. Manarez had gone to lie down, having charged Hebe to call her before she left Nicholas. It felt eerie to the girl, moving quietly through the sleeping hotel; a cat slunk by: there was the sense of catching something at a disadvantage, looking from behind at a scene meant to be viewed only from in front. At the foot of the stairs, down which she crept, a coloured servant with a flit-gun in his hand slept with his head on the bottom step, stirring a little as she slipped past. By the time the girl reached one of the long windows in the deserted dining-room, looking out on the garden, the waiting figure had moved from the tree to stand close alongside a wall, where she would be invisible from the rooms above. She came in without a word when the catch yielded, a ragged but commanding presence, and without a word Hebe led her upstairs, safely passing the sleeping figure again. From the front entrance, the voices of two night-porters could now be heard arguing cheerfully about the sharing of a tip.

When they reached Nickie's landing, Old Amy put a hand on Hebe's arm and turned her round for scrutiny, boring into her with eyes sunk deep in a skull-like head. For once Hebe felt with Mrs. Manarez: she too was awed by the woman, and disliked being near her. 'You his girl-friend, Missie?'

'In a way.'

When they came in, the boy had shifted himself with an effort, to lie with his eyes on the door, and all his heart was in them. He held out his arms. Old Amy gathered him to her as if he had still been the baby she had nursed. Between snatches of low-voiced talk she crooned over him in a sing-song voice, stroking his hair. Hebe could not hear what passed between them, but Nickie remembered her in a moment and said peremptorily over Old Amy's shoulder, 'All right, I shan't want you any more now.'

'I shall, my little fish. Let her stay,' put in Old Amy quickly. Her claw-like hand kneaded the muscles of his neck. In a very few moments he was asleep.

Old Amy settled him back in the bed and crossed to the other side of the room, beckoning Hebe, so that their whispered conversation should not disturb him. Again her eyes frightened the girl. This woman was not really old; depending on whether or not she meant well by someone, thought Hebe, she could be very good or very evil. The girl knew that she herself was safe, while Nicholas kept his affection for her: but also that she or anyone else would be cut to pieces by Old Amy without hesitation if the much-loved boy could get any benefit from this act.

'You going to help me get him away?'

'Away, where?'

'My place. My cabin in the Old Town first. Then up to the hills. Where he'll be well content — four days, five days, a week. Might be two. You know what's happening?' The eyes bored into her again.

'That he's dying? Yes.'

'You know how he'll die if you don't? All clean and proper in the nursing home. But lonely. And afraid.'

'Yes.' Louder than their words, Hebe could hear once more the thump-thump of her heart. 'He said of you, "I believe she could keep me alive",' she told Old Amy reluctantly. 'He really thinks that — thinks he'll be all right while he's with you.'

'Well, Missie?'

'All right, I'll help you.' Tears pricked the back of her eyes. 'If you behave yourself' — Whatever lay ahead, her part in taking the boy out of their care could not possibly be regarded by the older Manarezs as 'behaving herself'. Her plan had seemed marvellously real and near lately. Too real, too near, too easy: she might have known it could not happen like this. At the time of meeting the Quakers, she had not understood more than about half of what Lesley had said, when they talked near the beehive, but now she did: compassion could be the most compelling force in the world.

They took Nickie out of the hotel in his carrying chair through the full bustle of early breakfast time: his father was already away in the car, making arrangements for the boy's reception at the sanatorium: his mother still in exhausted sleep. With Hebe, who was taken for his sister, walking beside the sick boy, no one questioned where they were going.

15

THE COCKPIT COUNTRY

BEFORE they left the hotel, Nickie dictated to Hebe, who wrote with some difficulty, a note to his mother, saying that he was going to stay with his old nurse — 'Oh, better tell her, for a week. Then they won't be so keen to organize a search for me. So silly, they'd look, calling in police help! Another scandal to go round Port au Prince, if only a little one! — What fun this is!' They would be surprised, he told his parents, to see how much better he would be when he came back. 'Much better than if I went into the nursing home — Now let's go, before they come in to see me.'

'Nobody's going to come in,' Old Amy soothed him. 'We go when we ready, my little fish.' With Hebe acting as safe-conduct, so that she could come back openly into the Myrtle Bank, Old Amy went out into the arcade opposite the hotel and called in off the street one of the nephews of which, according to Nicholas, she had an endless supply all over the West Indies. He laughed weakly as he said it, confident that he was not going to die just yet. Not in Old Amy's care.

Outside the Myrtle Bank they turned right, away from the white man's town, and were at once deep in a slum area, in a maze of narrow streets twisting between rows of tin shanties, with sacking hung up in place of doors and their walls patched with pieces of rotten wood. These lairs were horrifying to Hebe at first glance, the change was so abrupt, and so ominous, but as something of a connoisseur of poor dwellings she reminded herself that hot-climate slums were not, rightly considered, slums at all — nothing like those in Greece: the difference being that no one had to live in them all the time, where the outside world was warm. The Jamaican weather would surely make it possible for her to exist outside, wherever they went.

This hope died when they reached Old Amy's place, a hut different from its neighbours only in that it was made largely from flattened biscuit tins, not petrol cans. 'You go in, and don't you come out again in daylight,' Old Amy told her, pushing her towards the sacking doorway. The two small rooms within had an indescribable smell, not only the reek of poverty and dirt and decay. 'Get that Obeah box out from wherever you've hidden it, Amy!' Nickie commanded. 'It stinks! You won't be doing any trade while I'm here.'

Old Amy laughed, the bubbling laugh which he had caught from her. 'You won't be here long, little fish,' she said, 'Tonight — tomorrow — soon as your Old Amy can fix for you to travel — we flit away up to the Cockpit Country.' But she took down from a high shelf in the gloom of the inner room a large wooden box, giving it into the care of her nephew, for the time being, with many warnings that it was not to be opened. 'Tell the people outside,' she ordered, as he carried it towards the door under a coat, 'we didn't bring a sick boy in here. They didn't see a chair. Nor us. Nor anything.' He nodded and went. Coloured people could be relied on not to give away their own kind, under white questioning: they would be particularly careful in this neighbourhood not to rouse Old Amy's anger.

What was in the box, Hebe never knew for certain: probably the feathers and entrails of a bird, Nickie told her when they were alone, along with an assortment of bottles for holding the blood: other things, like dried baby alligators or sharks' teeth, might be there too as part of a stock-in-trade, kept to impress those who came to consult Old Amy, but the bird and the bottles were the working tools. In theory, it should be a fine cock, killed ceremoniously at the right season by the Obeah woman herself, but in fact was more likely to be any cheap little bird from the nearby market. That worked just as well, with Old Amy, he said Out of the remains, mixed with earth, could be made the fatal little balls of which Hebe had already heard, signs of doom to be strewn about the path of the intended victim, where they would be fertilized for evil by the sun or moon-shadow of the victim falling across them accidentally. Without this contact they were ineffective, but once a man or woman found some of these things, evidently placed by an enemy, even if the shadow-touch were avoided with those which were seen in time, how was it possible to be sure that others, unnoticed, had not been made potent in this way? — Certainly, to Hebe, the air in the two rooms seemed noticeably fresher when the box had been out of them for a while.

But it was still stiflingly hot. Nickie did not appear to feel it. Before she went out, leaving them to their own devices for the rest of the day, Old Amy re-dressed him and Hebe in locally suitable clothes, in case someone like a rent collector looked in during her absence — one could not lock a sacking door. For him, an old, torn shirt was light enough as bed-wear, but for Hebe there was only a tawdry velvet dress so much too large that it had to be looped up, sweatily, round the waist, over a tightly knotted belt.

If asked, they were to say they were her sister's children. Their colour would attract no notice: Kingston slums teamed with skins of every possible shade. Indeed, Nickie appeared to grow more coloured in Old Amy's company: his boundless belief in her powers was entirely African.

In the dark, gruesome hovel, Hebe sat unoccupied while Nickie slept or rested with his eyes half open, drifting in and out of consciousness, very feeble but content. Why had she done this, she wondered, and could form no answer to satisfy herself, yet knew that she would make the same choice again if she had to. Would there be a hunt after them, she wondered, or would his parents accept that scrawled note in the way in which they accepted all his other wishes, as their law? At intervals she fed him with the milk and glucose they had brought along from the hotel, and in the end, overcome with weariness from the previous night, and the excitement of the morning, she slept fitfully, constantly roused by dreams of foreboding.

Old Amy came back at dusk with two more of her nephews, or young attendants, in charge of a small battered motor van, arranged for carrying loads of fruit. Some of the interior they ripped out, and stowed in her rooms. Old Amy seated herself on one of the light metal-mesh trays which had been left in its place, and very carefully Nickie was handed from his chair into her arms. Then the chair and the others were bundled in round them, as packing. She was immensely strong: all through the night, while they drove slowly up the central range of mountains, making for the wild jungle country in the west, she sat cushioning him in her thin, sinewy arms, and he lay peacefully against her dried-up breast and shoulder, as much at ease as he ever felt in the Manarez's finely sprung car. Trust in her made the journey possible for him to survive. The doors of the van were kept closed until they were well clear of Kingston, without having entered the white man's town on the way: when Hebe was almost sick with the mixture of heat and fumes (why had she come, why had she done this, why, why?) the driver paused in the plaintive, endless-seeming calypso of triumph which he made up about the kidnapping and sang as he went along. He stopped the van, opened the doors, and took down part of the side to give them more ventilation. Surely now they would be seen, recognized and reported, Hebe thought. There was still plenty of light in the sky, and they made an odd company, Nickie lying as though he were dead. But they met no one except a barefoot native girl in evening dress, trudging home from a dance with her shoes balanced on her head, above a much decorated hat, and she did not even glance back at them. Later they passed gangs of men burning banana-trash by the roadside, but these seemed dazzled by the light of their own fires. The drivers of the few other vehicles who overtook them waved an uninterested hand: Nickie must have seemed to them, she concluded, like a bundle of washing clasped tightly to the coloured woman in the back, or else, long trained by the white man in knowing nothing of what was inconvenient to know, if they suspected that here was a body being taken somewhere surreptitiously, they were very careful not to look again.

Some miles beyond Accompong they stopped once more, having

come as far as they could by road. Here, towards the summit of the mountains, all cultivation ceased and the riotous growth of tropical vegetation was as it had always been. Nicholas bore without complaint the pain of being taken from the van and put back into his chair, he said only in a tired child's voice, 'Is it far now?' and Old Amy touched his head, smoothing his hair, saying, 'Not far now,' and immediately he went to sleep again. Hebe knew nothing of hypnotism: cold fear of Old Amy grew and grew in her. For Nicholas it might be white magic: for her, Obeah was black indeed. And she need not have come. The idea hammered drearily in her head. This was her doing. For the first time, by her own will, she had worsened her condition. She told herself that she did not deserve to reach the Good Place.

For an hour or more the boy was carried by the nephews, or whoever they were, along a path which wound at times beside the base of bare, limestone cliffs, and at others became a tunnel through creaking thickets of bamboo. The ceaseless creaking and tapping of the canes, sounding as though unseen hordes of men and beasts were moving near them, intensified the feeling of solitude after a while, when it became plain that this noise was only the voice of the jungle, stirring in a light breeze. Outside, dawn had come, but no more than a green dimness filtered down to them in the rattling wilderness. This was the edge of the Cockpit Country. Soon they came to the end of the bamboos, and to a maze of pot-holes, some big, some small, filled with still denser vegetation and separated from one another by narrow limestone ridges, barriers of rock so twisted and jagged that to make two yards in any direction meant, as often as not, a detour of many hundreds. Hebe knew this place already at third hand: Nicholas had told her about it in the ship, during the long nights in which he could not sleep, when he talked of Old Amy. It was the background of all the stories he had loved hearing, over and over again, as a small child. Although he had never in fact been there before himself, the Cockpit Country meant security to him. But not to Hebe. This was the free land, he had said, granted to the Maroons and their descendants for ever by a defeated British government, two hundred years ago, as a gesture of honour at the end of one of the oddest and bloodiest of small wars: whole regiments of white soldiers had been swallowed up and disappeared for ever without trace in this weird region. Now that she had seen it, Hebe could well believe that: when she dropped the sack of stores she had been given to carry, and stopped to pick it up, the others had disappeared — and with them the path, too — by the time she stood up, ready to struggle on again. Terrified, she stayed where she was, calling loudly, till Old Amy came back for her, telling her fiercely to be quiet. The dark claw of a hand shaking her shoulder was the first she knew of the woman's nearness, so completely could the thickets hide anything or anyone a pace or two away.

'You get him taken away from me — before he must be — and you see what happens to you!' Hebe glimpsed again the woman who was not the Old Amy known to Nickie, but someone much more ruthless; and in the following days, when all three of them were together, with Old Amy at her gentlest as the boy's loving slave, Hebe never forgot that the other was also there.

In some of the cockpits, the stronger plants, struggling upwards, had choked the undergrowth to death, so that airless, dank caverns opened below thick layers of creeper: from these places rustlings and sighings were to be heard, in the quiet of the inner jungle, as though they were still inhabited by the hundreds of runaway slaves who had hidden there in days gone by.

'Mongoose!' said one of the carriers, when the chair was set down for a breathing space. 'Only mongoose living there now. Little, furry, brown mongoose. You thought snakes, eh?'

Hebe had indeed thought so. The young negro began making up and mouthing quietly, as they went on again, a mocking but friendly calypso about a silly, small white girl who went in dread of snakes in Jamaica, of all places, where mongoose had long ago eaten them all — a comforting impromptu in the circumstances, for himself as well as Hebe. Naturally, like everyone bred in the district, he knew beyond question that the sounds were made by duppies, a malevolent variety of ghost special to the West Indies: it was lucky for Hebe that she remained unaware how much commoner they were supposed to be, everywhere in the Cockpit Country, than mongoose, two of which ran across their path before the end of his muttered song.

Under a vast cotton tree they came to the end of their journey, Old Amy's hill dwelling. This was built into the base of the tree, between two of the sharp, plank-like buttresses which formed more than half of the side-walls, the huge trunk being the back. The buttresses had been prolonged with interwoven bamboos, and these had taken root wherever they touched the rankly fertile ground: the whole hut was a living thing, the open front — there were only three sides — was partly obscured by creeper; they had to tear their way in. Inside, covered with old tarpaulin, were several lead-lined trunks which protected from ants many sacks of stores — To this lair Old Amy retreated whenever the police in Kingston, or wherever else she operated, became over-interested in her activities.

Here the young men left them, as soon as they had put Nickie down just inside the hut. Without a word of goodbye, or of thanks from Old Amy, they faded back into the jungle, disappearing like shadows among other shadows before they had taken three steps through the shimmering, shifting curtain of fronds, just as their forebears had done, to the bewilderment of those who came to fight them. Hebe knew a pang of regret at their going: somehow, despite the way they could move through the jungle, making no sound, they seemed more part of the ordinary world than the sick boy in his deep, unnatural sleep, or Old Amy: at least one of them drove a fruit van by day, an excellently normal occupation, she felt. But she had chosen this, she reminded herself. She would see through to the end, then, the regrettable results of feeling sorry for anyone but herself. She sat down near the funnel-like entrance of the hut, to wait with patience for Nicholas to wake, or be awakened by Old Amy.

16

THE MAROON TALES

WITHIN the space of a few yards, for six days Hebe lived through a patch of time like no other she had ever known, sleeping just inside the hut, passing her waking hours outside but always in call. Occasionally she was told to do chores for Nicholas or Old Amy, but they were few; Old Amy was jealous of her, too, and preferred to do everything for her nurseling herself. The rest of her time Hebe spent idly watching, through a gap in the jungle wall, where a big flame-of-the-forest tree had recently fallen, the shifting of light and shadow over the Santa Cruz mountains, a few miles away on the other side of a valley.

In its fall, the flame-of-the-forest had dragged down with it a mass of clinging, matted, smaller growths: almost perceptibly, moment by moment, that window into space torn out of the enveloping greenery was being closed by the eagerness of other plant life, but for the moment light and air flowed through it, and Nickie could lie each morning with dappled sunshine flickering for a while over his pinched face. With the self-centredness of the very ill, he neither thought it strange that Hebe had come with him to this place, throwing away the compact she had stubbornly made with his parents, nor realized how she had changed from the person he still relied on not to mind what happened to him. Carefully and kindly she went on hiding from him her new-learnt pity. Of his parents, no doubt desperately anxious, whether or not they were searching for him, he did not appear to think at all. Once he said, nodding towards the gap, 'When that's shut up we'll go back,' but most of the time he seemed dreamily and passively content, unaware of the passage of hours. The ground fell away sharply in front of the hut, the gap in the surrounding jungle was below their eye-level, so that they looked down, as if from another star, on all that they could see of the world they had left behind, outside the narrow clear space round the trunk of the cotton tree.

Dawn came attended by humming-birds, hovering impatiently before flowers lazier than they at waking: noon was a white blaze of light streaming over the tops of the lower forests, cresting them with fire here and there, where other flame-of-the-forest trees stood and burned in scarlet blossom: evening made scents lie heavy on a wind puffing itself out into stillness, and brought a trembling, listening hush to the jungle-roof of the island, in which the last bird-calls sounded defiantly. But apart from the changing of the light, time did not exist.

Sometimes they lived by night, sometimes by day: sleep without distressing dreams came easier to Nicholas while there was light about him; the shadows closing in disturbed him, and then Old Amy would start a fire and cook over it one of the same-tasting meals which they ate at any hour: the boy liked this monotonous native food, which was mainly fruit and roots and sprouted grain. He had been living almost entirely on milk and medicines; now he began to eat again, occasionally, a mouthful or two at a time; and sitting with the firelight flickering upwards on to her face, hollowing her eyes, Old Amy would begin talking of the ways of her people, of the things they had done, perhaps in this exact spot, retelling endlessly to Nickie tales to distract him from pain, and prevent him from being afraid. The Maroon stories, brutal and terrible as many of them were, shone with a wild courage which made suffering companionable. Throughout these slow, soft-footed days and nights the three of them, in their small green cell, seemed not to be existing in the present at all: the future, since for Nickie there could be no future, they avoided mentioning: it was the past that became magnified, and close about them, and real.

The tales were told in no chronological order; the boy knew the historical background and could skip backwards and forwards in imagination, ranging over two hundred years, filling in the details of the period for himself; Old Amy could not be bothered to explain anything entirely for Hebe's benefit: it was some while, therefore, before she was able to piece the stories together into a consecutive whole — When Jamaica was in Spanish hands, menaced by the British who finally captured the island, the Spanish settlers had attempted to make their wretched slaves fight for them, against the invaders, by telling them that under the rule of the newcomers their treatment would be harsher; but for once cruelty over-reached itself: the slaves knew that it was not possible to endure more and live. The bravest of the men took to the hills, leaving their women and children in the slave-pens on the plantations, while they fought for their freedom and their lives in the Cockpit Country. It made no difference to them that their former masters were driven out; Britain was still a slave-owning country. Recapture, for a runaway, meant various forms of torture, as a warning to other slaves — branding, nose-slitting, appalling floggings repeated at regular intervals, or death. But year after year the band of desperate men still at liberty in the heart of the island became a greater danger to the welfare of the plantation owners: no master felt safe in dealing as he pleased with his human property while an overdriven slave could lift up his eyes and his thoughts to the hills. Expeditions of well-armed whites went up after the runaways: it was then that the Maroons earned their name, from their nerve-racking system of jungle signalling. Able leaders arose among them, notably one Cudjoe — Old Amy spoke of him reverently, as an ancestor but also as though he were a god — to organize a defence of invisibility which became a legendary horror to the slave-owners. A blowing of conch-shells, called Maroons, in the jungle on all sides of them, was all that the attackers ever heard of their quarry; and they saw nothing, if they turned off a path to pursue the noise, except a moving of fronds which might be the closing-in of a thicket after men had slipped through, or could just as well be no more than the way the lighter leaves fluttered and tapped in the faintest air. But when the white men returned to the task of smashing a track through the pot-holes, and the last-but-one in the line turned to speak to the fellow behind, he found no one there: then while he struggled to catch up the companion ahead, a dark hand stretched out of a bush at throat level as he passed, and that was the end of him, too.

To maintain this battle year after year, the Maroons instituted among themselves a savage discipline: Old Amy claimed proudly that they killed more of their own people than the white masters succeeded in doing, even after the planters, admitting defeat, had appealed for help from England, and the military arrived, to carry full-scale war into the hills. Detachment followed detachment, as their numbers faded away mysteriously among the sighing pot-holes and the horrible blowing of the conch-shells. Hebe's heart went out secretly to the bewildered white soldiers — no doubt well armed for their time but helpless against the jungle cunning of the Maroons — She had, however, the sense to keep quiet: Nickie had always been heart and soul with the Maroons.

Then came that part of the tale, or series of tales, which he particularly loved, and Old Amy lingered over, giving individual accounts that had been handed down with family pride for generations. Feeling secure at last in their fastnesses, the Maroons began creeping down at night into the plantations on the coastal plains, to steal their women out of the slave-houses in which they were locked, guarded by dogs and by white patrols with guns. No matter how strong the guard, and no matter what the penalty for a Maroon recaptured, singly the men wriggled their way, greased and naked to make capture more difficult, to lie against the walls of the pens, whispering to their women inside. It was not always easy to persuade the women to make the attempt at freedom: they faced the same penalty as the men, if caught, and they were surrounded by other slaves. The Maroons had no enemies more vicious than those of their own kind who dared not join them. There were betrayals and ambushes and heart-break, and much killing, but where the women were willing, time after time the men succeeded in cutting a way through to them and spiriting them back to the hills.

'Together,' said Old Amy, looking contemptuously at Hebe, representing the white race, 'we bred such fighters we kept you scared for fifty years and more. So long it took, that first Maroon war. And what you do, because you scared?' — The firelight, throwing its shadows upwards from the blunt nose and deep eye-sockets, made her back-tilted head look more than ever like a skull from where the girl sat: behind Hebe it seemed that the jungle crept closer to listen. She had an almost irresistible impulse to put out a hand, and get hold of Nickie's, but knew that he would not understand, loving these stories; instead she folded them tightly round her knees to keep herself from shivering while this evocation of valiant ghosts went on in the dead of the jungle night. 'You drove out our White Magic. All the good magic we brought from Ashanti in the slave ships. For making rain come and mealies sprout. Got to have many people together for that magic. You made a government order, not more than six slaves to meet together, for any purpose. Be flogged if they did. That way you hoped you'd stop us thinking and talking together of the Maroons. Maybe praying for them. Much good it did, posting up the notice of the order by the meeting houses, and around the plantations — most of us couldn't read. We got the flogging anyway, and so we learnt the order. And the white magic died. But the other — Obeah — that takes only one to make, in secret. Just one who knows how. So it goes on.'

She broke off to tell Nicholas prosaically that the price of a life in her line of business had recently gone up, like everything else since the war: fifteen pounds it was now, where it used to be twelve.

'And British law still takes no account of witchcraft,' she said scornfully. 'No such thing, they tell us. Can't be. So what they do when they catch one of us after a killing? Must get us locked up so we don't do it again. Why, they put us in prison, a good long stretch, for getting money on false pretences. There's the body. And somebody paid the fifteen pounds. Oh, never mind the body, it can't have died of Obeah, because there's no such thing. So —' Laughter, as unnerving as Dido's but more genuinely amused, finished the rest of the sentence for her. She went back to the tales of her people's resistance, which lasted triumphantly until the general freeing of slaves. 'And this land is ours,' she said. 'Ours.

You don't often get governments giving you land, even a poor bit like this, out of admiration.'

Twice, during their vigil by the sick boy, they were visited by local people who had somehow heard of her presence, or else, in their need, had come on chance, hoping for the luck of catching her at the hut, in one of her periods of cautious retirement — She had only been in jail once, she assured Nickie with pride, since she left the Manarezs as a nurse. 'Me, I work from a distance, see, little fish?' One of the visitors was a full blooded negro cane-cutter, an alarming pock-marked giant, swinging a razor-sharp machete, the other a half-caste girl of remarkable beauty, of the physically exquisite Chinese-Bantu-white mixture abounding in Kingston: in both cases they came laden with gifts of food, which added variety to the ordinary diet at the hut, and they did their business alone with Old Amy, going aside with her beyond the curtain of leaves to argue or plead. The girl was plainly terrified, and in tears when she left. Hebe envied her all the same; terrified or not, she could get away. She need not watch a dying lad, touchingly sure that he had won a reprieve, growing weaker hour by hour; nor watch herself, continually, lest she betray that she was moved, beyond tears.

Every day, Old Amy's power was more clearly manifest: she seemed to be holding Nickie alive by will: not only alive but in less pain than at any time since Hebe had known him, although the drugs which they had brought from the hotel were so nearly finished that they had to be used in much less than their normal doses. 'Missie' she continued to call Hebe, but there was neither deference nor courtesy in her tone: it sounded more as though she could not be bothered to recognize the girl's personality, by remembering her name.

'You want to marry Missie?' she asked Nicholas, on one of the boy's better days, when he was talking of everything that had happened on the voyage.

'Not particularly. Just for her sake. It wouldn't make any difference to me. But she'd get my money when I die. Only I'm not going to, yet. Get me to sleep now, Amy. I'm tired.' Hebe realized that if he had expressed a real wish to marry her, they would have been married at once, somehow, by Old Amy's contriving.

Once the woman left them by themselves for half a night and the first few hours of the next day, when, she said, stores were running low — although to Hebe there appeared to be plenty of food in the sacks at the back of the hut. Old Amy murmured the boy into a sound sleep before she went. 'It'll last till I'm back,' she told the quaking Hebe, but for once was wrong. Nickie woke, wanting water, while it was still dark. The drinking can was empty; fear had brought thirst to Hebe: afraid of Old Amy, when she was present, she was much more afraid of being left alone in charge of Nickie, with no recourse if one of his bad hours came upon him: she could not put him to sleep again. Compassion destroyed her self-assurance, she found. Suppose, in some way, she failed him now. It was bad enough, while he slept, to be alone to listen to the forest night — to listen with the night, rather. There was a feeling in her over-stirred nerves as though she and the night were each waiting for a move from the other. If she kept very still, and within the hut, looking out, she had more chance, she felt, of holding whatever the darkness hid at bay, not only for herself but for Nickie.

He seemed untroubled at finding Old Amy absent — 'She'll be back soon. She always did come and go suddenly like that,' — and insisted, when Hebe suggested he should try to sleep again, that he must have water first. Rare in this limestone region, a stream fed by a spring ran only about fifty yards away: the unfailing supply of good water was, in fact, the reason why Old Amy's lair had been built into this particular tree. Hebe went reluctantly, begging Nickie to whistle to her all the time, so that she could find her way back — the water itself was easy to reach: you simply turned down hill a little, and blundered ahead through the undergrowth till you felt your feet wet. But even after she had carried back safely at least half the water in the can, the impression persisted in her mind that somehow she had let the jungle in, on Nickie as well as herself, by leaving him alone for those few moments. She took his head on her knees, as Old Amy did, and stroked his hair in an imitation of her way of soothing him, but he grew more restless.

'When you're at school in England, will you think of me sometimes?' He gave a ghost of a chuckle. 'That much-classier-than-a-public-school school. Where others will be busy learning, and you'll be so much busier, forgetting.'

'I expect so,' she said.

'Funny, nice Hebe.' There was no more laughter in his tone. 'Anyone else would say, "Of course I will", or "All the time", or something like that. But you don't tell lies, do you?'

'I do when they're useful. You know that — My list of contacts in Salonika. I lied about it all the time.'

'Oh, the wonderful list! Wasn't even one name genuine?'

'They may have been. Every one, for all I know. The point was, I didn't know. So I pretended. But there's no sense in lying to you.'

Through their window in the leaves flickered points of light, far off in the darkness, where someone was burning banana-trash either very late or very early: they had no means of knowing which, Nickie's watch having stopped some days before. The fires seemed companionable; down there in that other world were fellow human beings at work; they watched for a while in silence.

'That man whose face you saw lit by the fire —' He spoke again abruptly. 'In the place where the *klepts* came.'

'Mihael. Yes. What about him?'

'Do you think he was satisfied, when he went out, that it just doesn't matter if there's a God or not?'

'I don't know, Nickie.'

'It doesn't, does it? It's like what you told me the other chap said. The one we saw in Athens. If there's nothing, I won't know. If there's something, I should think it'd be all right.'

'For you, you mean? Yes, I should think so. I expect Mihael just felt at last that it only matters about the living.'

'People bother so much, don't they, about what it'll be like after they're dead? Well, they know, really, don't they. I mean, they've been dead. Before they were born. And it was all right then.'

She said nothing, stroking his hair, trying vainly Old Amy's soothing massage on the muscles of the neck.

'Yes, it was all right then,' he said again. 'Kiss me, Hebe.'

She bent down over him, but could not reach his face without moving his head, and hesitated. 'Maybe I'll hurt you?'

'No. It doesn't matter.'

They kissed, childishly. He clung to her for a moment, and she felt his tears on her face. Then they began to talk again, and talked, very ordinarily, of Switzerland, and the house with the dogs, discussing nothing which they had not often spoken of, except his wistful desire, which struck her as absurd, to have known what it was like to live dangerously. 'Fancy, this is the nearest I've ever come to it,' he said. 'Just being here with you and Old Amy! Of course it was always wasted on you,' and in her new kindness she stifled the comment rising in her mind — that for her, too, there had been nothing before like this wanton endurance of fear.

Old Amy came back, when they were both asleep in the morning light, Nickie still lying with his head in Hebe's lap, and the girl leaning back against the hut wall. The woman started a fire to cook for them, but Nickie did not want to eat when he awakened, and she abandoned the effort: Hebe could make do with bananas, or nothing. Old Amy herself never seemed in real need of food, or rest.

'Tell us about the other Maroon war, the one later on,' he commanded, when the afternoon heat quivered outside the green gap — so narrow now that in another day or so it would be gone. Old Amy settled down at once, still with blood on her bare legs, Hebe noticed, from briars and the limestone edges over which she had scrambled, to recreate for him the old legends. These, of the second Maroon war, were more than usually grim stories of treachery on the part of ill-natured white planters, who resented, even after the passing of the law of Emancipation, the independent colony of blacks living on their own land, working for no one but themselves. Several of the whites, in league together, trumped up an accusation of stealing a hog against a Maroon, and a time and place was set for the leaders to answer a summons, coming down from their hills to discuss the incident in the white man's capital; but deliberately the date was arranged too early for the news to reach the hills and let the Cudjoe then ruling his people — probably a grandson of the first liberator — obey the court order within the time limit. He was thrown into prison as a hostage when he came, too late, and his people tried to rescue him: the killing began again — 'So we taught you once more, when you came against us up here, that you couldn't beat us in our own hills!' Old Amy told of the fizzling out of that war, but Nickie was dozing again before she had finished, and noticing this she stopped, did whatever odd jobs were needed around the hut, keeping an eye on him, and then took on again, while he was waking up from his cat-nap, as though there had been no pause in her narrative.

'Don't let's have any more of that war.' In the last day and night Nickie had become like a very young child who enjoys only certain parts of a familiar story. He could keep his attention on any subject for no more than a few minutes at a time. 'I want the bit about your own ancestor coming down at night to the slave-house, in the early days.' But he had drifted into sleep before she could reach the heart of the tale. For hours she sat quite still, not speaking, cradling the boy's head and shoulders, sending Hebe with a gesture for water and a fan of banana leaf to keep the flies off him. It seemed incredible to Hebe that anyone could stay so still for so long. Eventually she herself followed Nickie into sleep. She woke to see Old Amy methodically stacking the bedding under an old tarpaulin at the back of the hut. Nickie lay in his chair, his face turned away from her.

'You're not going away again, are you?' Hebe asked apprehensively.

'We both going. Tonight,' said Old Amy.

'Both? But Nickie —'

'He's dead. I told my nephew, have the van on the road tonight, just where we left it. And if we not come, tomorrow night too. Wasn't quite sure when we want it.' She straightened herself up, and made what seemed a great effort. 'Thank you, Missie,' she said.

A sense of desolation for herself: for him, an immense relief that the long ordeal was ended — the news brought Hebe not only these but the return of practicality: the recognition that now she must fend for herself once more.

The thought of what seemed an inevitable and terrible interview with his parents loomed in her mind all through the journey back to Kingston again in the fruit van — the passage had the same oddly invisible character which had impressed her on the way up to the Cockpit Country: then the bundle in Old Amy's arms had only looked like a dead body; now that it was one, in fact, the coloured people they passed, or met on the road, appeared to be even more taken up with their own concerns and carefully unobservant.

Nickie could not simply be deposited from the van at the door of the hotel. What would the Manarezs say, or do? If they had been held back from calling in the police to trace him when their boy disappeared, by the fear of thwarting a last wish, there was nothing to restrain anyone from any action at this stage if they felt vindictive. Nerves, petrol fumes and the heat of the van combined to make Hebe suddenly sick as they approached the town.

'You frightened, Missie?'

'A bit.'

'Of his people?'

'Yes,' said Hebe, leaning out again over the side of the truck.

'But we got to take him back to them. Leave my little fish in the hills and he get no Christian burial.'

'I know.' It was Nickie who had explained to her that most of the Obeah workers were also devoutly Christian. Old Amy herself wore a cross round her neck along with other charms. 'I'll be all right in a minute,' Hebe said, and told herself that this journey, however it ended, was not worse to endure than the sound of Yorkim rustling through the straw. Nor certainly, than the moment of knowing herself betrayed by Lesley, which had come to haunt her memory as one of the most shaking of all experiences, in some ways the saddest of the moments of swift growing. She had weathered fiercer storms than the one which loomed ahead. Never-theless the truck had to stop for several minutes, when her sickness became almost continuous.

'Look, I'll see to them,' Old Amy said, struck by an idea when they were in Kingston. 'Don't you come with us to the hotel, because maybe he wouldn't want you to.'

'Oh, thank you!' said Hebe, and was set down at Old Amy's lair in the black slum, to wait there while Nickie was given back to his parents.

The Obeah box had evidently returned to its usual place — Hebe did not need to go into the inner room to see, the atmosphere of both rooms was foetid; but she preferred this to the possibilities of her reception at the Myrtle Bank.

Exactly what Old Amy said to the Manarezs on her behalf Hebe never discovered. Not the lean, black figure whom she was expect-ing, but the florid and yet deflated one of Nickie's father pushed through the sacking doorway when she had been waiting for about two hours. He stood looking down at her with emotion. She scrambled up from the bed on which she had been lying and faced him.

'I would have liked his mother to see you,' he said mildly. 'But she won't.' Although his voice sounded old and tired, there was about it, as about the sagging figure, the relief which Hebe knew. He, too, was thankful now that it was all over. There was fellow-feeling between them, instead of the savage resentment she had expected. Vaguely she realized this, as soon as he began to talk, and the familiar clutch at her heart lessened.

'We understand our boy offered to marry you so you should have anything that was his when he died. But you refused. Although he told you, it's possible by the laws here. Stupid laws. I don't know why you said no — I don't ask. You must have known, with Nickie so ill, it could have meant nothing except getting money. Money that — ' He broke off with his old anxiety coming uppermost — was he approaching the point quickly enough? 'I daresay it seems odd I should be talking of money in connection with our boy's death. But you see, his mother — she can't believe you knew there was quite a lot in his name. Did you?'

'Yes.' She tried to comfort him, by telling him what she thought the most important aspect of Nickie's death. 'He didn't think he was going to die, you know, right up to the end. Not for quite a bit. He thought Old Amy could keep him alive.'

'In a way she did. And you, too. And he was happier thinking so. I believe that.' Apologetically, he went into a long self-justifying digression on the avoidance of income tax, assuring her that in business decent people did it all the time. 'Of course, we didn't know he was going to die so young — it was before he got ill that I deposited so much in his name. Capital additions, you understand — Now, well, his mother says you shouldn't have a penny. Old Amy wants nothing for herself — in some ways she's an extraordinary woman. But if he wanted you to have it — And I couldn't bear to take it back — If this was his last spoken wish — '

'You mean you're giving me Nickie's money? As if we'd been married?' said Hebe, almost aghast. To have a lifetime's ambition — even a short lifetime's ambition — fulfilled very suddenly was curiously frightening. Although she had no idea of the amount, here was undoubtedly the means to reach and experience the decorous levels of existence. Lying in the bottom of her mind was something the Professor had said, or quoted, but for the moment she could not recall it.

'Yes, and your passage to England — Oh, how can you stand this place!' he said almost pettishly, retreating before the smell to the doorway, where he stood half in and half out, throwing over his shoulder to her such details as the address of his lawyers, who would arrange the transfer on his instructions, and a summary of Colonial financial regulations, which would enable the money to reach her in England undiminished.

To be his to give away, in the boy's memory, was all that money could do for him at the moment, but at least it held off the full weight of realization, the exhaustion of his loss. Unpleasant as Old Amy's lair was, he seemed unwilling to leave it for the bleaker realities of the hotel, and stood in silence, looking out at the street swarming with lusty black life.

'No, no, take it. Just take it and go,' he said wearily when belatedly it occurred to her that it would be the proper course to thank him. 'And it'd be better if you didn't let us hear of you again. I mean that, mind. I'd like to think something in all this hell we've had — Nickie, my wife and I — I'd like to think it was going to do somebody some good. It'll be easier to believe that if we hear nothing more.' He lifted a hand in salutation, and then, at this last minute, after all the hours of tedious conversation Hebe had borne from him, said something which suggested that if he had not modestly clung to the things he knew about, for fear of being a greater bore, they might indeed have become good friends: he could have taken the Professor's place in her life. 'His mother's gone to church, to pray. How God must laugh, if the Thing in charge of the world's human enough to understand prayers, to find people going on thinking he's a benevolent spirit fit to be prayed to. When he lets things like Nickie's illness happen to children — to punish *us*, my wife says, for what we did when we were young! — Well, good luck, Hebe.'

There turned out to be between two and three thousand pounds in Nickie's account.

17

ACHIEVEMENT

'AND you are on your way to school in England? That will be very nice.'

'Very nice,' echoed Hebe, looking round with satisfaction. The little parlour behind the tobacconist's shop in Carcassonne was just as she had hoped it would be when she set out, not without trepidation, to call upon the aunt who had disapproved of Jean-Paul's escapade with the dentists — She was André's aunt, too.

The cat asleep before the well-polished stove, both of them as portly of their kind as Tante Marie herself, the bobbled tablecloth, the pampas grasses in a china stand, and the withered crown of *immortelles* under a glass cover, in memory of a husband — everything on the premises spoke of a highly settled existence. Half way between the splendour of the Grande Bretagne and the grim simplicity of the lair in the Cockpit Country, the atmosphere held something that Hebe had missed for far too long: it was cosy.

She had disembarked at Lisbon, instead of going all the way from Jamaica to England by ship, in order to pass through Carcassonne and make Tante Marie's acquaintance: and plainly, after only a few minutes' talk between them, it was an inspired course to have chosen — bold gamble as it had seemed when she landed.

They had not yet mentioned André, but that would come at the proper time. Tante Marie was asking her all the right questions, over cups of *tisane* made from the lime tree in the back garden. A woman of probity equal to her bulk, the tobacconist made it plain that she disapproved of Jean-Paul and always had, but since he was a relative after all, she was glad to entertain in this modest way someone who offered recent news of him.

Hebe's account of her association with Jean-Paul had by now

been more carefully edited than the story of her background given to the two kind ladies in Athens. Then it had been necessary to marshall her facts quickly; this time she had had a fortnight, between the West Indies and Portugal, in which to arrange them in the most favourable light. The facts were still facts: as Nickie had noticed, Hebe never lied outright if this could be avoided; but their outlines were progressively softening in detail. In time the tale would become quite unrecognizable, to anyone who knew the original happenings, although Hebe herself would still believe it. In the present version, Jean-Paul, her father and herself had been three of a party of travellers badly served by the agency responsible for their journey: there was, of course, no need to mention that the travel agent had been her father, but this new description of his activities had occurred to her in the ship: it sounded better than 'a seafaring man' and would be useful at school. She and Jean-Paul, she reported, had been much thrown on their own resources — she particularly, after the death of her father during the trip — and she was pleased to say that she had found Jean-Paul most resourceful. Tante Marie was equally glad to hear good of him for once. Perhaps, she suggested, he would now settle down properly, somewhere in the Middle East; and she led the conversation back to Hebe's own prospects. She was puzzled by the girl, and devoured by curiosity: was this Jean-Paul's young mistress? If so, it was impertinent of her to call. But Hebe's meek-looking clothes denied this. She had bought herself a new outfit in Lisbon, the plainest available, bearing in mind the much-studied illustrations to books about schools. Her models were many years out of date, but fortunately Lisbon had nothing which quite approximated to any of them, and no gym tunic at all: Tante Marie would not have liked the short tunic. To buy anything plain in Lisbon meant buying very expensively. Tante Marie's own ideas of suitable wear for an English schoolgirl were just as outmoded, dating from the time when the English were expected to look richly eccentric in baggy tweeds. Hebe wore her quietly over-sophisticated garments with confidence, and the result was, by accident, an impressive air of innocence.

'Is it a good school to which you are going?'

'Specially good, I understand.'

'But how can you know, if you have not yet attended it?'

'It was chosen for me by a very old American who is a millionaire and has a niece there.'

'Ah, indeed!' There was something disarming in the pleasure Hebe showed in the status to which she was about to become accustomed: it was the sort of pleasure that Tante Marie would have known herself, in the circumstances. She warmed further to her visitor when Hebe mentioned casually that she had already made sure, by cable from the ship, that the American had really been as good as his promise, and entered her name at the school with his recommendation to back it. To be so young and so business-like was formidable, in the best sense.

'And you will interview the principals by yourself, having no father and mother?' inquired Tante Marie. 'That is sad for you,' she said, when Hebe had agreed with composure, 'but never mind, I am sure you will manage very well, and create the right impression.' This girl was too good for Jean-Paul, no matter what her background.

Mutual approval grew so quickly that there was no jar in the conversation when the question came bluntly, 'And have you a *dot*, my dear, for when you leave? It is of course a pity that you should be all alone in the world, at your age. It will make it harder for you to "instal yourself" as you would wish. Or is a *dot*, as I think I have heard, not expected in England?'

'It is not necessary, but I have one,' said Hebe complacently, and to the raised, waiting eyebrow — there were decent and accepted limits to what Tante Marie would ask directly — she replied that there ought to be about a thousand pounds left over when she had done with school, as nearly as she could reckon beforehand the fees, and a reasonable living allowance.

Tante Marie selected a tooth to suck, and mused. Hebe felt shrewd eyes running over her, judging what she would be like in, say, two to three years' time, when it could be hoped that she would have filled out somewhat: and knew the verdict favourable. Apart from being what actually should remain, or thereabouts, a thousand pounds, she sensed, was just the right sum for a woman to bring to a marriage in this *milieu*: not too much, so that a wife might feel above her husband; enough to buy him a nice little business, such as a café. Whatever Tante Marie suspected she had been, Hebe could safely assume now that she was too valuable not to be kept in the family, if possible. She had no objection to being rated in this way: it was how she valued herself. The seal on her acceptance was set by no mercenary consideration, however, but by a happy chance remark.

Two customers interrupted their chat, and then a carter delivering supplies of tobacco. His horse wore a small straw hat, with holes cut through the brim for the ears. Hebe glimpsed the creature through the shop doorway and exclaimed with pleasure. 'I do like seeing things well looked after,' she said. 'Even though I'm sure a horse doesn't need a hat.' She was almost home, in security, at the house with the dogs! Rare as such a sight was in France, a horse with a hat was unthinkable in Greece, South America or any of the countries through which she had passed since leaving the Good Place where, no doubt, animals still mattered more than the human occupants. With tingling expectancy she counted on seeing its curious porch tomorrow, or the next day at latest — and here, like a welcome from afar, was this emissary of a pampered horse. None of this could she explain, to herself or Tante Marie; but she asked leave politely to run out and pat the beast.

Tante Marie beamed upon her, and followed more slowly, heaping majestic abuse on the carter for being late with her goods. Her last doubt was conquered by this evidence that Hebe, like herself, was someone who appreciated things not for what they were, but for what they stood for: this was innate respectability. She swept the girl back into the parlour, pushed aside the *tisane* cups, and produced two glasses of good red wine.

'I always let that man have a sound threatening,' she said, 'but in fact he will not lose my custom while his horse wears a hat. Not that I am immoderately fond of animals, you understand, but I do not like to think of their being ill-treated. I am quite sure, with you, that the creature does not suffer from the sun on its head. Would in fact prefer to have nothing round the ears. But I am just as certain that a horse which wears a hat is never badly used. And that is so nice.'

With comfortable prescience Hebe was aware of the next question, word for word, before it came, in the way in which places, never seen before, could be familiar in a dream-like fashion: 'Have you, by any chance, met my other nephew, André, who is also somewhere abroad?'

It was going to be all right! With a relative like Tante Marie on her side, how could it not be? Then why was it that there rose again in her thankful mind the slight, untraceable feeling of uneasiness which she had known before, when the news of her little fortune had been given to her — that something was missing, or was being lost?

The figure of the Professor recurred to her mind's eye, and totally irrelevant as it seemed, through her unusual memory for words and shapes and the pictures they conjured up, drifted something he had quoted from the same man: 'a great but now underrated poet of my own special period', he had called Tennyson — who had written of the 'plain eggs of the nightingale' and the music they hid.

Now it was something about silence, just as little understood by Hebe's mind, but felt with the nerves and the heart:

> So dark a forethought roll'd about his brain
> As on a dull day in an ocean cave
> The blind wave feeling round his long sea-hall
> In silence . . .

Perhaps this dark forethought, this breath of foreboding, touched her now only because there was, in fact, a cave not very far from the house with the dogs, which was held so closely in her thoughts.

In any case, it did not matter: the present moment was altogether too satisfactory for the sensation of chill to last long on the surface of her mind.

Through a daze of relaxation she heard Tante Marie's comments and questions flowing on, almost as if she had herself dictated them. 'But how remarkable . . . In Athens, you say, and looking well? . . . Only the other week, a card from him . . . A good type, that one, merely unfortunate, not at all *debrouillard* . . . A matter of time . . . When he returns, you must renew your childhood acquaintanceship — that would be charming.' And just before Hebe rose to go: 'Perhaps during your next holidays, if you would care for a few days in France — ? I shall then be staying with my brother and sister-in-law, who have a café in Lille. It could easily be arranged. . . .'

With greater finesse than she had deemed necessary over the *dot*, Tante Marie, as she was seeing the girl to the door, detained her for a moment to talk of the dangers which, she felt, Hebe must have met and no doubt surmounted on her travels: had there not been times when it would have been reasonable for a young girl to have feared for what Tante Marie described as her honour?

Hebe reassured her that though there had been such times, this, too, was all right. So far as she was concerned, her honour was indeed intact: she had done, or very nearly done now, exactly what she had set out to do. If by the word Tante Marie understood virginity, that was her affair and another matter. This, Hebe had quite deliberately lost, to a young steward in the ship, who resembled André. Rape was something she had always felt must be avoided at all costs, and in this she had succeeded: as a pleasure, she thought little of her recent experience, but it was bearable, and if you set out to make a career of marriage, it was only sensible to find out before too late what you were setting out to acquire.

When finally she took her leave, Hebe was kissed on both cheeks and left the tobacconist's with the knowledge that — barring accidents — she was as good as married to André already. Whatever entanglements he might get into abroad, he was not one to take such a serious business step as marriage without consulting his family.

Hebe turned her mind joyfully towards the fulfilment of her other ambition, to see again the Good Place.

* * * * *

Where the house with the dogs had stood, there was not even a hole, only a levelled space in a ruined garden, gaily filled with the pinks and yellows of the particular weeds which thrived on bombed sites.

Hebe stared at it for a long time, numb with shock, when she came to the end of the enormous round journey which had taken, in all, eight years of her life: England, South America, the Balkans, Jamaica, Italy, the Balkans and Jamaica again, and at last, once more, England. Afterwards she could not understand why it had never occurred to her that the Good Place and all it meant might easily be destroyed by war: perhaps because the existence of a Good Place had been so necessary to her, to bring her through, just as she had needed the idea of André, and the flame of respectability in the heart. For a long time she had accepted the possibility that her mother's relatives might not be anxious to take any further responsibility for her — that was all right: she could be responsible for herself — but not that they and the strong atmosphere which they had created could disappear for ever from her world.

Seeing her standing there, with an air so lost, a middle-aged woman on a bicycle stopped and asked if she had known the people in that house — eager, in the uneventful days of peace, to pass on the news that they had all been there when the place took a direct hit — yes, everyone who belonged to the house: bad luck, wasn't it? But this was a very thoroughly bombed neighbourhood. Oh, quite as bad as London and Coventry, although you didn't hear so much fuss about it. Hebe recognized her as someone she had known slightly in early childhood, but the woman, voluble in her pride of locality, paid too little attention to her to recognize the grown child. Hebe made some vague comment to avoid further conversation, and the woman went on. It seemed to Hebe that it was she herself, and not the people of the house, who had joined the legion of ghosts.

Something deserted her then, at the realization that there were goals which could never be reached — her faith in herself, and the courage to endure whatever that faith demanded. Still, it had served her well enough, this one-time belief that if you wanted something hard enough and long enough, it was almost bound to come your way in the end.

Soon, common sense re-asserted itself. Here was gain as well as loss. Without formulating the idea to herself in detail, she knew that this house had stood not only for security and a life of decorum and front doors, but for these things viewed against a slightly wider social background than they were likely to have at *Le Bien-Venu*. It belonged to a different world: perhaps it was as well, for her future satisfaction, that it had gone. The Professor had once pointed out to her a certain breed of ants of which only the queen and the males from which she chose a mate had wings: when the time came for the pair to construct a nest, they gnawed them off: wings would be only an obstruction while building underground — With the monkey-grimace which passed for a smile, he had pointed out, too, how wise this probably was on the part of the ants.

Henceforth, Hebe would keep her inward eyes still more strictly on practical matters, turning away from all wild longings to understand people and things which were no concern of hers, from the profitless streak of poetry in her own nature which had always run parallel with her earthiness. Emotion connected with a snake in the claws of a hawk, or with fish skimming over a tropical sea, was of no help in the efficient running of a business. There would be fewer and fewer, as time went on, of those disturbing moments of immense burning comprehension, when the whole mind saw, not only the eyes.

She turned and walked, a little less resolutely than usual, away from the place that could no longer be a sustaining idea, towards a future which, in the event, was to be much as she had planned it. Success would be hers, along the line she herself had chosen — improbable success, magnificently achieved, all things considered. Close ahead lay the moment, different only in detail from her imaginings, when she would enter by right a white school bedroom, and find there a buxom young girl of her own age who would look up and say indifferently, 'Oh, hello. You Laura Klee?' and go on banging herself vigorously on the chest with a hairbrush. 'Keep *cave* for me a minute, will you?'

'Keep what?'

'Look out and tell me if anyone else's coming!'

'Oh, that. Yes, all right.' Hebe had met the word when reading, but supposed it was pronounced 'cave'. 'What are you doing that for?'

'Getting out of being in the school play. They're giving out parts tomorrow. They always want me to be a man, and I look so silly in tights.'

'But I don't see why — '

'Because it makes a rash that looks just like measles. My dear child,' said the other with amiable patronage, 'what *do* you know?'

This question Hebe humbly and wisely left unanswered.

Further ahead, in the folds of the years, lay the moment when, in church, she would meet again the passage in the 106th psalm: 'He gave them their desire, and sent leanness withal into their souls' — and it would mean nothing to her, beyond the memory of when and where she had first heard it.

She would be bearing André's third child then, and have other things to bother about besides the echo of words — Nothing connected with the service preoccupied her, she read the Bible to while away the time: Hebe was never much of a church-goer, although it looked well to be seen there occasionally, and towards the end of a well-organized pregnancy there was little else to do. But the new waitress at the café was not shaping as she should, her manner with the customers was altogether too familiar. Just because the *patron* encouraged her — Hebe did not seriously object to that: André was often a little tiresome with new waitresses — there was no reason for that young woman to imagine she could scamp her work or presume on her position. Rising with the rest of the congregation and closing the book, Hebe decided that she would speak to her, after Mass: it must be clearly understood that no slackness would be tolerated at *Le Bien-Venu*, nor provocative talk, nor, certainly, any kind of impropriety in public.